BLIND HUNGER

Araminta Star Matthews

Dark Moon Books

DARK MOON BOOKS

Largo, FL

BLIND HUNGER

PAPERBACK EDITION

ISBN-13: 978-0-9787925-9-6

Dark Moon Books

An imprint of Stony Meadow Publishing

3412 Imperial Palm Drive

Largo, FL 33771

Visit our website at www.darkmoonbooks.com

Printed in the United States of America

Cover Artwork: Adam Sacco (Soulty)

Cover Design: Stan Swanson

Dedication

For Abner Goodwin,
around whom all my zombie—and more recently,
robot—apocalypse survival plans revolve.

Acknowledgements:

Few people realize how many people it takes to pull a book together. This book wouldn't be possible without the influence, support, and tireless efforts of the following people: Abner Goodwin, Amanda (Sigurdsson) Coffey, Rachel Robbins, Shawn White, Crystal and Michael Matthews, Rachel Lee, Tory Dresser, Joel Norris, Tracie McBride, Jennifer Word, and Stan Swanson. Thanks for making this possible!

Prologue

Nanologic Technologies and the Best of Intentions

Patricia pressed her head into the plastic cocoon-hood of her Hazmat suit before sealing it shut around her collar bone. She sucked in a breath through the fibrous mask that covered her nose and mouth as she pushed the code on the keypad next to the door. She walked inside and the pneumatic doors hissed shut behind her. The ventilators showered her with smoky, white air before the second set of doors opened into the greenhouse.

"Hi Pat," came the muffled voice of Miguel behind her. He held a clipboard in a gloved hand, and a sectioned gardener's box of soil samples in the other. His face was protected by a screened, hooded mask.

"Miguel," she nodded. "How are my babies, today?"

Clearing his throat, Miguel nodded. "Well, the babies are just fine," he said. "All the specimens in Sector Seven-B are showing significant responses to your Nanologic Serum. Nineteen out of twenty of the mature plants are technically and fully 'dead', but still producing viable fruit at a rate one hundred times faster than our control group of normal tomato plants."

Miguel paused, wishing he could scratch an itch just above his ear. "It's the most amazing thing. The plants are black and dry. The stalks crumble in my hands, but the tomatoes are plump, red, and still growing. I've already prepared the truck with samples for transport to our main site in Buckston."

Patricia smiled, the edges of her mask rising against her cheeks. "My serum works," she breathed. Her pupils widened, stretching against her blue irises. Excitement tingled up her spine, down her arms and into her fingertips.

"Did you say something?" Miguel arched his neck, leaning closer inside his suit to hear her better.

"No," she said, shaking her head. "I was just thinking how lucky we are to work for the company that is going to end world hunger."

Miguel chuckled. "You sound like Deidra in Sector Four A. You idealists make the strangest scientists. Still, I must admit that I'm pretty proud to be a part of this. If we can populate the world with plants that bear fruit up to seventy-five days after they've died, well—let's just say we can be prouder of this than Nanologic's *other* studies."

"Yes, Miguel. I suppose that's the truth, "Patricia said, nodding. "I'll check on those specimens immediately." She turned on her heel and walked down the narrow path between plant pallets toward Sector Seven-B.

As she walked, the folds of her plastic suit brushed against the plants arching out over the pallets on either side of the corridor. She knew that each pallet represented a different test group and so she was not surprised to see purple-leafed tomato plants bearing blueberry-blue tomatoes on one pallet across from the creeping yellow tendrils of a modified cabbage on the next. While she knew that every serum in this section of the Nanologic greenhouse was meant to improve the growth and development of vegetation in order to provide a more expansive food supply, she couldn't help but think no one would want to eat a blue tomato.

Turning the corner in the pathways that intersected the raised garden beds, she caught sight of Sector Seven-B, a pallet of tomato plants she'd treated with a serum of her own creation. Her masterpiece serum was a combination of modified parasites designed to expedite the nutrient-depletion of the soil into the plant and chemicals combined to trick the plant's "chemistry" into thinking it was still in its fruit-bearing stage even after death.

The result would be a tomato plant that would produce ripe and juicy tomatoes once every two days instead of once every ninety, and the kicker? It would grow them on the blackened, dried-out stalks of the plant long after the plant should have gone to compost heaven.

Sure enough, as Patricia drew closer to the pallet, she saw vibrant, baseball-sized red tomatoes hanging limply from the graying, yellowed stalks of a hundred or so dried-out plants. Her heart pumped hard against her chest. A peaceful smile pulled her lips toward her cheeks. Her grand opus, her serum had worked and it was a miracle.

Overwhelmed by her success, by her dream finally manifesting, her mind began to wander. She imagined herself delivering her acceptance speech in Oslo at the Nobel Peace Prize Award Ceremony. An exaggerated gentleman with a monocle straight out of a Dickens novel would ask her how it felt to create a sustainable food source for all humans on the earth. In her mind, she could see his white mustache bobbing under his stiff upper lip as his shaggy white eyebrows knitted together. At his question, she would redden, bat her eyes at the podium, and say softly into the microphone, "It was nothing. I was just doing my job."

As the imaginary applause filled her ears, Patricia's eyes scanned the field of delectable tomatoes so ripe and plump and red that her tongue started to sweat. Without thinking about the consequences, or the slap-in-the-face it would be to scientific procedure, Patricia's hand rose slowly from her body as if compelled by its own mind.

Overcome with excitement, her rubber-tipped fingers closed around one juicy specimen of tomato. The fruit freed itself from the withering vine with a hardy snap. No clipboard. No specimen container. No animal tests. All that spiraled through Patricia's mind was the sound of that applause, the deafening, rumbling thunder of an auditorium of thousands all slapping their hands together for her. In all the excitement, her science had disappeared.

With her free hand, she tore the seal of her Hazmat hood and lifted her mask. The fruit rose to her lips. The smooth skin of the tomato felt cool against the soft pink of her mouth. Her teeth met its surface, lightly piercing the skin. Cool, wet red juice sprayed over her tongue as the tangy taste of tomato flooded her mouth. She chewed quietly. A little of the juice spilled on her chin, but she did not stop to wipe it away. Her fruit, her baby, had grown up and it had all of her attention.

The only thing she noticed was the flavor of her Nobel Prize as the harsh white lights of the greenhouse faded into the background.

She didn't notice the tingling sensation in the soles of her feet or the palms of her hands. She didn't think of the unknown parasites and chemicals that may be injecting themselves into her salivary glands as she chewed. She didn't notice her blood thicken, or her vision blur. She didn't notice as Miguel turned the corner between the pallets, his mouth sagging open at the sight.

She didn't notice when, minutes after swallowing the first bite, her heart stopped beating and the blood in her veins turned as inky black as the stalks of the dead tomato plant beside her.

She didn't hear Miguel's scream.

CHAPTER ONE

Max

"What was that, you little punk?" Ronald slammed down his coffee cup, a few spurts of coffee sloshing over the side onto the table top.

Max looked at the floor in silence.

"Hey, you better smarten up, boy!" shouted Ronald as he flicked the back of Max's head with the side of his hand. "I asked you a question and I better get an answer."

Max glared at him from under the brim of his baseball cap. Threads of hay-colored hair stuck out in scraggily points all around Max's face. A band of freckles spread across his nose like Orion's belt, and tiny tendrils of peach fuzz curled over his upper lip and chin. He stood by the door, slouching in an oversized flannel shirt, with one hand looped loosely around the door knob and his other hand clutching a tired strap of a black backpack.

"I said, you're not my father," Max said quietly, setting his jaw to one side.

Ronald glared at the boy. "You're damn right I'm not your father. If I was your father, I'd have to kill myself just like he did." His voice rose steadily with each word, spit shooting from the sides of his mouth as he spoke.

"No. On second thought, I would take you out back with the trash. And everyone would thank me. You know why? Because everyone—" The man slammed a fist into the table top. Max flinched as the coffee cup bounced, splattering coffee onto the newspaper beside it. The murky brown liquid pooled together along the edge and began a slow drip off the side of the table.

"Because everyone knows what a punk you are!" Ronald raged on, his scraggily voice cut with what Max assumed was smoker's cough. "Because everyone knows you will never amount to anything. Your teachers know it. Your truant officer knows it. For Christ's sake, your mother and I sure as hell know it."

Bleary-eyed and frizzy-haired, Max's mother drifted into the kitchen. A cigarette dangled from her mouth with a half-inch cylinder of ash clinging to the end. Ronald stood panting, his knuckles white where he gripped the edges of the table and a red vein pulsing in an angry arch across his forehead.

Max stared desperately at the puddle of coffee collecting on the floor, afraid to look up, afraid to make a sound. He thought, if I can just stare at this long enough, *if I can just pay attention to this one tiny detail, maybe I'll disappear the way chameleons vanish into the background.*

"Shouldn't you be at school?" she asked, her voice croaking and rasping from a dry throat. As Max's mom spoke, the cigarette pasted to her lips bounced up and down. The cylinder of ash separated from the end of the cigarette and flitted to the floor. Max said nothing.

"Hey, boy. Your mother asked you a question." Ronald stood and made a move to walk around the table, before he was seized by a chest heaving cough. His hand rose to his throat and stroked it for a moment, before he twisted his body around the table and started after the boy.

Max looked up. "I was just leaving," he said quickly, turning the knob and opening the door into a bleak, gray morning. Half-hanging out the door, he glanced at the clock on the stove across the kitchen. It was already 7:15. He'd probably make it in time for first period history by the time the school principal was done plastering him with detention slips for missing homeroom. Max didn't mind detention, though. It meant more time out of the house and away from his mother's latest stupid boyfriend.

"Good," his mother said, turning her back on him as she shuffled barefoot toward the refrigerator.

Max stared at her back for a minute, blinking. He wondered if she cared about him at all. He felt as though she didn't even know he existed, or at least that she'd prefer he didn't. He stepped outside and slammed the door behind him.

"Bye, sweetheart," he said in a quiet, high-pitched voice. "I hope you have a nice day at school today." He sighed. *Whatever,* he thought as he swung his backpack back and forth to match his shuffle down the sidewalk.

CHAPTER TWO

Bryan, his Girlfriend, Rachel, and her Sister Kiley

Bryan watched from the window as Rachel eased her silver Volkswagen up to the curb in front of his house. The car jerked into park before the familiar horn honked, announcing her arrival. He grabbed his laptop case and school bag from the counter by the front door.

"My ride's here. Bye, Dad," Bryan yelled as he flung the door open.

"Hey, wait a minute." Bryan's dad trotted toward him, his wallet in hand. He paused a few feet away from his son, and bent an elbow over his mouth as a dry, raspy cough sputtered from his lips. He wiped the back of his hand across his lips.

Bryan paused at the door and turned around. "You all right, Dad?" he asked.

Straightening, his dad fumbled in his wallet and pulled out a twenty dollar bill. "Do you need some lunch money today? I know I forgot to get bread at the grocery store last night."

Bryan switched his bags to one hand and gratefully accepted the money. "Thanks, Dad! That's awesome."

His dad lifted an eyebrow. "You will spend that on *lunch*, right?"

"Of course, Dad. I'll get Rachel and me a couple of hamburgers, or something."

His father tried to grin, but his red rimmed eyes gave the man's face a sickly hue. Bryan's shoulders tensed, bracing for what he knew would come next. His father patted his shoulder.

"I think—" the man began, but his voice seemed to catch in his throat. Bryan waited for another coughing fit, but his father just swallowed as the muscles in his face shifted visibly under his skin. "I think your mother would have really liked Rachel."

Bryan forced a smile to his face. "Yeah," he said. He looked at the ground. "She's waiting, Dad," he said after a pause. "I gotta go."

His father snapped himself from his reverie. "Of course," he said, clearing his throat again, the pads of his fingers massaging his neck just below the Adam's apple. "You have a good day at school." He paused for a second before wrapping his arms around his son in a big, bear hug. "I love you, son."

Bryan dropped his bags and returned the hug. "Sure, Dad. I love you, too. Thanks." Scooping up his bags, he turned to walk off the stone porch. "See you tonight," he said, jumping off the last step onto the driveway.

"Not tonight, Bryan. I've got that business trip to Chicago, remember?" He covered his mouth again as the cough seized his chest. His eyes clenched shut as he sputtered and hacked into the crook of his shoulder.

"Are you sure you should be going to Chicago like this, Dad?" Bryan asked, hesitatingly. "You need something?"

"No, son. I'm fine." His father coughed once more into his elbow, then ran a palm across his forehead. "I just wanted to be sure you remembered I was flying to Chicago today. That's all. It's a quick business meeting; that's all. I'm sure this is just allergies anyway."

Bryan raised an eyebrow, but knew better than to question his father's resolve. "Oh. Yeah. Okay, Dad. Sorry I forgot. I guess I'll see you, um, Saturday then?"

His father nodded solemnly. "Yes. I'll see you Saturday. If you need anything, Helga will be in Thursday. Let her know if you want anything special for dinner. I'll leave some money in your room just in case."

"Sure thing, Dad." Bryan paused and eyed his father. "Are you sure you shouldn't just call in sick? I could stay home and make you soup or something."

"Nice try, Bryan. Don't you have an algebra test today?" said his father, cocking his head to the side.

Bryan grinned. "Geesh, Dad. You've got a better memory than my laptop. Yeah, yeah. I have an algebra test today that I am completely prepared to take. I really was just looking out for you, pops."

"Right," said Dad, returning the grin.

Bryan waved the twenty dollar bill as he took a step backward. "Thanks again."

"Behave," said his father just before shutting the door.

"Like hell," Bryan whispered through his grin as the door clicked into place. He turned back to face Rachel. She rolled her eyes as he sprinted toward the car, the drawstrings of his navy hoodie bouncing against his chest as he ran.

"I thought he'd never let you leave," she muttered as Bryan slid into the passenger seat.

"I know," he said as he leaned in to greet her with a kiss. As his lips approached hers, she cleared her throat and tipped her head toward the backseat.

Bryan didn't even look. "Hello, Kiley."

"I don't know why you have to kiss my sister every single time you see her," Kiley grumbled, fixing her darkly penciled eyes coldly on the back of Rachel's seat. She crossed her arms over her chest, and slid her index finger under the black fishnet glove on the opposite hand. Her black lips pursed.

"I mean, that's a lot of saliva to be sharing every single day. And don't even get me started on what kind of mad germs you two are exchanging. Ebola virus, anyone?"

Kiley's eyebrow cocked as she stared darkly at Bryan through the rearview mirror. She continued, "My friend Molly kissed Derek behind the bleachers at a football game last week—not that either of us would ever be caught dead at any event featuring blondie, cheerleader losers and sunshine-yellow pompoms, mind you, but Molly was absolutely insistent that her new nugget had to hand out towels or something for some ridiculous detention he supposedly got for wearing a Flying Spaghetti Monster t-shirt to school and upsetting the adult collective. Whatever. Loser if you ask me. Cuz you know what happened to Molly?" Kiley paused for effect. Her eyebrows lifted high on her pale face and her head cocked to the side. "Now Molly has Mono. No joke."

"Okay," Bryan said cautiously.

"What if you caught leprosy and your skin started to rot and your nose fell off while you were kissing or something? That's what can happen, you know. That's how diseases are spread, Rachel. Through mucus membranes, like the inside of your mouth."

"Kiley!" Rachel said sharply, fixing her sister with a glare in the rearview mirror. "That's disgusting! Leprosy? What the hell is wrong with you?"

Bryan turned to put his book bag on the backseat beside Kiley. She looked at him passively, curling a strand of strawberry hair behind her ear. She had colored the tips of her hair jet black with a Sharpie the night before and a few streaks of black smudged the tips of her fingers and ear. Noticing the stain on her fingertip, she thrust her hand under her thigh.

"She's just jealous," Bryan said, his eyes fixed on Kiley but his head tipped toward Rachel in the driver's seat.

Kiley raised her eyebrows and lifted her chin. "I so am not. And it could happen, you know. I saw a whole documentary about leper colonies in Hawaii on television last week. It's an infectious disease, sis. That means it is catching. That means you *could* get it from kissing!"

"We are not going to give each other leprosy, Kiley. I doubt there has ever been a case of leprosy in Greendale." Rachel pulled out of the driveway and onto the street as Bryan buckled his seatbelt. "Ever," she added, ice frosting the edge of her voice.

"You don't know that for sure. You don't even get good grades in history. History is the only subject that matters." Kiley pouted, turning her gaze out the window to stare at the steely grey sky. "History is where I belong. And besides, Greendale has had plenty of infectious diseases."

"Such as, Ms. Know-it-all-Dark-and-Dreary?" sneered Rachel. She sniffled and wiped her nose with the back of her hand before returning it to the wheel.

"Um, see? You just infected the whole town with your boogers, Rachel."

"Or just anyone who drives my car, *sis*. So really, just me."

"I'm kind of curious about these infectious diseases Greendale is known for, Kiley," said Bryan, casting a nervous glance at his girlfriend in the driver's seat. He tried to signal her with his eyes, but she just kept driving, her eyes fixed on the road.

"What diseases have you learned about?" he asked at last.

"Well, there was this cholera thing in 1861 that wiped out half the town. Miss Snellar, that's my history teacher, she told me that it was because a family froze to death on the far side of the lake and nobody found them until spring.

"It's like this thing I saw on the History Channel about rotgut whiskey where all these medical doctors in the Victorian ages, or whatever, were trying to practice on dead bodies but they couldn't get any, so all these grave robbers started stealing bodies and stuffing them in barrels of whiskey so they could hide the body when they delivered it to the doctors, right? Only after they delivered the dead guy, the grave robbers didn't want the whiskey to go to waste so they totally drank it. Sick, right?" She grinned, eyes glittering.

"Anyway, everyone got sick from all the dead body germs. Dead bodies, by the way, are called cadavers which I think is a totally delicious name for them. Like hors d'oeuvres, or something yummy." She licked her lips for emphasis and smiled smugly when Rachel, who had been glaring at her through the rearview mirror, shuddered visibly and averted her gaze.

Kiley went on. "So this family just rotted in the town's drinking water when everything thawed out, and that's when everybody got sick. Just like grave robber whiskey barrels. All these *cadaver* bits flaking off and floating around in the water. Blood and viscera—yeah, that's an SAT word, Rachel. You should know it if you want to go to college the year after next. It means guts, Rachel. Guts. Just spilling out of their bodies and melting in the sun and getting all torn apart by the fish, and—"

"Kiley, enough." Rachel's voice was flat and cold.

Bryan swallowed hard as he stared out the windshield, his hand absently rising to cover his stomach. The streets were bare and a thin layer of frost glistened on the grass along the edge of the road.

"I'm sorry I asked," he mumbled.

"Looking a little green, lover boy," whispered Rachel, grinning.

"I notice you're not," he said sharply.

Rachel shrugged. "You live with the Queen of the Underworld back there, you get used to it."

Kiley chipped the tips of her black nail polish pretending to ignore Bryan's obvious queasiness as she carried on. "And then there was some smallpox outbreak in the nineteen hundreds. Miss Snellar told me it was the worst epidemic of smallpox to ever happen in America. They say some kid brought it back with him from visiting his aunt and uncle in Chesterville and cuz Greendale is totally a valley, all the germs just pitched their tents right in the middle of town. She said it killed a third of the kids in Greendale under the age of ten. The Vatican even sent a special group of nuns to come assist with the victims on account of St. Michael's being a new parish. Can you imagine? An entire fourth grade class, wiped out?"

Rachel rolled her eyes. "Don't be such a freak."

"Don't be such a cheerleader."

"What does that even mean?" asked Rachel.

"It means you don't have to be so sun tan lotion and pep rallies, all the time, sis. Death is a part of life. And besides, if you keep trying to tan in those hyper-hot tanning beds the way you do, you're going to die, too. Your skin is going to get all crocodile-leathery and you'll evaporate into a dry, dead husk. So deal with it, cheerleader."

"I'm *not* a cheerleader," Rachel warned.

"It's time you came out of the locker room," Kiley said solemnly. "I'm sure Mom and Dad will accept you. You're their daughter, and they love you."

"Perhaps it's time you climbed back *into* the coffin, sis."

Silence filled the vehicle for a moment.

Bryan turned in his seat to look at both Rachel and Kiley. Kiley's head slowly tipped toward the pane of glass in the door. Mumbling something under her breath, a splotch of mist spread and receded in seconds near her mouth.

"Oh, I don't know," said Bryan, his gaze deliberately fixed directly between both Rachel and Kiley. "I think history is kind of interesting, don't you? And coffins are, um, okay sometimes." He tried not to remember his mother's funeral so long ago, but the long, sleek mahogany casket cluttered his vision. He squeezed his eyes tightly shut and gulped. Forcing himself to speak, he added, "Wasn't that famous actress, what's her name, Sarah Bernhardt, I think–anyway, wasn't she famous for sleeping in a coffin?"

Tapping the steering wheel with her thumbs, Rachel pretended to ignore him; but, Kiley stole a glance at Bryan. He caught her gaze in the rearview mirror and returned the smile, watching as a blush of crimson rose to her cheeks before she quickly averted her gaze.

"Yeah," Kiley said, her voice soft as dust. "I think you're right."

Chapter Three

Sage

Sage rubbed gritty sleep from the corners of her eyes as she sat up in bed. It was early and the dim sunrise cast streaks of dust around her room. The six foot tall bookshelf in the far corner seemed slashed by cat claws of shadows and light. The home chemistry kit spread out on the desk next to the shelf always reminded her of a mad scientist's lab, the beakers and test tubes glowing iridescent in the dark.

Tucking her chin length blond hair behind her ear, she swung her legs over the side of the bed and stood up. Her hands moved quickly over her flannel nightgown, straightening out the creases against her body, before turning back to the bed to grab Squiggly. Stifling a yawn, she unzipped the hidden zipper in the back of her sock bunny and wiggled her index finger inside. She felt the hard, smooth surface of the Swiss Army knife her uncle had sent her from the base where he was stationed in Korea. Clinking softly against it was a half-dollar-sized compass around which was wrapped a length of transparent fishing line.

Sage carefully zipped up Squiggly's back and wrapped her arm under its woven armpits. She pulled it softly against her chest before heading to the kitchen for breakfast.

The kitchen was bright—too bright for such a dark morning. Her mother, dressed in a white linen dress and sporting green and sea foam blue beads woven into the braids of her mocha hair, stood with her back to Sage in front of the stove.

"Sage, my little warrior, do you want your veggie facon pan-fried or nuked?" Sage's mother did not turn to look at her daughter standing in the hallway. She pushed a bamboo spatula across the frying pan in front of her rapidly, swaying her hips as she cooked.

"No facon for me, mom. Just toast today, I think." Sage's bare feet slid over the polished wooden slats of the kitchen floor as she made her way to the glass-topped table where her father sat scrolling the mouse of his laptop with one hand, a cup of steaming tea in the other.

"No facon?" her father asked, raising an eyebrow. "Are you feeling all right? You aren't sickly like your dad this morning, are you? Tofu bacon is your favorite."

"I'm fine, Dad. I just want toast with jam today, that's all." Sage set Squiggly on the table beside her hand-woven papyrus placemat. She dangled her legs in front of the high-legged chair, swinging them back and forth above the floor as she glanced at her parents. She studied her father as he ran his fingers absently through his mop of peppered black hair with a sigh.

"What are you working on today, Dad?" Sage glanced at him curiously.

Her father paused, his gaze drifting out of focus above the monitor of his notebook. He tapped a contemplative thumb on his chin. "Well, Sage. I guess you could say I'm writing my soul for the Greendale council individuals who seem to think that trash bags stuffed with autumn leaves and grass trimmings and sent to the local landfill is somehow better for the environment than composting—at least, for apartment renters. They've passed a rule that anyone who is renting their home cannot compost on their property per town ordinance." He pursed his lips, staring at Sage ruefully. "How myopic is that?"

The left corner of Sage's mouth turned upward as she cocked her head to the side. "Myopic?"

He grinned weakly, his lips pulling against the rosy glow of his cheeks which were flushed red with fever. "Today's word, little warrior. Got a guess?"

Sage tipped her head back. "Hmm." She mentally scanned her mother's book shelf, stopping on a book near the top. Something by Thomas Moore, was it? "Utopia is a perfect society, right? So, the adjective form of that word would be utopic? No. Utopian? I give up. Is myopic the opposite of utopian? That doesn't sound quite right."

He leaned back in his seat, crossing his arms over his chest for a second, rewarding her with a smile. Leaning forward, he tousled her hair and said, "In this case, it's pretty darn close. What did I do to deserve a little genius child like you, sweetheart?"

"Don't leave her hanging like that, Ben," Sage's mother spun her hair over her shoulder as she turned from the toaster to glance toward the table. "Sage," she said. "Myopic means near-sighted."

Sage smiled. "Oh, I get it."

"What?" Her mother and father asked in unison.

"How it's the opposite of a utopia. You know, to be nearsighted about throwing away leaves and stuff that is biodegradable. In utopia, everything would be paradise; so, people would know they had to compost."

"That's my girl," her father said, a smile spreading across his face. His eyes glinted as she smiled back at him.

Her mother walked to the table, carefully setting a blue stone plate on Sage's placemat. "Two pieces of unleavened rye bread at your service," she said with a mock bow. "And what can I bring my tiny queen for jam?"

"I'm not tiny," Sage shot back. Her mother laughed.

"You'll always be my little bean sprout, Sage. You know that."

"More like the sacred Hindu cow, sweetheart," her father added. "Revered by our most ancient cultures as sacred, never to be eaten by mere mortals such as we."

"Strawberry Rhubarb, please," Sage interrupted, ignoring her father's cow reference. She'd found that, in times like these when the man started waxing poetic, it was easier to just pretend like she didn't hear him.

Her mother ran her fingers through her daughter's hair. "I should have guessed," she said, turning toward the pantry. She scanned the shelf for a minute, turning jars label side out so she could read the scrawling, handwritten names. After selecting a ruby-red jar with an illegible label, she walked back to the table and set it beside Sage. "I can't tell if this is Strawberry Rhubarb or just plain Strawberry. Is that okay?"

Sage nodded as she spun the metal cap off the container. She used the edge of a butter knife to pry off the brass lid that was jam-glued to the rim of the mason jar. "Is it okay if I bring Squiggly to school with me today?" she asked.

Her parents exchanged looks. Her mother lifted her eyebrows before folding her arms. Her father nodded slowly.

"What sort of contraband are you smuggling today, Mr. Sock Bunny?" asked her father in an affected voice aimed at the stuffed rabbit.

"The usual. If I'm going to be a scout, I figured I should have supplies. Like Jack London. Or Tom Sawyer."

"Well, that's sound logic for my little warrior. I suppose you're planning an adventure? I think it is best that you be prepared for anything." He turned to her mother. "Don't you think so, Deidra?"

Deidra bristled, but bit the inside of her lip in an effort to hide it. Her gaze fixed above Sage's head as her eyes glossed over with memory. As if on auto-pilot, she answered mechanically, "Yes, but you need to remember that even though we try to teach you that authority is questionable and rarely ever right here in the sheltered world of our own, personal home, in the world outside—"

Sage finished for her, "in the world outside, authority can hurt and having a knife in school is illegal."

"Actually, I was going to say, sometimes authority will save your life." Deidra grinned, tousled Sage's hair, and sat down.

Sage looked at her mother for a moment before continuing. "I know, I know. It's just that I was reading *Huckleberry Finn* last night and I was thinking how Huck could have survived a lot better on the river if he had a Swiss Army knife like the one Uncle

Joel sent me, and a compass to find his way back home again, and some fishing line. So I thought, I should pack Squiggly up with a few of these tools for myself. You know, in case I build a raft and leave on a river-bend adventure."

"In that case," her father said. "You should have a flint and one of those survival manuals, too. And just where do you expect to be rafting in the middle of November?"

"Like London's 'How to Start a Fire'?" Sage asked.

"Which doesn't actually teach you how to start a fire, Sage, but it isn't a bad read," Deidra said, her eyes glowing with pride. Her mother picked up Squiggly from the table and gave him a squeeze. His blue and pink stripes crinkled under her whitening fingers as she prodded the plushy bunny.

Ben leaned forward in his seat. "Can you feel any paraphernalia?" His eyelids sagged around his bloodshot eyes as he sniffed. "I mean, she's a little young for that, don't you think?" asked Ben with a sly grin. Deidra tapped him playfully with the back of her hand.

Sage looked nervously from her mother to her father and back to Squiggly. *What are they talking about?* She thought.

Her mother frowned at Ben, pulling her eyebrows together. "It's not like she's stashing a pipe in here. She's a little young to go challenging the marijuana prohibition, don't you think?"

"Really, dear?" he asked, shrugging his shoulders weakly. "You were about her age when you started—" Sage's mother sliced through the air with a sharp, telling look. Ben fell silent.

Placing Squiggly gently down on the table, Deidra squatted down beside her daughter so that her head was at the same level as Sage's. "Sage, biscuit, don't you worry about authority. You're a minor. Even if they find your knife, they won't do anything to you except impose a few detentions and a call to your parents. Besides, your father and I are just looking for a reason to home school you again. I'd be homeschooling you right now if I didn't have this crazy job, you know. Anyway, don't you worry, sweetheart. It'll be fine. I promise," she said. She tweaked Sage's nose as she rose.

Silence blanketed the room. Sage stared at the open jar of jam for a moment before thrusting the butter knife clutched in her hand deep into the gooey redness. She pulled out a chunk of fruit and pectin and plopped it on the center of her toast. The jam spread in clumps over the crispy bread.

Staring at the tufts of red, she was reminded of the time she fell off her bicycle on a family bike trip in the mountains. A sharp pebble had sliced into her knee, penetrating the skin about an inch deep. She'd needed stitches when they reached the doctor's office, she remembered, but what was most amazing was the way the blood and tissue seemed to separate. Slowly, as if parting an ocean, the skin pulled away from itself and blood began to seep out a droplet at a time until a rich red layer coated the entire knee. She had watched in fascination as the blood separated into two different pools—one dark maroon, the other a surreal fire engine red. That color—that ruddy coagulating mass—came to mind as she spread the jam across her toast before biting into it.

Ben's raw, scratchy voice cut through the silence. "You still haven't answered me. Could you feel anything?"

Deidra bit her lower lip and sucked in a deep breath through her nose. "Not really. The secret compartment is pretty well surrounded by stuffing, but I am worried about the zipper. If you roll the bunny around in your hands long enough, the zipper kind of feels like a wire running through the back. If they feel that, they might find the hidden bag."

Ben reached for the rabbit. Turning it over in his hands a few times, he dropped his head for a moment to clear his throat then tossed the bunny back onto the table. "I think she'll be fine," he said. Turning to Sage, he added, "Just be careful not to take it out of your book bag during class. The last thing you need is to have your belongings confiscated by the proletariat bureaucrats who call themselves 'school administrators'." He cast a woeful glance at Squiggly. "They'd probably torture the poor hunny bunny until he gave up his secrets. Poor little guy. It'll be the rack for you." He coughed into his hands, his entire body shaking as his chest tried to heave out whatever gummy bits were clinging to the inside of his lungs.

"Ben!" Deidra said sharply. She turned to Sage, squatted again, and placed both hands on her daughter's shoulders. Startled, Sage paused mid-bite. A splash of ruby-red jam smeared across her lips as a half-moon shaped piece of toast hovered near her mouth. Her eyes were wide.

"They don't torture stuffed animals at Greendale Elementary School," her mother comforted her. "I have every confidence that Squiggly will not be subjected to anything horrific, no matter what secrets he may be guarding. It's Greendale Elementary, not Guantanamo Bay, darling."

Sage blinked. With eyes still fixed on her mother's gaze, she slowly began chewing her toast again. "Sure, Mom. I know," said Sage, winking at her mother between bites. "Besides, Squiggly's brave. He wouldn't give up any secrets, anyway."

Deidra's eyes probed Sage's. She pulled her daughter closer to her, looking at her face from all angles before releasing her grip on the girl's shoulders and returning to a standing position. "I just needed to be sure, Sage. The last thing we need is psychological damage instilled by the prospect of torture being inflicted on my daughter's best and only friend."

Even though Sage knew that it was the truth, she still had to stifle a flinch at the sound of the words "best and only friend." Since Sage had moved to Greendale a year ago for her mother's new dream job ending world hunger and enhancing the world's food supply at Nanologic Technologies, Sage had been hard-pressed to make friends. It didn't help that, before arriving in Greendale, she and her father spent long days at home together where he home-schooled her between freelance writing gigs.

For some cloudy reason, home-schooled kids were not well received by the other nine-year-olds in town. When she first arrived, there were a few girls who had been friendly enough, sitting with her at lunch, talking to her on the playground, but as soon as one of them found out she had been home-schooled prior to coming to public school, they avoided her as if she had an infectious disease.

Sage wasn't too bothered by the way her schoolmates left only one seat in the back of each classroom for her to sit in, or how she was always left to work with the teacher when it came time to work in pairs during science. But, every time she tried to say hello to someone and was greeted with a strained, tensed "hello" followed by an audible sigh, Sage couldn't help but long for her first home in New England.

Chesterville had been a quiet town where most of the youth were home-schooled and attended a charter school for music, art, and physical education. With a population of barely 300 at its peak, the town had been filled with more waterfalls and forest paths than any place she had read about in her dad's National Geographic's. It had been her personal Garden of Eden. The town had only one restaurant which doubled as a bed and breakfast, and the owner's daughter, Amanda, was Sage's best friend. They had been nearly inseparable, and though they wrote letters to each other every week on homemade stationery (and covered the envelopes with stickers and doodles of friends holding hands), and they emailed each other as often as they could, it wasn't enough to satisfy Sage. Amanda only had access to a computer on the commune about once a month, and Sage wanted to write to her all the time. She missed Chesterville and Amanda more than she ever thought possible.

Her father's voice cut through her reverie, snapping Sage back to the breakfast table. "It's almost time for school, Sage. Finish your toast and get dressed so we can pack you up and ship you out."

Sage gulped down her bite of toast. "Yes, Dad." She dropped her nearly finished toast onto the plate, and her mother picked it up.

"Are you sure you're finished? You didn't eat very much," her mother said, bringing the plate up to eye level as if somehow the close examination would reveal the exact weight of the food Sage had eaten.

"I'm not hungry," said Sage, swinging her legs around and scooting off the chair. Immediately, her mother pressed her cool hand to her forehead, checking for fever.

"You're not sick, are you, my little warrior?" she asked with a hint of worry. "Everyone at the greenhouse has some kind of super flu virus right now. There's some mean bugs scampering around this town."

"Yeah, I bet she has the same virus that is working its way through my body, hm?" Ben pondered, shifting back in his seat. His watery eyes leaked at the edges. Sage cringed at the crust around his nose.

"I feel fine. I don't think I'm sick," said Sage. "Just tired. I think I should go to bed early tonight." Sage was fibbing. She wasn't tired; she was sad and missing her best friend. But she didn't want to worry her mother anymore than she already had. Moms were sensitive that way.

"All right, kiddo," her father interrupted. "If you're healthy, then you have to go to school. Chop, chop!" he said with a clap. As he brought his hands together, Sage caught sight of a tiny welt on his left wrist, which he'd kept hidden under the table for most of breakfast.

"What happened to your wrist, Dad?" asked Sage, concern cutting the edge of her voice.

Ben glanced at his wrist before slowly sliding it back into his lap, under the table. "Oh, that?" he said. "Nothing. Just a scratch, really."

Deidra frowned at him. "What scratched you?" she asked.

"Nothing," said Ben, shifting in his seat. "It was nothing. I was in the natural food store and some elderly woman scratched me when she reached over my arm for the organic tomatoes. Really, it's no big deal." He grinned sheepishly.

"You should have told me," said Deidra, sighing. "It looks infected. I'll get the tea tree oil."

As Sage walked out of the kitchen toward her bedroom, she cast a backwards glance toward her father. He lifted his shoulders with his hands out as if to say, 'what did I do?' Sage shook her head. *Parents*, she thought.

CHAPTER FOUR

Max and His Sick Friend

Max stomped along the sidewalk, head hung low. With a fallen oak tree branch in hand, he let the end of the stick clatter against the slats of the white picket fence in front of the Burgess house. A few flecks of dried white wash flicked off the slats. He sneered at the exposed wood. "Serves them right," he muttered to himself.

When he reached the end of the Burgess' fenced front lawn, he flung the stick into the street and stuffed his hand into his pocket, digging deep. The cigarette he had stolen from his step father was still there. His fingers felt around the paper shaft. It was unbent and still in one piece. He dug further. His lighter was still there, along with his retractable switchblade. He had stolen it from his real father a few years before he died. It had remained his constant possession ever since. If the school had found out he carried it, he might have gotten suspended again—or worse, expelled—but Max made a habit of avoiding detection. The idea of being at home all day with his mom and her boyfriend disgusted and terrified him, so it was common sense not to get caught breaking the big, suspension-worthy rules. He kept to himself, avoiding the jocks who would try to provoke him into a fist fight just to prove they were Alpha Males.

As Max turned the corner of Wing Street, Rick Sigurdsson, a neighbor who was a firefighter, came out of his house to collect his newspaper from the front lawn. Rick's job always reminded Max of his father's job in the military saving lives and rescuing people from danger and death. That is, before Max's father slipped off the deep end and committed suicide. Either way, Rick was cool and he was nice to Max even though most of the police department thought Max was a delinquent, and they were just waiting for the boy to cross the line into real-crime territory so they could arrest him and haul him off to the county jail.

"Hi Mr. Sigurdsson," Max said with a smile and a wave.

Last summer, Rick had paid Max to mow his lawn every week with one of those human-powered push mowers. Afterward, he would always invite Max in for a tall glass of milk and a cheese sandwich while he poked around his wallet for the twenty dollars to pay him with, about double the going rate for a lawn the size of Rick's. Max knew Rick felt sorry for him, but it didn't matter. The food was always a nice perk, and the older man wasn't too hard for the boy to figure out, either. Not like most grown-ups. The firefighter would always have this sagging look on his face, as if a clothespin had clasped the skin between his eyebrows and pulled his features upward.

Everyone in town knew that the man had lost his wife and son in a car accident the previous year, so Max kind of figured Rick was nice to him because he felt bad for him. The hand-me-down clothes which were two sizes too big on Max coupled with the unkempt mullet that clung to his head made it obvious that the boy wasn't exactly the star of the show at home. So, when Rick began inviting Max over to watch sporting events, the boy always found a way to sneak out of the house and visit without his parent's knowledge. Then the firefighter and the teen would lounge on the couch all afternoon, drinking root beer and eating popcorn as they shouted at the referees making bad calls. It was always the highpoint of Max's week.

Today, however, it did not appear that Rick was having any fun. His face was ashen: paper white in the cheeks and forehead, but black as pine pitch beneath the eyes. His nose was rubbed so red and raw, Max could see the cracks where blood had started to seep through the skin even from where he stood at the end of his buddy's driveway.

Rick returned Max's wave weakly, as if his arm were suspended by a marionette string controlled by some unseen operator hiding on the rooftop. The smile fell from Max's face.

Jogging up the driveway, Max asked, "Are you all right, Mr. Sigurdsson?"

Rick held up a hand as if to stop the boy from coming closer, but Max kept running toward him. He stopped about two feet in front of Rick, who recoiled slightly in response, covering his mouth with his hand.

"Just got a little case of the flu, I think." Muffled by his hand, Rick's voice was ragged and weak. "You should stay back, Max. I wouldn't want you to catch this, too. It's not much fun." The man tried to smile, but was racked by a long, rasping cough that visibly rattled his chest. When he withdrew his hand from his mouth, Max could see the unmistakable splotch of red that had collected there.

"Is that blood, Mr. Sigurdsson?" the boy asked incredulously, leaning forward to get a better view of Rick's hand.

"It's nothing," said Rick, thrusting his hand into the pocket of his bathrobe. "Don't worry about me, son. " Rick looked up and down the street. "Shouldn't you be at school?"

Max knew the man was trying to change the subject, but he didn't argue the fact. He looked at the ground. "Yes, sir."

"Well, why aren't you there, then, my young friend?"

"Guess I'm running late again."

Even with his chapped and cracking face, Rick managed to look as stern and disappointed as possible. He peered down his nose at Max. "You're going to end up with another detention. Is that what you want?" His brow creased as he absently wiped under his nose with the back of his hand. "I'm on call today, sick as I may be, Max. I'd hear on the scanner if the truancy officer should pick anybody up. You know what I'm saying?"

Rubbing the toes of his sneakers together, Max pressed his lips together. He recognized the tone that Rick had taken as disappointment, but it sent a bubble of contentment rushing up through Max's body. He shivered slightly. It reminded Max exactly how his father used to talk to him before he was gone. How he'd get so disappointed when Max would get caught doing something wrong. How his eyes would start to sparkle as if he was about to cry.

"Yes sir," Max said with respect. "And, no sir. I don't want detention."

Rick pulled his shoulders back. "Then perhaps you'd best be getting off to school then, okay?"

"Yes sir," said Max. He turned to leave, but stopped short, an idea dawning on him. He looked back over his shoulder at Rick. "Is it all right if I stop by after school to, you know, help you with anything? I could clean up for you while you get better, or make you a can of chicken noodle soup, or something."

"Sure, Max. Just make sure you tell your mother so she doesn't worry," said Rick. "To be honest, I think I would appreciate the help. I'm just not myself, today."

"Thank you, Mr. Sigurdsson." The boy smiled and gave a quick wave, then jogged down the driveway and along the sidewalk toward school. He was probably going to be late. Maybe he could slip into first period without being noticed. His history teacher was, after all, kind of a flake.

CHAPTER FIVE

Kiley

Rachel pulled the car into the circle in front of the middle school. Kiley grabbed her backpack, swung open the car door and, without a word to her sister, slammed it shut. She walked slowly around the rear of the car as it pulled away from the cul de sac. Glancing at the passenger side door, she caught a glimpse of Bryan. He waved. Immediately, a storm of ravens fluttered wildly inside Kiley's abdomen. Her lips curled into a smile as her cheeks reddened slightly. She looked at the ground.

Bryan is so crazy smart and hot, she thought. *I don't understand what he is doing with my extra-crispy, side of cocoa butter sister. He's not even as old as her. Isn't the boy supposed to be the older one?* She paused, the tip of her combat boot toeing the gravel in the ditch beside the circle. *That's why he'd be perfect for me. I'm younger and prettier and way cooler. And at least I didn't get my fashion sense from that sad and pathetic pastel preppie store with the creepy, talking mannequin commercials.*

"The pleather and stripey socks goth store is way cooler, my sister, the sheep," she whispered in the direction her sister had just driven.

With a sigh, Kiley stepped onto the curb and plodded toward the bike rack where she and her friend, Emma, usually met before school. Looking up, she saw the rack was completely empty. Usually there were at least six bikes chained between the metal bars of the rack, and sulky Emma would be leaning against the back of it, texting all those lucky tweeners who had their own cell phones—unlike Kiley whose mother thought she was too young for that sort of thing.

But Emma was not at their usual haunt today. In fact, no one was. The place was eerily deserted.

Twisting her head slowly from side to side, Kiley scanned the campus for a sign of her friend. Her mouth went slack. The yard around the school was empty except for a single pigeon bobbing its head in the gutter, looking for food scrapings and cast-offs.

The muscles in Kiley's face tightened, her eyes squinting. *Where is everybody?* She thought. A tickling sensation like a spider crawling quickly up her spine caused her to shudder, her shoulders rising slightly. Turning her gaze to the brick stairway leading up to the front doors of the middle school, Kiley caught sight of a lone piece of crumpled paper rolling tumbleweed-style across the brick and stone walkway. She reached for it, chasing after it as the paper scuttled along the ground until her hand came to rest on it. She wrestled it from the wind's grasp.

Standing upright, she unfolded the note. An ink-doodled sketch of a teacher in the bottom corner caught her eye. From the scribbled messy bun and fuzzy cardigan, the image was unmistakably Miss Snellar, the seventh grade history teacher at Greendale Middle School. Next to the image was a hastily scribbled phrase inside a caption bubble like the ones people drew in comic books. The speech bubble coming out of her mouth read, "Oh boo hoo. I'm too sick to teach and all the substitutes are sick too, so you all have to spend the day running laps in the high school gym." Below the drawing was the poorly-lettered phrase, "School sux."

"That's odd," she said, her voice seeming to echo across the empty campus. She glanced at her watch. The number 7:55 blinked up at her. *School hasn't even started yet. And this can't be from yesterday, because I spent the whole day in an in-school suspension in the library for spitting on Thomas's breakfast sandwich,* and—she let the thought trail off. She hadn't noticed anything about merged classes yesterday, and she certainly would have noticed if a whole class of students marched past the library doors in the middle of a class period. In fact, everything had seemed perfectly normal yesterday—apart from the fact that she'd spent the day isolated from the rest of her classmates, alone with the librarian, reading vampire novels hidden in the fold-out of an oversized science textbook.

Suspicion crept up the length of her neck. She tried to brush it away, swishing a few strands of black-tipped, red hair across the nape, but the tiny threads of fuzz that coated her skin tingled there and she shivered.

"I am *not* creeped out. I am *not* creeped out," she repeated under her breath. "I am the Queen of Creeps. Nothing scares me except bobbleheads, and I don't see any of those around here right now." She took a few deliberate steps toward the front doors to the school.

As she started walking up the stairs, something occurred to her. *Why would they merge middle school history with the high school phys ed, anyway? Were they doing historical reenactments of battle preparations, or something ridiculous?* Kiley grinned as she imagined a room full of her classmates donning Civil War regalia and performing calisthenics in the high school gym until the gym teacher clapped her hands together and shouted "Change up!"

Her smile quickly faded, though, as a new thought occurred to her.

How can everyone be sick at the same time, though? As if the answer hung in the air above Kiley's head, she reached a hand beside her ear and closed her fingers together as if to grab it.

"Smallpox," she said, her eyes glazed as she gazed into the distance. Inadvertently, her black-nailed fingers rose to her neck and began scratching the surface of the skin over her collar bone as she walked.

Kiley reached the top of the stairs and stood before the double doors. The hallway behind the doors was dark. Her fingers stopped scratching at her red-streaked neck and moved toward the glass of the door window before halting abruptly.

"Was smallpox spread through touching stuff?" she asked the air.

She closed her eyes. "I'm *not* creeped out," she said with some authority before she finally cupped her hands to the glass and peered inside. The hall was deserted. She tried to turn the handle, but the door was locked and only shook on its hinges as she tugged. A nervous, hollow feeling swept through her, pinching the nerves inside as dryness in her mouth prevented her from swallowing. She closed her eyes as a mouthful of stomach acid shot up to the back of her throat. She gulped it down.

Definitely smallpox, she thought, closing her eyes and leaning on the door for support. Her free hand rose to her neck again and recoiled dramatically at the sensation of the warmth rising from the red welts she'd caused while scratching. Her head jerked to attention.

"Oh. My. God or Goddess," she said out loud. "There's the rash." Her mind raced. *I can already feel the heat and tenderness from the rash developing on my skin. Soon I'll be overtaken by fever. And—and just a minute ago I was about to vomit. It's too late. I've got smallpox. I'm done for.* She lifted the back of her hand to her forehead in a silver screen, silent movie pose and gulped hard.

"I'm already delirious," she moaned., her eyes closing. She slid her hand down her face and touched the skin on her neck again and remembered the scratching from minutes before. Straightening her posture, she snorted at herself and looked around the school porch to see if anyone was watching.

"Where is everybody?" she shouted as she turned to face the campus. She glanced at her watch again. 7:58. "Not that I'm complaining, milquetoast school officials who may be within earshot, but shouldn't school be starting now? What the *hell* is going on?" She placed deliberate emphasis on the curse word, certain that any adult who might be lingering about would slap her with a detention at the sound of it.

But nothing happened.

She dropped her gaze to the toe of her boot where the leather had split and scarred from kicking tree stumps and rocks in the woods behind the school.

"That's what I'd like to know."

Kiley jumped at the voice, and spun on her heel. Standing doubled-over at the waist with his hands resting on his knees was Max Sheldon, the biggest waste of breath in her class and possibly the last person she wanted to see that morning.

The boy struggled to catch his breath. "I just ran around the entire building. The place is locked up tighter than the White House." His chest heaved as he spouted out the words. He looked over his shoulder to the hill that connected the middle school to the high school campus. "I was just about to walk up to the high school to see what was going on when I saw you trying to get in. I mean, if school is canceled, I do have things I could be doing." He sucked in a deep breath and rose to an upright position.

Kiley's upper lip pulled backwards against her teeth. "Like killing squirrels or shooting heroin, or some other delightful trailer park activity?" The moment the words passed her lips, she regretted it. She could see the cloud rolling over his face and she bit the inside of her lower lip, determined not to apologize. *Never lose face*, she thought.

If he was right and there wasn't anybody at the middle school, then things were definitely weird. Max might be her only source of companionship at the moment. *Strength in numbers, after all.* Her mind whirled. Dropping her gaze, she reconsidered the need to apologize. As she opened her mouth to say the words, she was cut off.

"I thought Lady Death would get her rocks off sacrificing squirrels to the Earth Mother, or whatever," Max said, his back stiffening.

"I worship Bast, the Egyptian cat goddess of the undead, freak," she said coldly. "Not that a backwoods billy like you would know who Bast was, or anything. I mean, you'd have to crack a book sometime to figure it out."

A frown pulled the corners of his mouth hard against his face. "We don't have to be like this," he said. "I didn't mean to say—I mean, I was just trying to be nice before you got all snarky with me. There's no one around you have to impress by being mean to me, and I'd rather just be nice to you." He lifted his hands palm up the way people in the movies do during a bank heist when the robbers stick guns in their faces.

Kiley blushed, her eyes dipping down to stare at gum someone's shoe had mashed into the brick of the stairs. Sheepishly, she apologized. "I'm sorry. Goth, you know? Mean kinda goes with the eyeliner." She grinned, searching Max's face for a sign, but the boy remained motionless. "Guess that was a dumb thing to say," she said at last.

Max relaxed. "Do you want to walk up to the high school with me?" he asked, his voice flat and low like the electronic voice of a computer reading over a page of text. Poker-face voice. It matched his personality making him hard to read which, she figured, might be one of the reasons for his reputation around school as a tough guy. But something in his eyes, a sorrow that glittered there like a rain-streaked window pane, moved her. There was a small crack in Max's cold façade and she saw herself reflected there. And just like that, she trusted him.

Taking a deep breath, she filled up her lungs before letting out a sigh. Without moving her head, her eyes scanned the campus lawn one last time. Still no sign of Emma. No sign of anyone. She made up her mind on the spot.

Gulping audibly and straightening her back, she flung her backpack over her shoulder. "Sure. My sister and her boyfriend just drove up there, anyway. They usually make out in the parking lot awhile before going inside, so if we hurry, we might catch them tonsils-deep in a little tongue action."

Smirking, Max turned toward the hill, thrust his hands in his pockets, and began walking. Kiley followed close behind.

CHAPTER SIX

Bryan and Rachel

Patting the dashboard as if it were a compliant puppy, Rachel eased the silver VW Golf into a spot in the high school parking lot. "Good girl," she said, giving the dash a final pat. She shifted into park and turned off the ignition. She cleared a tickle from the back of her throat and sniffled discreetly, then turned toward Bryan with a sly grin on her face and leaned in to kiss him. Just as their lips were about to make contact, however, Bryan's head jerked sharply to the right. She pulled back.

"What the heck, Bryan?" she protested as she whacked him in the chest with the palm of her hand.

"Dammit, Rachel. What are you hitting me for?" he asked, rubbing his chest.

"I was trying to kiss you, loser, and you didn't even notice. You were all like 'oh, I'm too cool to be kissed by *you*,'" she said, affecting a whiny, sing-song voice for the last part. Without hesitation, Bryan leaned in and planted a soft, quick kiss on her lips, startling her.

"Is that better?"

"Much."

"Good," said Bryan, pulling away from her face. "Now that we have that out of the way, can you look around at this parking lot for a second and tell me what's wrong with this picture? What time do you have on your cell phone? Because, I thought it was just about eight o'clock, but by the looks of this parking lot it feels like we are way early, or way late."

Rachel snorted. "Whatever," she said, reaching for her bag. As she fumbled through the confines of her fake Coach bag, she said, "I think some people shouldn't look gift horses in the mouth. I think some people should be excited to realize they might have extra time to spend alone with their girlfriend." She found her cell phone and pulled it out. Cocking an eyebrow, she added, "In a parking lot. With no one in sight. Possibly for hours. Just the two of them. No drama queen sister in the backseat yapping on about diseases and death." Her voice clicked on each syllable, stressing every sound for effect.

Grinning, Bryan swiped the cell phone from her hand. Flipping it open, he said, "I got a gift horse for my fourth birthday from my mom. It was a great gift horse. Palomino. Dad had a stable built for it, and everything. I brushed it every day, and you know what? No one ever looked that thing in the mouth. Except maybe the Vet, I guess, but I was never there for that. What does that even mean?" The time on the cell phone read 8:03 a.m. He held it out for Rachel to see. "We're not early, Rachel. We're late."

She plucked the phone from his hands. "Well, you don't have to *look* in my mouth, hottie. You could just slink around it with your tongue."

"Like this?" he asked. He dropped his tongue from his gaping mouth, crossed his eyes and made a groaning noise. "I'm coming to kith you, Barbawa," he added with a lisp as he tried to press his tongue against her cheek.

"Gross," said Rachel, playfully pushing him away. "You are such a freakazoid weirdo sometimes, Bryan. Maybe you're the one related to Madame Gothy Freak, and not me. What the hell was that? Some zombie movie, right?"

Bryan licked the side of her face and grinned as she frantically wiped it off with the back of her hand while she repeated "Ew, ew, ew."

He leaned back. "As much as I would love to continue tonguing my girlfriend in the parking lot, it is kind of weird that no one is here, don't you think?" he said. "We should go up to the high school and check things out. Maybe there's a note on the door or something."

"Yes. It'll read: *Dear Bryan and Rachel. School is closed today. Please take this opportunity to make-out in the shed behind the school. There will be a quiz on proper oral hygiene next Thursday.*"

"Uh, or it might say: *Danger. Gas Leak.*" He raised both his eyebrows.

"Fine," she groaned. "I think I have this stupid cold that's been going around anyway. I wouldn't want you to catch my germs," Rachel sulked.

"Baby, I *live* for your germs. Give me leprosy, or give me death."

Rachel laughed. "God, she's such a freak, right?"

"I dunno," Bryan said with a shrug. "She's just a little lost, I guess."

Rachel rolled her eyes and decided to change the subject. "Maybe school is canceled. My mother told me that they canceled school in Brighton a few months ago because some maintenance workers discovered asbestos in the ceilings. It was an all of a sudden thing, too. Like, everyone was in school and then, poof. They were all sent home. Just like that. No warning. No mass hysteria. No blaring alarms or people jumping up and down, waving their arms at students trying to get inside. No muss, no fuss, no—"

Bryan interrupted her. "I get the point, Rachel. Maybe you should call your parents and ask them to check the news. Maybe they could log into the school's website and check if school was canceled and we just didn't get the memo. Then they could call us back."

"Damn. I wish my parents hadn't shut off my cell's internet connection," she grumbled, as she punched her home number into the cell. "You update your social network page just fourteen times during school hours, and suddenly they're all *Oh, Rachel. Uh, that's not an appropriate use of your time, Rachel.*" Her head shook from side to side as she affected a deep, sarcastic voice before pressing the phone to her ear.

The phone rang six times. Bryan could hear the mechanical voices of Rachel's parents humming incoherent words before a beep blared through the phone's small speaker.

"They weren't feeling good this morning," Rachel offered. "They've probably called out sick from work and turned the ringer off." She thrust the phone into Bryan's hand. "Try calling your dad."

His hand wrapped dumbly around the phone. "I can't. He left for Chicago on a business trip right after you picked me up this morning. Probably at a security checkpoint at the airport by now. I could call the housekeeper."

"Just try your dad anyway. He hasn't had enough time to get to the airport already. Even if he's there, he probably hasn't made it through the security line yet. It takes forever these days. He might be able to check out the news in the terminal."

"Fine," Bryan sighed. He punched in the numbers to his father's cell phone. The sound of his father's voice rang cheerfully in his ear as the phone went straight to voice mail. "No luck. Voicemail." He held the phone up for Rachel to hear.

She frowned. "All right," she said. "Let's walk up to the high school then, and see if someone's there. Maybe your precious sign is posted on the door, lover." She pulled the handle and pushed the car door open. "Come on."

Looping his bag over his shoulder, Bryan opened his door and stepped out. He still clung to Rachel's cell phone as he slammed the passenger side door closed. He thrust the phone absently into his pocket.

The Greendale High School parking lot was at the top of a steep hill, surrounded by a cluster of trees. Orange and red leaves clung to the branches as a cool autumn breeze scuttled through them. As it was still early in the school year, the foliage was too thick in some places to see past the bend in the road or down the steep hill toward the middle school, but from where they stood, Bryan and Rachel had a view of the lake at the bottom of the hill on the opposite side of the school. The path leading up to the school was clear of all but a few staggered trees and park benches, caged trash cans and bicycle racks. There wasn't a soul in sight. No teachers and no students. Not in the parking lot or near it. Not on the path to either school, nor on the path through the mini-forest to the gazebo where the cheerleaders and football players met to sneak cigarettes and the occasional joint.

"Maybe we should check on your sister before we head up to the school," Bryan suggested.

Rachel placed both hands on her hips, resting her weight on her left leg and thrusting her right hip forward. She let out a harsh sigh. "Just which one of us are you more interested in, Bryan? Me or my sister the vampire? You want her to bite your neck? Is that it? You into the kinky stuff?"

Before he could stop himself, Bryan laughed, but Rachel's stance didn't budge an inch. Even her face remained stone rigid. He shook off the laugh, and said, "Are you serious, Rachel? Your sister is like, what? Ten? Give me a break. This isn't Lolita, Rachel."

But it wasn't Rachel who responded to him.

"I'm twelve, thank you very much." Kiley's calm voice rang out against the stillness of the high school campus as she and Max crested the hill and walked toward them. Drawing closer, she added, "Besides, Bryan, you're only fifteen."

"Almost sixteen. I have my permit," Bryan snapped.

Kiley continued, ignoring him. "We're like, 2 ½ years apart. My *sister* on the other hand is almost eighteen. What do you two see in each other? Do you get kicks out of washing her dentures each night and cutting tennis balls for the bottom of her walker? She's like thirty compared to you. You don't even have classes together. You're like her pet. Completely whipped." She made a whipping motion with her hand and punctuated it with a swooshing sound effect. "She's only into you because you do whatever she tells you to do and you have a lot of money which you spend on stupid presents for her, like diamond earrings? Or that ultra-thin laptop? What do you think she sees in you, Bryan? A lapdog. That's what." Deliberately avoiding his gaze, Kiley set to work straightening imaginary wrinkles in her black, puffed-sleeve blouse.

Bryan stared at her, mouth dropped open. He couldn't remember a time she had ever spoken to him with such authority, not to mention the thinly disguised disgust in her voice. She was Kiley. She was his girlfriend's little sister. Sure, she wore pants with hundreds of safety pins through them and put on black lipstick before going to the thrift store, but she was innocent.

Childlike, right? If there were a person more benign and sweet than Kiley, in spite of all her gothic veneer, he had yet to meet her. He stared at Kiley for a moment then turned his head toward Rachel, who stood with a smirk on her face.

"Hey," he retorted. "I'm not your lapdog. And she knocked you, too. Are you really just a gold-digger, Rachel? Is that all you see in me?"

The smirk vanished, and Rachel turned on her sister. "Yeah. What the hell business is any of that to you, Coyote? I buy him presents, too. And I don't care if he's younger. He's the hottest boy in school." She stole a quick glance at Bryan before returning her gaze to her sister. "Or are you just jealous? Is that it? Does itty bitty Kile E. Coyote have a crush on my boyfriend?"

The sound that came from Kiley's mouth was somewhere between a cough and a laugh at the sound of her childhood nickname–" Kile E. Coyote". Refusing to meet her gaze, she said, "Sure. Whatever."

Max cleared his throat. "Excuse me, but if we're done with the cat-fight, pissing contest, do you think we can talk about how the world seems to have vanished in the time it took me to get from my neighbor's house to the school? I mean, your dysfunctional family soap opera thing is entertaining and all, but am I the only one who thinks that the Houdini act both schools have pulled is just a little weird?"

"Do I know you?" Bryan asked, crossing his arms over his chest. "Are you a friend of Kiley's?"

Kiley snorted. "So not. This is Max Sheldon? Stayed back twice? Beat up that sophomore jock kid last summer because he spilled his Big Gulp on Max's jacket? Come on. Everyone knows Max."

A slight smile rose on Max's lips as he eyed Kiley for a moment before looking at the ground. "I didn't mean to fight that kid. He stained my only nice shirt. That's all."

"Yeah, well you won, didn't you?" asked Kiley before turning to face Bryan again. "He's like a total badass, Bryan. So I'm thinking you don't want to piss him off."

"Look, I didn't mean any offense to your little friend, Kiley. I'm just trying to say that we shouldn't jump to conclusions,"

Bryan said. "I mean, there has to be a logical explanation for this, right?" His eyes pleaded with Rachel's for a sign of recognition or support. She opened her mouth to speak, but only a squeak came out. She coughed and cleared her throat. Bryan looked at her with concern, but she smiled at him and shook her head.

Ignoring her, Kiley asked, "Who's jumping to conclusions? Max didn't say anything about why there's nobody here. He just said it was weird. And it is weird. Don't you think?"

"Well, whatever the hell is going on, we're not going to find out by standing around here all morning arguing." Rachel sniffled as she started up the path toward the high school's main entrance. "Are you coming, or what?" she asked when no one followed. Max and Kiley exchanged looks. He nodded meaningfully at her, and they started up the hill as well, a few strides behind Rachel.

Bryan stood there for a moment, watching the others walk, a feeling of discomfort washing over him. Tingling at his scalp just below the hairline and traveling down his spine like a thousand insects playing leapfrog on his back, the sensation set the muscles in his shoulders and hips twitching. His eyes focused on a red leaf curled like a cupped hand as it finger-walked past the car beside him near the tree line around the parking lot. Straightening his head, his mouth went dry and slack. As if on cue, a sound issued from the wooded area behind him. He turned his head toward the noise.

He wasn't sure what it was. A screech? A bird? A monster emerging from the closet of his imagination? Had he really heard it, or were his nerves playing tricks on him? Bryan looked up toward the others for a sign that they had heard the noise too, but they continued walking, growing smaller in the distance, without interruption. Rachel's arms swung widely at her sides. Kiley clung to her backpack, clutching it to her chest like a stack of books, and Max walked with his hands thrust deeply inside the pockets of his oversized trousers. Whatever Bryan might have heard, he was apparently the only one who had heard it. They were only a few dozen feet in front of him. How could they not have heard it? He looked around one last time, then hurried up the hill after them.

CHAPTER SEVEN

Sage

The clean morning light flowing through Sage's bedroom window had dusted away the room's shadows and returned it to full color. She walked to her sliding closet door and traced a finger along the branches of the Tree of Life mural her mother had painted when they first moved in. Gripping the handle camouflaged by one of the branches, she opened the closet door and switched on the closet light from the drawstring connected to it. The closet was immediately filled with the rosy hue of the light bulb.

Sage selected a pair of light blue jeans and a short-sleeved, blue shirt. She discarded her pajamas and put on the fresh set of clothes, topping it with a deep purple, felted cardigan with embroidered flowers for the pockets. She slid her feet into a pair of knee-high, stripey socks, tugging them up over her calf while she braced herself against the jamb for support. Grabbing Squiggly from the bed where she'd thrown him earlier, she carefully nestled him in the left pocket of her sweater.

Silently, the latch of her bedroom door scraped ever-so-gently against the door jamb, and the door swung open. The motion of the door was so quiet, so slow and deliberate, that Sage didn't notice it. What she did notice, however, was the sudden itch at the back of her neck, the tingling sensation that something somehow was not quite right.

Slowly, the girl lifted her head. The blunt-cut ends of her blond hair brushed against the nape of her neck, just below her ears, and amplified the tingling sensation that crawled over the skin of her neck. For a second, Sage focused all of her attention on the sound, listening so carefully she imagined she could feel the tiny hairs inside her ears vibrating with the sound waves of some scarcely audible noise. Her eyes narrowed and her breathing slowed as she concentrated hard on listening.

Was it just her imagination, or had she heard something? Why did she suddenly feel the sensation of cold steel slicing through her abdomen? Absently, her fingers fumbled through the pocket of her cardigan until she found the folds of Squiggly's back. Pinching the zipper between the pads of her index and middle fingers, she carefully began unzipping Squiggly's secret pouch. She was not fully aware of what she was doing. Was she going for her Swiss Army knife?

Why would I need that? she wondered, but she did not stop searching until her fingers closed around the tiny, plastic handle, and the fingernail of her thumb pressed into the crescent moon latch of the knife blade. Without changing her stance, she slowly rotated her neck to the right as she cast her gaze over her shoulder.

The door to her room was still in its slow-motion swing, the knob poised to bounce into the protective stop fastened to the wall. With fear trickling through her bloodstream and frosting her arteries from the inside out, Sage expected to see a clown or something at least equally terrifying standing in the hallway, so she was pleasantly surprised when the familiar silhouette of her father appeared instead. It wasn't until she took a breath of relief that she realized for the first time that she had not been breathing for several seconds.

"Dad, you startled me," she admitted, staring at him warily as the adrenaline from moments before still coursed through her blood. "I'm almost ready to go."

Her father's head was bowed slightly so that the pupils of his almost glowing eyes seemed to be looking up at her. Her relief in seeing him seemed to be in direct conflict with the illogical fear still lingering in the pit of her stomach. Her veins still felt sickly cold and her eyelids still twittered as if they had minds of their own. Some instinct within her told her to keep her eyes open and remain observant and ready—for what, she didn't know. Even her hand continued its intuitive caress of the knife, as her thumb nail nudged the blade free from its handle. *What's wrong with me,* she thought. *This is my dad.*

Ben stood in the hallway, blocking Sage's path He seemed oblivious to her presence as he stood there unmoving, save for the shallow heaving of his chest. His hands hung loosely at his sides, fingers splayed like a cat's paws. The only sound was that of his breath, ragged and labored, as if he had just come in from a run. Or was that Sage's breath she heard?

"Dad, is everything okay?" Her voice wavered. *Why am I so afraid? Something's wrong. But this is Daddy.* Sage's mind raced. Logic battled emotion. The memory of her last advanced biology class the year she'd been home-schooled flickered in the back of her mind and she knew her cerebral process and her central nervous system were at odds with one another, each unwilling to give up control. Her mind rationalized that her father was a safe person, while her gut told her he was dangerous.

The silence seemed to swallow the room as Ben ignored her. Sage imagined she and her father were trapped in the belly of a whale, bouncing deafeningly about in the void as her father stood there, unmoving, without so much as a nod in her direction.

"Daddy, please answer." Sage started as her mother appeared in the hallway from the direction of the kitchen. Sage bit her lip.

Ben took a step toward his daughter, but Deidra was too quick. Wielding the wrought iron frying pan she had used that morning for facon, she brought her arm up hard and fast against the back of Ben's skull. Sage heard a sickening crack and the metal of the skillet sent an echo twanging through the room. He fell, face-first, his head bouncing against Sage's springy mattress before jerking to the hardwood floor below.

Sage screamed.

Deidra dropped the skillet with an ear-splitting bang and stepped quickly over Ben's fallen body. Kneeling in front of Sage, she grabbed her daughter by the shoulders and shook her until the screaming faded. Tears streamed down Sage's face as she turned to face her mother. There was blood on her mother's arm and a streak of it across her forehead. As the red inked in her eyes, she looked to Sage less like her mother and more like an irrational monster. A patricidal demon.

Deidra wept, and thin streams of red icing rolled over her cheeks.

"Sage, you have to listen to me." Deidra's voice was high-pitched and wavering as if a scream hovered around the edges of her voice box. "Your father– he–I don't know what happened, he just—" Deidra turned to look at the body lying on the floor, but her vision was blocked by the bed between them.

When her mother turned her head, Sage could see a fresh, jagged gash along the side of her neck. She also noticed four parallel slashes under her mother's chin that were so deep she could see the blood pumping up from within. Sage's eyes widened as she held her breath.

Deidra's fingers tightened on her daughter's shoulders. "Sage, your daddy is sick, okay? I don't know what is happening, baby, and it's hard to explain to you. He just turned on me in the kitchen. Out of nowhere. Just like yesterday at the green–" Deidra let the sentence trail, her gaze drifting downward.

"Your father," she said, pulling a hand away from her daughter's shoulder and touching a tentative finger to the wound in her neck. Her finger recoiled at the wetness. "He bit me." Her gaze drifted to the floor. Pausing only for a second, she stood quickly and grabbed Sage's backpack from where it sat on the floor beside the bed.

"We've gotta go," she said. "Now." She tossed the bag to Sage who barely had time to respond and catch it. Blood glistened bright red against the pale skin of her mother's arm. A damp halo of blood stretched from the armpit of her dress to her waistline where blood had dripped, or sprayed, along the side of her mother's body.

Gripping the wrinkled straps of her backpack with whitening knuckles, Sage stood unmoving. "I don't understand," she said quietly, her voice barely above a whisper. "This can't be happening."

When her daughter failed to move, Deidra's face raged red as the tip of a blazing thermometer. The veins in her cheeks and forehead seemed to rise to the surface of her skin, pulsing in time to the beat of her heart. Before Sage had time to react, the back of Deidra's hand struck the side of Sage's head hard enough to spin her around. Tears burst from Sage's eyes as she ran her fingers gently over her stinging face. Her mother had never struck her before.

"Well, it is happening, and you better listen close! Pack your damn bag because we have to get out of here right now." Deidra's voice echoed loudly, and Sage had to push her fingertips into the pockets of her ears to keep them from throbbing. A steely hand gripped Sage's upper arm hard, ripping her hand away from her face. The girl refused to meet her mother's gaze.

"Now is not the time for a rebellious streak, little girl. I said now," her mother said, pushing Sage across the room toward her closet. Sage steadied herself on the edge of her desk. A quick glance at her father confirmed he was still passed out on the floor, half-blocking the doorway. She was relieved to see his chest moving up and down with his rapid breathing.

Aware that her mother's eyes were trained on her, Sage started filling her backpack with whatever her hands happened to pass over, trying to stay calm under the watchful eye of her mother, who now seemed to have transformed into an unidentifiable monster. Sage fought to keep the tears from her eyes. She was still reeling from the fact that her mother had hit her. She'd never struck anyone before that Sage was aware of, and now she'd hit her own child. Barely realizing what she was doing, she plucked a sewing kit from her desk and stuffed it in her already heaving bag. She grabbed a random book from her bookshelf, a handful of clean socks, a pair of pants and a nightgown. When her bag was full, Sage zipped it quickly and thrust both her arms through the arm holes, tightening the straps so that it was secure on her back.

"I think I'm ready," she said. "But shouldn't we get some help for Dad? I think you hurt him badly."

"Don't worry about your dad right now, okay? He's fine. He'll be fine. Just do as I say right now," she said."I just need to get the keys to the jeep."

Deidra walked around the bed toward the fallen body of her partner, the father of her child. Sage pressed herself against the closet door as her mother passed. Squatting, Deidra plunged her hand into Ben's side pocket, rocking his body in the process. A short groan drifted up from his upturned body. Deidra immediately stopped digging and held perfectly still.

Slowly, Deidra turned to face her daughter. She mouthed the words "go now" without so much as a whisper. Sage stood frozen, her breath coming hard and fast. She couldn't believe what was happening. In the short moments it took Sage to walk from the kitchen to her bedroom and get dressed, her father had attacked—no, he had *bitten* her mother? Scratched her face with his fingers? And then, he had walked down the hall to Sage's bedroom to—to what? Attack her next? To bite and scratch her? But, this was her daddy. This was the man who put Bandaids on her knees when she fell off her bike. The man who read storybooks to her every night, acting out all the characters and bounding about the room as he read. This was the man who had never, not once, hit Sage to discipline her or scare her or, well, anything. And now, he was lying on the floor of her bedroom. His breath was ragged and a slow pool of blood cradled his head. And, what's worse, her mother—her peace-loving, organic, vegetarian, animal-rights-activist mother—was the one responsible for it.

Sage's silent reverie was interrupted by a faint hissing sound coming from Deidra's direction. The girl shivered when her mother mouthed "go" once more and jerked her head toward the doorway. With her free hand, Deidra pointed toward Ben's pocket and made a steering wheel motion. Sage nodded.

Her stockinged foot slid tentatively across the hardwood of her bedroom floor as if her feet and her head had different ideas about what she should do. She watched her father's supine figure as his chest rose up and down rapidly. Somehow, the image of him breathing, the simple thought that he still had air in his lungs, was a comfort to Sage in spite of all the bloody evidence on her mother's face and clothes.

As Sage inched closer to her parents, a strange thought crept into the corners of her mind. *What if–What if Dad hadn't really attacked Mom? After all, Dad was awake a moment ago. He could have told me something bad, something that Mom did. Until she knocked him out, of course. What if Mom, for whatever reason, attacked herself and–and Dad was on his way to protect me—just like Mom was maybe pretending to do?* It was a startling thought, and it was just as unlikely as the scenario her mother had proposed when she barged into her bedroom and knocked her father out with a frying pan. It was all just too much, but she couldn't ignore the possibility, and as soon as the thought popped into her head, her eyes drifted warily to her mother's face. Deidra stared at her intently, her eyes glistening.

Sage quickly snapped her eyes back in front of her, afraid that, somehow, her mother might be able to see the doubt in them. That she might somehow recognize her daughter was contemplating the feasibility of the impossible scenario before her. As the girl's feet slid carefully toward her mother's crouching form and her father's nearly lifeless body, Sage paused for a moment, trembling slightly. Her eyes drifted carefully toward her mother's hands. One of them was hidden in the confines of Ben's pocket, but the other was clearly visible as it rested on her straining knee. From the corner of her eyes, Sage strained to see her mother's fingertips. Was that blood caked under them? Or was it simply blood that had stained them from touching her neck moments earlier?

Sage knew she couldn't be sure.

Her father's body lay in the alcove of the doorway, blocking the entrance. If Sage misjudged her step, or if her legs weren't long enough to stride over her father's torso, she might land precisely in the middle of his splayed legs and rouse him back to consciousness. *On the other hand,* thought Sage, *if I were to accidentally step on him and wake him up, maybe I could learn the truth about what is really happening, and if necessary, he could get me away from Mom.*

Her eyes darted to her mother's face again. Deidra's mouth was open, her head nodding from the intensity of her heavy breath. Around the irises of her mother's eyes, Sage could see an eclipse—of blood forming.

The fear that spread through Sage was nearly crippling. Should she blindly trust her mother and leave her father behind to—to what? Suffer? Die? Or, should she pretend to stumble, accidentally planting a foot on her father's thigh or back, waking him up? And what then? What if he really had been violent? What if he really had attacked her mother in the kitchen? Would Sage be safe from either of them? Her mind was reeling. These were her parents whom she loved effortlessly. How could she even answer such questions? Nothing seemed real. It was all just too hard to believe, let alone understand.

Lifting a leg, Sage let her foot dangle in the air for an instant before allowing it to drop neatly between her father's limp legs. A quick glance at his chest revealed no signs of movement, but his breathing seemed to have slowed from its labored, jagged pace. *Was he simply unconscious? It was as if he were in a deep sleep. Was he dreaming? Was she dreaming?*

Before Sage had time to consider her next move, Deidra dropped her knees silently to the floor and positioned herself to hoist Ben up slightly. Without further hesitation, Sage pulled her other foot cleanly over her father's body to the floor between his legs and shimmied along the polished wood grain, careful not to nudge her father as she moved. It was a slow process, but a moment later, she had made it past her father's sprawled body and into the hallway.

She turned, but as she stepped away, she twisted her head to watch as her mother tipped Ben's body to the side and shoved her hand roughly into the pocket of his lounge pants, tipping his body up and away from the floor. Sage's eyes were drawn to her father's back.

Something was different.

Only a moment ago, she had noticed his back moving as his body labored to fill his lungs with air. But now, there was no movement. He was still as stone.

Is he holding his breath? Sage tried to imagine why he would hold his breath when suddenly it dawned on her that he wasn't holding his breath at all.

He was dead.

"Mom," she shouted, tears filling her eyes. Deidra jerked her head up, her hand sliding quickly out of Ben's pocket as the corners of her mouth curled upward. Coiled in her hand like a cluster of precious gems was Ben's keychain. A triumphant smile lingered on her mouth as her gaze shifted from the keys to Sage's face.

Her triumph was short-lived.

Ben's head jerked upward from the floor, his neck pivoting toward Deidra who was still smiling at her daughter. At the sight of her father's face, Sage's mouth dropped open and a glass-shattering scream echoed from the depths of her lungs. How could he move? He was dead a moment ago. He wasn't *breathing*.

His face was ashen as if completely drained of blood and the veins in his face and neck protruded darkly against his now pale, waxy flesh. The whites of his eyes had turned jet black, as if filled with old and poisoned ink. In the short moments her father had lain face down on the floor, his lips had cracked and split open in a vertical line from the divot of his nose to the point of his chin, creating an awkwardly gaping mouth. What was left of the skin that hung around his mouth was bloody and almost burned at the edges, as though acid had been thrown in his face and had begun eating away at the pulpy flesh, turning the once-pink membranes of his gums to a bluish grey. A dull whine escaped from his throat unlike any human sound Sage had ever heard, reminding her of tigers from the zoo. The sound startled Sage. She dropped her backpack and pressed herself back against the wall as if she was hoping to disappear through it.

As Deidra caught sight of the terrified expression on her daughter's face, her lips twisted with fear and she recoiled from her partner. Without hesitation, Ben opened his gaping mouth and clenched his jaw around his partner's forearm. Blood burst from the sides of his mouth as his teeth penetrated her soft skin. Deidra's scream rang out harmoniously with the high-pitched shriek of her daughter. The man jerked his head backward, tearing a chunk of bloody flesh from the arm of the woman who had mothered his child. A tendon and a scrap of muscle tissue stretched from her arm to his mouth like strands of drool and blood gushed sickeningly to a widening pool on the floor between them.

Unable to tear her eyes from the scene, Sage's gaze bounced from her father's horrific face to her mother's desperate eyes. Sage watched as the woman's eyes rolled back, a pool of blood visible around the bottom of her eyes like a saucer of red syrup. Her body swayed back and forth once before she collapsed with a thud face flat on the floor. The keys she had been holding bounced from her hand and skittered into the hallway.

Ben sat still, almost as if in a dream, as he lazily chewed the muscle fibers of Deidra's arm, seemingly unconcerned by the jingle of the keys as they bounced against the floor, or by Sage's shrill screaming as it echoed through the startling still hallway.

CHAPTER EIGHT

Bryan, Rachel, Kiley, and Max

"Hey!" Bryan called as he hurried up the grassy hill after the trio. "Did you guys just hear that?"

"Hear what?"Kiley asked, feigning indifference. She placed a hand on her hip and tilted her head as she waited for him to catch up to where she was standing.

"That weird roaring noise that just came from the woods over there?" Puffing with exertion, Bryan caught up with Kiley who now lingered at the back of the procession. He thrust his hands into his pockets, elbows turned out as he sucked air deep into his lungs.

Kiley rolled her eyes. "Let me guess. You have a treadmill in your bedroom that doubles as a towel rack, am I right? Try hitting the gym once in awhile."

"I have asthma," mumbled Bryan as he retrieved his inhaler from his pocket and sprayed a blast into his mouth.

"Do I look like your nurse?"

"Why are you suddenly so mean to me?" he puffed.

Kiley shifted uncomfortably, looking at the ground. "I dunno. I guess I just didn't like hearing you call me a child, or whatever. I am so not a Lolita. That book isn't even very good."

"You've read it?" he asked.

"Sure. Last summer. I read all the time. Unlike my preppie sister who thinks reading is for nerds."

Bryan smiled. "Yeah. Guess she thinks I'm a nerd."

Max had stopped walking and wandered back to meet Bryan and Kiley. Rachel barreled straight up the path toward the high school entrance.

"What's going on?" asked Max as he drew nearer.

Kiley huffed and turned back to Bryan. "Now you're just making creepy forest noises up to scare me," she said. "Just because the school is all Mary Celeste all of a sudden, you think you can spook me with ghost stories? Get real."

Max's head tilted slightly to the left as a look of confusion filled his face. Catching the squint of his eyes and the tension in his lips, Kiley shrugged. "Mary Celeste was a cruise ship, or something. You know? The one full of passengers in 1872 that was discovered in the middle of the ocean, floating around completely empty?"

Max blinked at her.

"The funny part was, nothing was missing," Kiley continued. "You must have heard this story. Don't you have Snellar for History? They found like two thousand barrels of alcohol untouched?"

Max shrugged.

"Well, it certainly makes it pretty believable that spooky things must have happened to them, right? I mean, if I were a pirate, I'd steal the liquor. Wouldn't you?"

"Unless it was rotgut," offered Bryan.

Kiley glared at him.

"You drink?" Max asked flatly, ignoring the inside joke.

"What?" The question caught Kiley off guard. She shifted nervously, stealing a sideways glance at Bryan who was staring straight at her. She felt a flush rising in her cheeks, and she swallowed hard, trying hard to push down the redness growing on her face. "Well, I am hardcore, you know. Hello? Black lipstick."

"Avoiding the question?" asked Max beneath his breath, loud enough only for Kiley to hear.

"Well, no, I guess. Whatever. I just meant—well, it might be worth money, is all. I mean, that's what pirates do. They steal valuable stuff. Alcohol is stuff with value. Pirates would steal it, right?" And at that point, she wasn't even sure how they'd ended up talking about the stupid ghost ship.

"Um, yeah." Bryan said, irritation saturating his voice. "I'm not trying to spook you with ghost stories, or any other SyFy Channel crap. Just—seriously, all right? I heard a goddamned noise in the woods. It was weird and creepy and freaking scary as hell and I don't know if we should really be here right now. Okay? Am I clear? Are you understanding me at this point, or do I need to drag you down to the woods and have you hear it for yourselves?"

Sighing, Kiley stared at the ground.

Max, unmoving, asked, "What did it sound like?" His voice was calm and smooth, as if he dealt with abandoned schools and strange noises in the woods every day.

Max's calm demeanor seemed to relax Bryan. His breath slowed and his shoulders loosened. "I don't know," he said. "It sounded like a screech, maybe? Maybe a growl mixed with a screech?"

Max nodded. "And you think it came from the woods over there?" Max waved a hand toward the parking lot and the woods beyond it.

"From in the woods almost directly behind Rachel's car, I think."

Shuddering, Kiley looped her thumbs inside the straps of her backpack and pulled her hands together over her heart as if praying. "You guys are really creeping me out. I've seen all the scary movies, okay? I know that it's the group of unsuspecting teenagers that are always attacked by the evil axe murderer or resurrected camper or the demon summoned from the—hey, you guys didn't read out of any demon summoning books this morning, did ya? Even as a joke? Because I wouldn't be afraid if you did. I'd be fine. I mean, there is nothing in the woods. We're all good." Kiley's lower lip trembled slightly.

"This from the Queen of the Underworld?" Bryan said with a cocked eyebrow. "I thought you'd jump at the chance to team up with the army of the undead, Lady Darkness?"

Kiley scoffed. "Yah," she said, rolling her eyes. "Cuz this is a movie and you're totally testing my Gothiness right now, right?

Whatever, Bryan. I'm not the one wetting my pants over some defenseless bunny rabbit hippety-hopping over fallen twigs on the forest floor, lame-o." Turning her back on him, she stomped up the hill.

"It's probably just a bird. Maybe a kingfisher." Max turned away from Bryan and followed after her. "I wouldn't worry about it," he called over his shoulder. "It's not like we're dealing with a mysteriously abandoned school, or anything unsettling like that."

Bryan watched them as they strode slowly toward the school, a lump forming in the back of his throat. He glanced uneasily at the woods behind him, his eyes skimming over Rachel's car alone in the parking lot, and he gulped.

"Hey guys, wait up," Bryan yelled, running to catch up with the two younger kids. Bryan came up beside Max and walked shoulder to shoulder with him as they lurched up the hill. Leaning toward him, he lowered his voice. "You and I both know it isn't a kingfisher—kingfishers don't growl or screech. So, what's your game, kid?"

Without looking at him, Max responded in a low voice. "Listen. God only knows what's happening right now, but the last thing we need is a couple of girls freaking out because you heard a noise in the woods. Or even *us* freaking out over it. I say we just get up to the high school and see if anyone is there, and, if there is, maybe we can find out what's going on."

"And if nobody's there?"

Max stopped and turned his head to face him. "If they're not there, then we go inside anyway and find a TV or something that can tell us what's going on."

"How will we get in? If no one is there, it's probably locked," said Bryan.

Max grinned.

"Hey!" Kiley had turned back to face them, a hand perched on her hip. "What are you two lovebirds whispering about?"

Bridging the few strides that separated them, Bryan put a hand on Kiley's shoulder. "Don't worry, Kiley. Everything is going to be fine." He pointed at Max and then scratched his head. "Uh—"

"Max," the boy offered.

"Max and I are here." Bryan patted her shoulder consolingly.

Rolling her eyes, Kiley sighed loudly. Affecting a Southern accent, she lifted the back of her hand to her forehead and faked a swoon. "Why, I do declare I have always depended upon strong men to take care of me. Whatever would I do if you two knights in shining armor were not here to rescue me valiantly from the bunnies in the woods and a day off from school?" She peered up at Bryan.

"I had no idea what a snarky brat you could be, Kiley," said Bryan coldly. "I'm so glad we're having this time to bond. It will save me the trouble of being nice to you."

"Whatever," Kiley retorted, blinking rapidly and trying to recover as her forehead wrinkled with anxiety. "I don't need you to be nice to me, jerk nugget. I just want someone to tell me what we're still doing here. I mean, it's pretty obvious there's nobody at school today. Shouldn't we consider this is a good thing? Why are we sticking around?"

Bryan straightened. "I don't know," he said. "Why *aren't* we going home?" He directed the question at Max.

Shrugging, Max said, "Go ahead. But I'm curious." He turned back up hill. The green double doors to the large brick building were in plain view now. Max strained to see if the light in the windows was coming from the inside or reflecting from the gray sky outside.

Kiley stood with her arms crossed over her chest and her mouth twisted to the side. Bryan looked her in the eyes. Pinching his lips together in a sympathetic smile, he let a wisp of air out of his nostrils. "Sorry, Kiley," he said. "My Dad's on a business trip, anyway. I'm alone until our maid comes in on Thursday."

"So?"

"So," he said. "We might as well see what's going on, right? I mean, aren't you curious?" He reached his arm out, resting the palm of his hand on her shoulder again. She wished he wouldn't do that. It made her all squirmy inside. Her skin got warmer when he touched her and tingled under his hand. She jerked away, pushing her lips tightly together. "Fine," he said with a shrug. "Do whatever you want. I'm going to check the school out."

Bryan turned back toward the school. Max was only a few yards ahead of him up the hill. He took a few steps to catch up.

"Wait," Kiley grumbled. Bryan paused, turning back to look at her.

"What?" he asked, a hint of irritation in his voice.

"Where's my sister?" Kiley said, trying to see up the hill. At the sound of her question, Max stopped walking too and looked around the campus. Bryan spun back toward the school, creases of concern wrinkling the smooth, young skin around his mouth and eyes. The trio looked in all directions, but Rachel had disappeared from sight.

"Where did she go? She should be at the doors by now, right?" Bryan spoke quickly, his voice betraying a twinge of panic twisting up his stomach. He arched his neck back toward the direction of the woods, as if somehow she might have doubled back without anyone noticing. Somewhere in the back of his mind, he knew that wasn't possible, but he looked anyway.

"Relax," said Max. "She probably went inside already."

That made perfect sense to Bryan and a wave of relief washed over him. He broke into a slow jog up the hill while Max followed at a slower pace. Kiley shuffled along behind them, casting a longing look over her shoulder at her sister's car.

"Wish *I* could drive," she muttered. "I'd so be at home right now."

As they crested the hill and set foot on level terrain, they walked briskly toward the school. The wide cement stairs leading up to the school were empty, but that was not abnormal for a school day. Once the morning bell rang most students slipped inside quickly and it was well after 8:15. In spite of this knowledge, there was still something that disturbed Bryan. The closer the trio drew to the school, the more whatever it was eluded his grasp and tickled the back of his mind. His eyes narrowed as a growing sense of dread swept through his body.

"My Spidey sense is tingling," he said as he approached the steps.

"Meaning what exactly?" Kiley asked, reaching out a hand to touch him. As her hand came close to his back, she thought better of it and let it drop to her side. A sideways glance at Max told her that he had observed the action, but he looked away as her face turned toward his.

"I'm not sure," Bryan admitted. "Just—well, something feels wrong, you know?"

"I know," Kiley agreed. "Something here is very, very wrong."

CHAPTER NINE

Sage

Sage pulled herself over the short rock wall that ran along the wooded area between her house and the high school. As she dropped to the opposite side, her dirty, stockinged feet—shoes were the farthest thing from her mind as she had run from her house—slammed hard into a tree root. Pain shot up the length of her shin. Her breath was ragged, rattling in her lungs as her heart heaved against her ribcage. A distant sound, somewhere in front of her she thought, cut through the ringing in her ears and she paused. Her head jerked to the right as she held her breath. Low, in the distance, she could just make out the hum of voices.

Is there someone at the high school who can help me?

Gulping in a lung full of fresh air, Sage looked toward the trees in front of her. Even though they hadn't been in town long, she remembered the school parking lot was somewhere up ahead, beyond the cluster of birches and pines that separated her suburban street behind her from the school ahead. The corners of her eyes watered as her eyebrows knitted together. For the first time since she had escaped the horrors at her house, she felt something akin to hope.

She was just about to plunge ahead when she heard another sound and froze. The sound threatened the stillness of the woods surrounding her and shot terror like a lightning bolt through her spine. She forced the tears away from her eyes. It was the sound her father had released earlier that morning, that sickening, vibrating howl that seemed to bounce off the walls of her room.

Only now, it came from in the distance somewhere—as if someone or something was on the prowl.

The image of her mother flickered through her mind and she squeezed her eyes shut.

No. It can't be her, she thought. *I have to get to high ground. I have to get some help.* Her eyes popped open and she stared straight into the trees ahead.

Fear gripped her, but with it came a positive reaction. She felt her body filling with a spark of red hot adrenaline. The pain in her shoeless feet and the rattling in her lungs faded into the background like the hum of a muted television as she forced her body forward at breakneck speed. If there were people at the high school, then that was where she wanted to be. As long as they were—well—regular people.

CHAPTER TEN

Bryan, Kiley, Max, and Sage

"Help!"

The wind carried the desperate cry to the three kids standing near the school's front doors. Instantly, heads jerked in the direction of the call, scanning the terrain for the source of the sound.

"Help!" the scream repeated as a small figure appeared from behind Rachel's car. "Is someone there?"

"It's a girl," breathed Kiley, staring intently at the figure as the child ran clumsily in their direction.

"What's wrong with her?" asked Bryan as he turned towards Max.

Max shrugged. "What are you looking at me for? I know as much as you do. Do I look psychic?"

"More like *psycho*," Kiley said quickly. "Burn. But you *are* the one who's been acting like our unassigned leader since my sister, um, found a way inside, I guess."

Bryan squinted as the girl clamored up the grassy side of the hill using her hands and feet to climb with the speed and agility of a cat. He had never seen her before. The three of them stood motionless. "Should we help her?" Bryan suggested.

"Like how?" asked Kiley. "Do you want to go down there and carry her up the hill, or something?"

"No. I just meant—" Bryan frowned. He huffed a breath of exasperation as he shook his head. "But she *was* yelling for help a minute ago. Assuming this whole thing isn't some elaborate fire drill orchestrated by the entire school district, she might actually need some help. Besides, maybe she knows something about whatever it is that's going on around here."

Striding forward, Max said coolly, "Wait here. I'll check her out." Before Bryan or Kiley could react, he quickly bridged the distance between himself and the girl. Digging his heels into the divots in the hill, he was able to keep his balance without even bothering to take his hands from his pockets. Kiley found herself gazing admiringly at him as he slid gracefully down the hill. Then, she caught herself and shook it off. She felt Bryan's eyes on her, but refused to return his look.

A dozen yards down the hill Max intercepted the young girl. She was moving at least as fast as he was if not faster, scampering like a human spider across the grass. She didn't bother to slow as Max reached her and she would have passed him if she hadn't slipped in the dew of the morning grass. She gasped and clambered to her feet quickly. "We need to get inside!" she urged.

"What?" Max mumbled as he moved toward her.

"We need to—get—inside—now!" she repeated as she gasped for air. Her backpack lurched up and down her back, threatening to heave itself over her head and she struggled to maintain her balance as she grabbed for the straps.

"Hey, wait up," Max insisted as he braced his right leg into the hillside. Sliding his left leg forward, he offered the girl a hand. She slapped her hand into his and, letting him take most of the weight, pulled herself up to him. Hand-in-hand, they shimmied quickly back up the hill.

As they drew closer, Bryan and Kiley were able to see the girl more clearly. She had blond hair cut snugly below her ears. Across her forehead was a streak of dirt that matched a dirt stain on the back of her right hand. Kiley squinted at the girl's other hand. There was a smear of something red and flaky. The older girl knew that stain. She'd used a similar color as lipstick by piercing her fingertip with a safety pin and spreading the red liquid over her lips, allowing it to dry dark and red as the day wore on. It was blood.

"She's not wearing any shoes," Bryan whispered in amazement. Kiley's eyes dropped to the girls' feet. Sure enough, her feet were shod only in filthy stockings that were so covered with dirt and grass that it was impossible to make out their original color.

As Max and his new companion reached level terrain, the girl slowed down. She panted heavily, bending forward at the waist. Max still held her left hand, but her right hand made its way to the small of her back. As she stepped gingerly forward, her knees trembled, and her legs seemed as if they would buckle beneath her at any moment.

"Are you all right?" Bryan asked, leaping forward and reaching a hand to help steady her. Grasping her wrist in his hand, he swung her arm over his shoulders and hunched over to help her over the last few steps.

Swallowing another gulp of air, the girl struggled to speak. The journey up the hill had nearly been too much for her and she struggled to simply hold up her head. Bryan and Kiley knew she needed to catch her breath, but, at the same time, were impatient to hear what she might have to say. Max stared at her calmly.

"Looks like you've been running for a while," Max said coolly. "What are you running from?"

The girl shook her head, the blunt ends of her hair flouncing around the sides of her face. She pointed at the doors of the school. As if the group of kids were an orchestra and the little girl was their conductor, the trio turned their heads toward the doors of the school in perfect unison.

"You want to go inside?" asked Bryan, but Max had already taken the cue and was striding toward the front doors. He tugged on the handle, but the door wouldn't budge.

"Locked," he said, his hand still clutching the handle loosely.

The girl's eyes widened for a moment before her head dropped forward, hanging limply from her neck. Her chin rested hard against the crook of her collar bone. Kiley patted her shoulder tentatively.

"It's going to be okay," Kiley said awkwardly, but the girl shook her head.

"I don't think it's ever going to be okay again," the little girl mumbled so softy that Kiley barely heard her.

"Is somebody chasing you? Did someone hurt you?" Kiley asked. "My sister has a cell phone. We can call your parents or the police or somebody." Even as she said it, it dawned on her that she still didn't know where Rachel had disappeared to. And, if the door to the school was locked, then how could her sister have gotten inside? And if she wasn't inside the school, then where the heck was she?

Bryan looked toward Max with panic in his eyes as he realized what Kiley was thinking. He scanned the campus once again for a sign of Rachel. Nothing. Not a living thing seemed to move in any direction they looked.

Kiley pulled her hand away from the girl. "Where is she, guys? She's gotta be around here somewhere. Rachel has never been this quiet a day in her preppy cheerleader life." Kiley looked imploringly at Bryan. "Do you have your cell? You can try and call her." He stretched out empty hands, answering her question without uttering a word.

Their silent exchange was interrupted when a piercing screech ricocheted through the air. The sound was guttural and vibrating like an aria, but more primal, like a frog's echoing wails. The blonde girl's head jerked up, her eyes bright orbs of terror as every muscle in her body went so rigid her skin seemed to vibrate with the tension.

"That." Bryan said angrily, pointing the index finger of his right hand toward the ground for emphasis. "That is the noise I was talking about. Now tell me you didn't just hear that!"

Before anyone else could speak, the little girl turned to look at him. Her pupils were the size of black glass marbles as she searched the bottom of the hill for the source of the sound.

"We need to get inside. Now," said the child. Her voice was strong, powerful, commanding. Too commanding, perhaps, for a nine-year-old. Max was so taken by the presence of the young girl, he almost forgot the school door was locked and reached for the handle again. He looked at her apologetically.

Reaching into her pocket, the girl fixed Max with a cold and determined look as her fingers wiggled under the folds of her cardigan. She pulled out a long limbed, pink and blue striped, stuffed cat and tossed it through the air at him. It bounced lightly off his chest before he caught it with both hands. He turned the stuffed animal over in his hands then looked at her with raised eyebrows.

"What am I supposed to do with this? Snuggle my way into the school?" he asked, holding the stuffy away from his body as if he were holding an infant's dirty diaper.

"There's a hidden zipper that opens into a secret compartment. There's a Swiss Army knife in there. Not your standard issue," the girl said. "Pull the pick out of the back and extend the piece that looks like a bent prong." She fixed him with an unblinking look, her mouth a neat line of pink. "Ever picked a lock before?"

For a minute, Max toyed with the idea of acting offended. Then, he let a grin rise to his face. "Sure," he said. "No problem, kiddo."

"Good," the girl commanded. "Then quit smiling and get cracking. I don't know how much time we have." The girl turned to face Bryan and Kiley. "You two keep watch at the ends of the stairs to make sure none of them are coming from the sides of the building. I'll take middle position to protect the center of the hill."

Kiley blinked, the left corner of her mouth pulling back into her cheek. "What the hell are you talking about, juice box? I want to know what's going on. Like, first of all who are you? Where did you come from? How old are you anyway? And why should I be taking orders from a Happy Meal? I barely listen to my parents. Why should I listen to you?"

The little girl spun around to face Kiley. Her expression was even, lips together, cheeks slack. Her eyes, earlier glossed over with a dreamy haze, were now sharp and piercing. She pulled a slow, deep breath into the bottom of her lungs. When she spoke, her voice was perfectly calm. "My name is Sage. I'm nine and a half. And you should be taking orders from me for three reasons: first, I know what's going on here. Second, I was home-schooled until we moved here which means I probably have a broader skill set than you do even if you are older than me, because I'm pretty sure I was studying college level material before I was forced into this local joke of a secondary school. And, on top of that, I lived with my parents for two years on the River Valley Commune where we survived off the land. And the last reason—and probably the most important—is because if you don't do exactly what I say, you'll be dead before lunchtime."

Kiley crossed her arms and glared down at the child. "Broader skill set . . ." she began, angrily. "What the hell kind of a phrase is that? Are you calling me stupid? For your information, Fruit Snack, I'm at the top of my class and I have straight A's in History. I have spent every summer vacation reading about two books a day since I can remember, and I used to go camping every summer in *Maine* where there are still more trees than people. And what difference does it make, anyway, if you can survive off the land? This isn't *Swiss Family Robinson*; this is a *high school*, kitchen spice."

Sage let a short breathy laugh out of her nose. "Clever," she said sarcastically. "I have never heard that one before." She looked at Kiley, then really looked. From the toes of her boots to the arches of her black-penciled eyebrows. "All right," she said. "We don't have time to argue about it right now, so I'm going to have to ask you to trust me." Her eyes pleaded with Kiley. "Please," she added.

"Why?" she asked icily. "Give me one reason why any of us should trust a Care Bear like you? Genius or not, you're still a lunchbox, and it's hard to take a lunchbox seriously."

Sage bowed her head, letting her gaze linger on a tuft of grass that had been kicked up by Max when he helped her up the hill. "You should take me seriously," she said. Her voice was low and sorrowful. "Because I just killed my parents."

CHAPTER ELEVEN

Sage

Sage's screams echoed down the hall as her feet slid backwards along the floorboards, her back and arms pressed against the wall. Her father's skin was blanched white and covered with a thin film of sweat that glistened in the dim light from the hallway. His blood-filled eyes were locked on Sage as his grey mouth worked over the pulpy end of Deidra's arm. He slurped loudly as he sucked skin and blood past his lips and over his teeth. A guttural sound emanated from his stomach as if it were growling with hunger pangs. Sticky, red blood oozed from the torn flesh around the ugly wound in the arm, dripping over the wrist bone and down the fingers of the hand.

A pool of blood grew beside his feet as he sat with his legs crossed lotus style. The blood flowed freely from an artery in her mother's arm that had split open when he ripped it with sickening ease from her body.

Sage wanted to check and see if her mother was still breathing, if there was some chance that she might be alive, but she didn't dare take her eyes off her father for even a second. Sweat trickled coldly along the curve of her armpits. Her screams had long gone hollow in her throat as she stood there against the wall of the hallway breathing spasmodically. How she managed to keep down her breakfast she had no idea, although nausea nibbled around the edges of her stomach just the same.

Mustering the courage to peer around the door jam, she craned her neck away from the wall and to the left. As her eyes rolled over the figure of her father, she watched his head jerk away from his bloody meal, his chewing mouth pausing as he did so.

She froze.

His iris-less eyes seemed to lock onto her as the arm he was munching dropped to his lap. He twisted his head as if listening intently, waiting for the slightest sound. Sage stood completely still, silently begging her breath to slow enough to stop her chest from heaving. A moment later, he grunted, retrieved his bloody snack from his lap and tore another chunk of flesh off with his teeth.

Acid shot up through Sage's esophagus, spilling a tablespoon of vomit into the back of her throat. She managed to swallow down the pool of puke before slowly turning her eyes in the direction of her mother. She could barely make out the top of her mother's head, the woman's long hair reddening darkly as blood pooled around her head. It was impossible to tell from this angle if her mother was still breathing.

Very slowly and carefully, Sage slid her heels from left to right as she inched along the wall. Her toes scrunched and flexed so slowly that a cramp stiffened her pinkie toes. She bit her lip to keep from crying out. She wanted to reach down and work out the cramp with her fingers, but she knew that even the slightest movement from her might catch her father's attention. What she did not know was how he would react to it. And that's what scared her most. Would he forget the object of his current attention and come after her? Would he try and eat her, too?

She stifled a shudder as she edged her way along the wall. Her arched neck and extended head remained rigid as her hips slid along the wall a fraction of a centimeter at a time. And she knew she couldn't just turn and run for it. She had to see if her mother was alive. Not only because she needed help, but also because she knew she needed to escape and her mother seemed the best option for that to happen. Her eyes lingered for a moment on her father as he absent-mindedly chewed a flap of skin.

Tears swelled up at the corners of Sage's eyes as she tried to imagine what could possibly have happened to turn her father from a loving, laughing, living man into a monster in a matter of minutes.

Could there be something in the water? Something he ate? Radiation from his laptop? Is there a cure? Is my father the only one, or are there more? Is everybody's father turning into a—a what? A zombie? Is my father a zombie? Am I going to turn into a zombie? Questions raced through her mind at break-neck speed. But she didn't have time to sort everything out at this moment. Her top priority had to be getting away from her father without—without being eaten. She could sort out such things as doctors and cures and yes, even hope, later. Now, she just needed to escape. With her mom, if possible.

After several long minutes, Sage had finally positioned herself at an angle in to the doorway of her bedroom that allowed a full view of her mother's collapsed form without alerting her father. He sat, seemingly quite content, as he smacked his lips, still gnawing away at flesh and bone. Her knuckles whitened against the wall as the pads of her fingers tensed against the tiny bubbles of paint that clung to the sheetrock. Straining, she stretched, trying to see if her mother's chest was moving or not. From this new angle, she had a perfect view of her mother's body, but the shadow cast by her bed lay like a grey blanket over her fallen mother's form.

Mommy, thought Sage. *Please, please get up.* A tear slid past the corner of her eye, rolled over her freckled cheek, and nestled in the crook of her mouth before falling off her chin. She tasted salt. *I can't do this without you!*

As Sage stretched her neck further away from the wall, the exertion from tensing muscles nearly made her knees buckle. If only she could get close enough to make sure. Did her mother have the car keys in her other hand? Had she simply passed out from the intensity of the pain from having her arm torn off, or had she bled out completely? What would she do if her mother was dead?

But somewhere deep inside her bones, she knew, and clarity swept over her. The butterflies ricocheting off her ribcage eased as the tension in her shoulders drained away. The whites of her knuckles bled into soft pink as her fingers eased slowly from the wall.

If she's dead, then I'll have to leave without her.

Just as the thought came to rest like a heavy weight planted squarely on her shoulders, she realized she hadn't blinked in quite some time and her eyes felt dry. Her vision was tingling and red at the edges. With a quick glance at her father, who still sat chomping through a bit of arm gristle nearly at the wrist, she allowed her eyelids to drop for just an instant. No sooner did her eyelids come to a peaceful close than, through the haze of her eyelashes, she caught a glimpse of movement from the direction of her mother's body. Startled, her eyes popped open and, as they did, her left foot slid out from under her, knocking her knee hard onto the wood floor. Pain shot through her leg as icy shards shot up through her calf and thigh.

In that instant, her father paused his feast. His fading eyes flickered in her direction before locking into place.

Her eyes trained on her father, Sage brought her hands slowly to the sides of her right foot and planted her front fingers on the floor like a tripod. She pressed her left foot into the wall, angling her body toward the bathroom, ready to break into a sprint at the slightest hint of movement from the creature who had once been her father.

He stared at her, his black tongue lashing out from between his frayed lips and darting over his bloody teeth. The cracks of his mouth bled and oozed as he gnashed his teeth, snarling. A growl rumbled low in his throat. When he opened his mouth, a primal, vibrating screech squealed from the back of his throat. He lurched forward resting his weight on his fists and his knees. His hands were glossy white, as if they had spent the last hour housed inside a pair of stretched rubber gloves. The black of his veins, etched darkly against the whiteness.

Sage caught sight of the cast iron skillet her mother had earlier dropped near the door. No sooner did her father lurch forward than Sage lunged toward it. As the creature pounced into the hallway, Sage grabbed for the skillet, ducking under his outstretched arms. Her hands closed around the pan's narrow handle as she tucked her shoulder and rolled to the right so that she landed lying flat on her back. Her father leapt toward her, gnashing his teeth and missing her by a millisecond as she slid her feet out from between his grasping hands. He turned his head toward her as she scrambled to a standing position. Opening his bloody, horrific mouth, he let out a loud, inhuman screech.

"Daddy," Sage begged, tears streaming down her pink cheeks. Her mouth twisted into a painful sob. Instinctively, she shifted her heels so her weight rested evenly on her legs with the toes of one leg pointed in her father's direction, the other pointed at a ninety-degree-angle behind her. The father-monster pushed off with his heels and lunged again, his mouth open wide and his red, glistening teeth poised to chomp down on contact.

As he flew toward her, she gripped the frying pan between both hands like a shield and pressed off with her back heel, lunging forward on her front foot. His head collided hard with the frying pan, knocking them both off balance. She toppled backwards at the same time as the man collapsed against the opposite wall. Sage kicked her feet against the floor, skidding. The frying pan had rebounded hard against her chest and she struggled to breathe. A sharp pain shot through her ribs as she sucked in a chest full of air.

Her father lay slumped against the wall across from her. The top of his head was crushed in. Scribbles of red-soaked, grey brain matter oozed out where his skull had cracked in a few places, reminding the girl of a time she'd been at a friend's house while they were cooking ground beef in tomato sauce. Blood drenched the front of his face and his shirt. Had she done that or had she simply added to the damage her mother's earlier bash had created?

Without warning, vomit rose up her throat and spewed out of her mouth, splattering across on the floor, mixing with the blood already there. The acid burned the sides of her mouth as her abdomen heaved a red and orange, lumpy fluid onto the floor. Wiping her mouth with the back of her hand, her eyes drifted to the frying pan which lay upside down near the contents of her stomach. A puddle of brain matter clung to the back of the pan like curly, grey noodles. Sage's abdomen heaved again and a sputtering of acid-laced breath flooded her mouth. There was nothing left to come up, but her stomach muscles still continued their mission.

Light-headed, she scrambled to her feet, her shoulder bouncing against the wall. She stepped over her father's slumped body as she stumbled into the bathroom in a drunk-like stupor.

Standing over the white porcelain sink, her head lolled on her neck as she glanced at her reflection in the mirror. Blood streaked across her mouth from where she had wiped the vomit from her face. Her mouth slack, she dropped her gaze to the back of her hand. A streak of blood stained her pale skin.

She turned on the faucet. The pipes hummed to life as cold water flowed from the tap. She cupped her hands beneath the stream and leaned forward, her abdomen pressing against the cool of the porcelain as she splashed water into her face. She rubbed her hands viciously against her skin, scrubbing the area around her mouth once, twice, then again.

As she looked at herself in the mirror, water rolled off her chin in pink droplets from where blood had mingled with it. She leaned close to the glass, eyeing her reflection closely. Her pupils were like two discs of obsidian, so wide and round that they nearly eclipsed her iris, leaving only a sliver of blue halo around the black pool. She blinked.

Pulling away from the mirror, she thrust her hands beneath the water flowing so cleanly from the faucet, allowing it to splash around her hands and wrists as she rubbed them together. The streak of red—her father's blood or her own, she didn't know—slowly disappeared under the gush of water. Although her hands somehow still felt dirty, she twisted the faucet off and patted her hands dry against her cardigan.

As she turned to leave, her eyes widened as her sight honed in on a welcome figure. Her mother hung in the doorway, a shadow draped over her familiar form like someone had cast a black, gauzy sheet over her body as she looked at the bloody stump where her arm used to be, reaching for it with her free hand. Her movements were uncoordinated and jerky, as if she were sleep-walking. She took an uneven step and lumbered further into the hallway.

"Mommy!" Sage cried out, her arms spread wide for a hug. She took a step, preparing to run across the hallway.

At the sound of Sage's voice, however, her mother's head jerked to attention and she took a faltering step toward the bathroom. The hall light cast a sliver of light across her mother's face and Sage recoiled. Her eyes were dark with blood and her skin looked like white rubber stretched over black inky veins.

The smile slid from Sage's face.

Cocking her head to the side, Deidra opened her mouth wide as a vibrating screech belted out. A much too familiar screech. The woman lunged down the hallway toward the bathroom. Without even thinking, Sage slammed the bathroom door and slid the latch swiftly into place. Deidra slammed hard into the door and it rattled against its hinges. Sage recoiled against the bathroom sink as her mother, if the creature outside could still be called such a word, pounded repeatedly into the door frame.

Tears once again threatened, but Sage gritted her teeth, and a cold determination straightened her spine. With soldier-like efficiency, she spun on her heel, squatted in front of the bathroom sink and flipped open the cabinet. She pulled out a bucket containing several bottles of cleansers and first aid liquids. She unscrewed the cap of the drain-unclogging solution and emptied the liquid into the bucket. She then added bleach, Hydrogen peroxide and rubbing alcohol.

As each bottle gurgled its contents into the bucket, she scanned the room for weapons. Her eyes locked on the curtain rod. Could she use it as some kind of a pole or joust, perhaps? Drive the end into her mother's abdomen and lunge forward until this new monster was wedged against the wall?

No, she told herself. *I'm not strong enough for that.*

Her eyes moved over her father's safety razor. *Too small.*

The toilet plunger. *Too ridiculous.*

The toilet. *Too heavy.*

But even as she thought these things, her mind rolled over the memory of a martial arts movie she had watched with her parents where a fighter had been cornered in the bathroom. He had removed the cover to the toilet tank and used it as a weapon.

As the last of the chemicals splattered into the bucket, Sage stood up. She lifted the tank cover off the toilet and tested its weight in her hands. As the door continued to rattle on its hinges, Sage tried a few test swings of the basin lid. It was heavy, but she liked the way it swung itself against her own weight, almost taking control of her body with each swing.

She knew she'd have to time it perfectly. With the heft of the porcelain tank lid in her small hands, she was apt to drop the thing if the creature outside were to bump her arm or her hand. Sage's mind swam in a sea of images of what was about to happen. She imagined how the scene would play out, scanning over it with her mind like a computer testing a code for bugs.

A screech reverberated off the bathroom door as Deidra lunged against it again. One of the door pegs shimmied upward, ready to give against the strain of the repeated batterings.

"This will have to do," Sage said aloud, leaning the lid against the wall. She hoisted the bucket onto the ledge of the bathtub and carefully climbed up to position herself beside it. Then she grabbed the industrial sized conditioner bottle from the shelf inside the shower and emptied its contents on the tiled bathroom floor. Checking that the path to the doorway was clear save for the conditioner, Sage braced herself.

On the next impact of Deidra's body against the bathroom door, Sage wrapped her hand tightly around the brass doorknob and counted off "five . . . four . . . three . . . two . . . one . . . "

Without hesitation, she slipped the latch and turned the knob at almost the exact moment that Deidra plunged into the door. The door smashed open and her mother tumbled through the entry. Her limbs wind-milled through the air as she tried to maintain her balance, but she quickly lost the battle and flopped to the floor. She thrashed against the slick, frictionless floor, sliding through the conditioner mess without any semblance of traction. She screeched loudly, scrambling to get up, hindered and off balance by her missing arm.

Sage dumped the chemicals into her mother's face, bucket and all then leapt lithely to the entryway where the floor was not yet soaked with the slippery conditioner. The chemicals began to work their acidic magic on the already grey flesh of her mother's face, forcing the woman's eyes to pinch tightly closed. Wasting no time, Sage grabbed the lid with both hands and swung her body in a hard, fast arc. The lid collided hard against the side of her mother's head. Sage cringed at the sound of the bone crunching beneath the porcelain. Deidra screeched as fresh blood spattered against the bathroom walls.

Realizing she couldn't build up enough force to strike hard enough with the porcelain lid again, Sage dropped the lid and ran.

She slowed just enough to grab her backpack as she careened past the kitchen doorway and around the kitchen table, skidding to a halt in front of the door leading that connected to the garage and her only means of escape to the outdoors. She glanced uselessly at her shoeless feet as she turned the knob. She pushed the door open and stepped down into the garage. Deidra had escaped from the bathroom and was lumbering down the hallway. Sage slammed the door shut, leapt over the low railing of the garage stairs and ran to the back of the garage to where her parents' tools were neatly arranged on the wall.

Sage glanced over the toolset as her mother fumbled with the door. Her eyes came to rest on the ski set hanging on the wall. She grabbed one of the ski poles, tested the tip for sharpness, and then braced the handle end of the ski pole against the solid bottom shelf of the workbench so that the point of the ski pole angled up. As the door flung open and a one-armed Deidra leapt over the stair railing with both feet spread wide, Sage mustered her courage to remain standing until the very last minute.

Deidra lunged at Sage. Just as she did, Sage dropped her weight, kneeling on the ground with her hand gripping the ski pole tightly. Deidra rammed into it full force, the point of the pole penetrating the skin and skull of her forehead as it plunged sloppily into her head. She hung there for a moment, blood streaming freely down her face, before she toppled in slow motion and plopped lifelessly to the floor.

Without checking to see if her mother still moved, Sage released her grip on the ski pole, flung her backpack over her shoulders, and bee-lined for the garage door. Hitting the switch to the garage door opener, Sage didn't wait for it to completely open, but rolled beneath it and ran into the street at top speed.

An ear-piercing squeal echoed behind her, but she didn't look back. She veered to the right running wildly down Ash street and toward the small wooden path that led from her neighborhood toward the high school. Perhaps she would find someone there that could help her. After all, schools were supposed to be safe places for children. Right?

Chapter Twelve

Sage, Kiley, Max, and Bryan

Bryan blinked at the girl, speechless. Max looked off in the distance, his face free of expression. Only Kiley seemed to have words for the child.

"What do you mean, 'you just killed your parents'?" Kiley's voice was uneven as she nervously chewed at a fingernail.

"I mean just what I said. My parents are dead. Or at least my dad is dead. My mother is most likely dead, though I think she's been chasing me which is exactly why we need to get inside that building and figure out our next move." Anger suddenly flooded Sage's voice as she glared hard at Kiley. "Maybe it doesn't make much sense, but if you want to live, you'll listen to me and do exactly as I say. We don't have much time."

The two girls stared at each another, eyes locked and unblinking for several seconds before Kiley finally broke away. Bryan stood dumbfounded, his mouth hanging open.

Shaking her head, Kiley spoke. "We are not seriously going to listen to a psychopathic child, are we? What is this? *Pet Sematary?*" Kiley fixed Bryan with a strained glare, seeking his support. "I think we just need to find my sister and get her to drive us all home. And maybe escort this child to a psychiatric hospital along the way."

Sage leapt off the cement stairs and lunged toward Kiley, who took several steps backward. Sage followed her and, pulling her shoulders back, pressed her face forward, inches from Kiley's own.

"You aren't listening," the younger girl said, her voice rising to a near scream. "My parents are dead because they freaked out and turned into–I don't even know. Zombies, maybe? And the entire town has vanished. I didn't see a single person on my way here. The schools seem to be closed, but nobody knew it was going to be closed today. Not *one* of you, or you wouldn't be here. And you think you should go home? You think you are safe anywhere?" Sage was panting with exhilaration. She crossed her arms over her chest.

"We need to get inside," the girl continued, a calmness easing the tension from her shoulders as she spoke. "It's a school. There will be food, water, television, radio and computers with internet access. I say we get inside, find out what the heck is going on here, and *then* try to figure out where we should be going or what we should be doing. At least that's my plan. Do you have a better one?"

Kiley's lips whitened as she pressed them together. Leaning forward, she said in a low, mean voice, "I'm not going anywhere with you, without my sister. And I don't think I believe you, anyway. It's a ridiculous story. A Vanilla Wafer like you overpowering two industrial-sized, zombie parents? It's like something out of *Evil Dead*, only without a stunning Bruce Campbell to carry the script and shoddy special effects." The two girls glared at each other, each poised like cobras ready to strike.

Stepping forward, Bryan pressed a hand against the shoulder of each girl, forcing them apart. "Listen," he said. "I hate to break up this cat fight, as ridiculous as it would be—Kiley, you're almost four years older than this girl. What's wrong with you?"

Kiley curled her upper lip and shook her head at him.

Bryan went on. "But, if you'd care to end your staring contest, you might see that Max is holding the door to the school wide open. So, why don't we all just go inside now and find some help. I think we have enough problems without you two tearing each other's eyes out."

Sage released a long, deliberate breath. "I'm sorry," she said. "This hasn't exactly been my best day, and it isn't over yet. I feel like I have to act while I can. I'm sort of numb to everything now, but I'm afraid if I stop to think about what I've done, I—"

" I'm still not going anywhere with any of you until I find my sister," Kiley said, crossing her arms over her chest.

"Look," Bryan said, offering a compromise. "I'll go look for Rachel, but I'd feel a whole lot better if the rest of you would just go inside. You can wait by the door, then we can lock it again when Rachel and I come back. But at least if you're inside, you'll be safer than standing around out here."

Kiley scoffed. "You don't seriously believe that Greendale has been taken over by zombies, do you? Didn't you call me the 'Queen of the Underworld', or whatever? I think that means I'm the expert here, and I hate to break this to you, Linus, but there is no Great Pumpkin. And zombies are not real. And, sadly neither is the Easter Bunny or Santa Claus. Tough news, I know. But, you can't believe this garbage."

Bryan glanced at Sage out of the corner of his eye, then walked swiftly toward Kiley, swung his arm around her shoulder and walked her a few steps away from the door. Lowering his voice, he said, "I don't know what to believe, right now, Kiley; but, the simple fact remains that this little girl is covered in dried blood and running through the woods without any shoes. Just let me go look for your sister and then we'll deal with the girl and whatever else is going on. Deal?"

With a scowling glance at the child, Kiley finally nodded. "Fine," she said. "Come on, Spice Girl. Let's go inside and let our dashing hero do his knight-in-shining-armor thing while we peasant girls gaze on admiringly from the window."

Sage glanced at Bryan then walked with Kiley toward Max. She held out her hand to the boy.

"What?" Max asked.

"My Squiggly?"

"Your what?"

"My stuffed bunny." She motioned toward his pocket. "And all of its contents, if you please."

Max nodded. "Oh, yeah." He pulled the stuffed animal and the Swiss Army knife from his pocket and handed them to Sage. "Here you go, kiddo."

The young girl looked at her Swiss Army knife and then at Bryan, the strain of conflict raising her eyebrows high on her face. "You really should have something to fight with if you are going to stay out here," she forced herself to say. The memento meant a lot to her. Perhaps now more than ever.

Bryan shrugged. "I'm sure I'll be fine," he said.

After a moment, Max pulled something from his pocket and tossed it underhand to Bryan. It tumbled through the air as Bryan instinctively put his hands out to catch it. The handle of the switchblade knife bounced into his palms. He looked at Max.

"Just in case," Max said with a shrug, his expression stoic.

Bryan nodded. "Thanks, man." He thrust the knife into his pocket.

Sage looked at Max. "Does that mean you believe me?" she asked.

Max shrugged again. "You mean, do I believe your parents turned into monsters? Sure. Why not? My parents have been monsters for as long as I can remember." He smiled, thrust his hand out to hold open the door and motioned for her to go inside. She nodded and stepped over the threshold and into the high school lobby. Max stepped in after her and let the door click shut behind the three of them. He turned and faced Bryan through the window, pressing a thumbs-up sign to the glass.

Bryan nodded and raised a hand to Max before turning back toward the empty, grass-covered hill. Sighing, he marched down the steps and swung to the left of the school building, intending to walk around the outside. He wasn't convinced they were actually in danger, but he prepared himself for anything, his hand gripped tightly around the knife in his pocket. Zombies? Not likely. But something sure wasn't right.

Rachel probably just reached the door, saw that it was locked and she walked around the building to find another way in, he thought. But his fingers tapped against the side of the knife in his pocket as a sense of unease trickled cold sweat under his arms and down his sides.

CHAPTER THIRTEEN

Bryan and Rachel

The high school was an oddly shaped building. Having started out as a one-room brick school house in the early 1800's, the lobby of the school was the oldest part of the structure. As the town expanded over the years and the need to accommodate more students arose, additions were built around the original room. The result was a hodge-podge of rooms shaped like a series of Tetris blocks wedged neatly together with gaps of free space on nearly every side. From a bird's eye view, the building with its gaps resembled a six-pointed star with rectangular ends instead of points.

The gaps between walls and sections served as gardens, each with a nature-themed name and stuffed full with flowers and trees, park benches and metal waste baskets. The gap gardens also served as a great make-out place for hormonal teenagers before school started. Currently, the school was large enough to accommodate all 900 Greendale high school students as well as another 112 students from neighboring towns too small to support a school system. That was a lot of secret kissing.

As Bryan rounded the front corner of the building, he half expected Rachel to leap out at him from the Sunshine Gap Garden, which cut a narrow, alley-like swath through the southeast edge of the school. Rachel was not the type of girl to shudder at the ghost stories her sister liked to tell at dinner, or lift the blanket over her head on dark and stormy nights. She didn't believe in those hokey poltergeist hunters on television, and things like vampires and werewolves made her laugh more than tremble. She was the type to scare others, not be scared by them; and so, as Bryan traversed the edge of the building, he prepared himself to be startled by the popping of an air-filled paper bag or a scary-faced Rachel lunging into his path from the shadows. She'd laugh, then he'd laugh and everything would return to normal.

It did not happen that way.

Peering into the Sunshine Gap Garden, Bryan saw no movement save a lone sparrow, its tiny head tucked protectively beneath its wing, preening. He let out the breath he had been holding, leaned left and right and inspected the area thoroughly. Was she hiding in the juniper bush? Was she under a park bench? But there was no sign of her, or for that matter, anyone.

Straightening his back, Bryan turned toward the outer wall of the building. From his vantage point atop the plateau, he could see pockets of morning mist rising off the wide expanse of lake behind the school. The lake was quiet, unrippling—a serene reflection of the motionless school which, by this time, should be bustling with students knee-deep in their first period classes.

Bryan grinned as he realized he should be taking an algebra test right now. *Instead, I'm walking around an abandoned school trying to find my girlfriend and carrying a knife because a possibly-homicidal nine-year-old child suggested I needed protection.*

He glanced down at the tiny handle in his hand. Carefully, he flicked the switch and a six inch blade projected from the base of the handle fast as a blink. *And this is my protection. A glorified can opener.* He thought, his grin widening as he flicked the blade back into its handle with a push of the button. His grin vanished as quickly as it came when a pulsating, hoarse shriek rose from near the bottom of the plateau close to the lake.

Bryan shuddered. *Perhaps I do need protection, after all,* he thought, and closed his fingers around the handle of the tiny switchblade, the pad of his thumb resting gently on the release button.

As he walked through the Moonlight Gap Garden, he bristled
at the thought of Rachel lying in wait. He tried to distract himself
from the tension by reflecting on how they had first met.

She was a year ahead of him in school, and, by rights, should
have been two years ahead if she hadn't needed to repeat her
sophomore year. Kiley and her sister were from the neighboring
town of Fox Hills and, before she got her driver's license, she had
an hour bus commute to school. While Kiley had been adept at
completing homework by ignoring the heaves and bumps of the
back country roads the bus traversed, Rachel spent her time
nestled in the back of the bus with her friends, stealing swigs of
bourbon or cheap tequila from a poorly mixed Mountain Dew
bottle one of her friends had spiked.

The first time he saw her, she was leaning over the water
fountain in the science wing, her long red curls hanging like a
curtain backdrop behind the cool, silver metal of the fountain.
Her eyelids closed slightly as she puckered her lips to draw water
from the spout. From the way she was leaning over, Bryan could
see the curve of her small breasts under her teal sweater. When
she pulled away from the fountain, she popped up quickly, her
hair and breasts bouncing. As she swung her hand behind her
head to straighten her hair, she turned from side to side and
caught sight of Bryan staring at her.

At first, a look of disgust rose instinctively to her face, but she
squinted for a moment. Her lips dropped open, and she smiled
at him slightly, looking down at the ground then back up into his
eyes. At that moment, the bell signaling that the next class would
start in thirty seconds blared through the hallway and she was
lost to him in a throng of students rushing to get to their classes.
It would be only a short week before they'd meet at the fountain
again, only this time she'd have an intricately folded note with
her phone number written inside it as she rose from the stream
of water, hair dancing softly over her back as she did.

The image of Rachel's long red hair swishing past her
shoulders clung to his mind as he made his way through the
Moonlight Gap Garden. Pressing his shoulder against a brick
wall, he whipped his head around the corner quickly, scanning

the night-blooming garden. No sign of Rachel. *If she's waiting to scare me*, he thought. *Maybe I can scare her first.*

As he turned the corner toward the back of the building, he caught sight of the maintenance shed behind the school. He had done his freshman year community service on school grounds and was familiar with the shed. Large enough to fit a couple of parked school buses, the shed was the home for gardening tools, grounds-keeping supplies and two tractors, one rigged for snow removal and the other for grass cutting.

The slam of a wooden door against its frame echoed toward Bryan, as if the sound waves had been carried over water. A flash of movement near the entrance on the far side of the shed caught his attention. While it moved too quickly for him to be sure, the flash of brown and red was probably Rachel's hair and sweater. Bryan took off sprinting. How she could play games at a time like this never ceased to amaze him, though that was part of the reason he enjoyed her company.

But right this instant, it was beginning to piss him off.

"Rachel!" he shouted as he barreled toward the shed. "Rachel!"

Puffing slightly with asthma as he jogged, he approached the corner of the building which stood kitty-corner to the jagged back wall of the high school. Bryan swung his arms wide as he strode around the corner. A breath of relief slipped past his lips as his eyes filled with the sight of Rachel's figure. She stood facing the entrance to the shed, her sneakered feet pressed into the gravelly, tread-worn path that led from the back entrance of the high school to the shed door. Grass grew up in tufts around the doorway. Browning leaves from a nearby birch tree scuttled along the ground behind her feet in the icy November breeze.

"Rachel," he said, approaching her. She remained motionless, her curly red hair blanketing her back to her waist. He reached out a hand. "Rachel. We've been worried. Why did you take off like that?" He placed the palm of his hand on her shoulder, "Your sister—" He was abruptly cut off as Rachel spun on her heels to face him. Her hand closed around his wrist in a steely grip.

"Ouch," he said, his eyes dipping to her crushing fingers. Her hand was the color of ash. Scrawling, inky lines of veins popped up on her hands and fingers. His eyes continued up to the cuff of her sleeve and over the hills of her sweater to her face. The once freckled skin of her rosy cheeks was now pasty white, glistening with iridescent dew. Black veins framed her face. The whites of her eyes had been replaced by the deep burgundy of blood that pooled there and her irises were as black as her pupils. She opened her cracked, blood-encrusted mouth to reveal smoke-colored gums gripping crimson-stained teeth. Just beyond her, Bryan could make out the half-eaten remains of what looked like a small dog or puppy, its severed, furry limbs matted with sticky red blood.

He twisted his hand in her grasp, swinging her arm in a wide circle as he pulled his wrist against the connection of her thumb and fingers, the weakest point of her grip. Her hands made a snapping noise as he ripped his hand away from her clutching fingers. As she lunged forward, her mouth gaping, Bryan shifted his weight to his heels, arched his back and, grabbing her wrist at the same time, spun her around away from him. Jamming his free hand into her shoulder, he pushed her to the ground. A sickening snap of tendons popping inside her shoulder sent his stomach lurching as, appalled at his reflexes, he stumbled backwards away from her.

Unbothered by the dislocated shoulder jutting out from her neck at a twisted angle, Rachel glared at a wide-eyed Bryan and lunged upward with both arms stretched out in front of her. Instinctively, he grabbed her wrist, spun around again, and slammed his palm into her other shoulder, using the velocity of her lunge to slam her frighteningly hard, face-first into the shed door.

Gasping, Bryan's mouth dropped open as he stared at his monstrous girlfriend. She whirled and, dropping her jaw wide, let out a trembling, vibrating scream.

"Rachel, please," he pleaded, but deep inside he knew she could no longer hear or understand him. She dove at him again, this time hunching over wrestler-style and positioning her hands and head like a battering ram and colliding hard against his abdomen. The force of her impact sent them both sprawling to the ground. A shot of pain spiraled up Bryan's spine as his back slammed against the gravel-covered ground. Rachel lifted herself quickly, straddling Bryan as he lay there half-dazed. Spreading her brittle lips, she opened her mouth wide and lowered her face as if preparing for a kiss. He knew, however, that a kiss was the last thing on her mind. Or what was left of her mind.

Bryan thrust his left fingertips hard into Rachel's esophagus, her fragile trachea crunching under the pressure of his fingers. It seemed to have little effect on her, though, as she snapped wildly at his fingers with her glistening teeth. He wrapped his hand around her throat and locked his elbow. He desperately held her head away from him as his right hand reached in panic for the switchblade inside his jacket pocket. Hooking her fingers into claws, Rachel swiped through the air at his face. He rolled his head quickly to the side, her fingernails missing his left eye by the length of an eyelash.

Bryan's fingers closed around the switchblade. Withdrawing it quickly, he pressed the blade release with his thumb and drove the six inch blade with all the force he could muster into the side of her face. The point of the blade connected with the soft tissue around her left eye, sliding easily past the eye socket and dislodging the eyeball. The eyeball loosed itself from the mess of string connecting it to the inside of her socket. The severed, gooey orb dropped onto Bryan's forehead. A spray of ocular fluid and blood spewed from the cavity where her eye had been, dousing Bryan's face with viscous liquid. Reflexively, he closed his eyes as he pressed the curve of his hand into Rachel's throat and, straining all the muscles in his abdomen, forced himself upward. She fell backwards off his hips, hissing as she rolled around on the ground.

They both got to their feet. Bryan lunged hard and fast at Rachel, his shoulder slamming into her ribs, tackling her with such force that her feet lifted off the ground. He drove her into the wooden slats of the shed door so hard that the wood splintered at the hinges, breaking under the impact. She went careening on her back, skidding against the shards of broken wood along the floor of the shed as Bryan used his hands to reduce the shock of his impact. He tucked and spun as he hit the ground, rolling to the left and bouncing spryly to his feet.

As Rachel struggled to stand, Bryan whipped around and ran along the interior wall toward the gardening tools. The creature plunged ahead, leaping around the snow tractor and barreling full force toward Bryan. His hand no sooner closed around the handle of a pair of gardening shears than her icy fingertips dug sharply into the crook of his neck, jabbing into the flesh just below the collar bone. Clinging to the handle of the long-bladed gardening shears, he used the closeness of her body to his advantage and, arching forward, he pulled her toward his body as he sprang up, jamming the back of his head into her face.

He dropped to a squat, spun on the balls of his feet and bashed his forehead into her face. Black blood spurted from the sides of her nose which now hung at a sickening angle on her face.

"Please don't do this Rachel," Bryan begged. Hot, salty tears gushed from the corners of his eyes and rolled down his cheeks. Unrelenting, she opened her mouth and pressed forward teeth-first. Tiny droplets of grayed saliva dripped from her canines. In an instant, he had the gardening shears angled open in front of him. Just as she thrust her head toward him, he pushed the shears forward hard and fast. The blades of the shears tore through the soft, sallow flesh of Rachel's neck, blood spraying out from both sides. Mustering all his strength, Bryan jammed his hands together.

Rachel's teeth gnashed as a whining, whimpering noise whistled from the bottom of her crushed throat. Bryan shut his eyes tightly as he pushed the handles of the blade together with even more force. The blades moved with a shuddering, jarring sensation like a paring knife slicing through steak. With one final heave, the blades cinched to a close.

Bryan inched open his eyes. A mauve haze hung at the corners of his vision where blood had spattered his face. For a moment, her lifeless head rested on the blades of the shears, her face still contorted with rage and her teeth poised to bite, before it tottered to the left and tumbled to the ground. Her knees lost their rigidity, and her headless body, still spewing oozy red and black liquid down its front, toppled forward. Bryan stepped out of the path of the lifeless torso a split second before it could embrace him with its still flailing arms.

Panting heavily, Bryan tossed the garden shears to the ground beside the fallen body. He lifted his hands in front of his face. They were drenched with Rachel's blood.

His girlfriend's blood.

He looked blankly around him, blinking slowly and deliberately. As if on autopilot, his head swung from side to side. Spying a dusty rag lying on a table, he leapt over her body with two long steps and retrieved it with mechanical movements. He wiped the blood from his hands and wrists before using the back of his hand to wipe his face. Blinking blood from his eyes, he threw the rag to the ground, His eyes glanced over her body which had fallen outside the entrance to the shed, with only her feet still inside the rough-hewn room. He avoided looking at her head, which had landed a few feet beyond her neck on the ground between the shed and the school's back door. Stumbling, he stepped over her and moved to walk around the school without looking back.

CHAPTER FOURTEEN

Kiley, Max, and Sage

"So what happened to your parents, anyway?" Kiley asked, plopping on the floor in a half-lotus as she eyeballed Sage warily.

The high school was dimly lit by the grey, November light of an overcast day as it seeped in through the wide windows that surrounded the lobby. To the left of the lobby, the picture window looking into the main office was pitch-black. Max stood with his face pressed into the glass of the vertically-rectangular window of the front entrance. Sage took a seat on the floor next to Kiley and eyed the shadowed hallway on either side of the main office nervously.

"I already told you. I killed them." She blinked. "At least I think I did," she added.

A chill ran up the length of Kiley's spine. "You keep saying that. It's really creepy. I'm all for Addams Family shenanigans, but even they had a fairly functional family unit. What you're saying gives me a full-on, toe-curling wiggins. You shouldn't mess around."

"Are you saying you don't believe me? Listen. Just a little while ago I watched my father tear off my mother's arm and eat it right in front of me. Then, he tried to take a bite out of me, so I bashed his head in with a frying pan. Then, my one-armed mother, whom I thought was dead, attacked me and I had to split her head open with a ski pole. There. Are you satisfied or should I draw you some diagrams?" Sage slumped, her shoulders sagging. All at once, bulbous tears began streaming down Sage's face, dripping from her chin into her lap. Sobs rocked her body and she pressed her hands against her face.

Kiley flinched. The kid had seemed so hard and strong, a force beyond her pint-sized frame. Tears were the last thing Kiley had expected. She looked to Max for help, but he only pressed his face harder against the glass. She watched as a tiny bubble of mist formed around his nostrils on the window pane. It seemed she was on her own, and comforting others wasn't exactly goth-girl's forte. Tentatively, she reached for Sage's shoulder, allowing her palm to rest there for a moment before she patted it up and down.

"There, there," she said hesitatingly. Sage hunched away from her and cried. The sorrow that poured from her drifted in waves that nearly knocked Kiley out. The weight of this child's grief was not that of rocks but boulders, and Kiley suddenly felt compelled to roll them off the poor child's back and scoop her up in her arms. The animosity she felt earlier vanished in an instant. She flung her arms around Sage's slumped shoulders.

As she lay there with her arms draped over the poor girl, whose body shook with tears, the image of Kiley's own parents flittered through her brain. She imagined her mother lying on the kitchen floor in a puddle of blood. She envisioned her father hunched over, a wound in his chest. She even imagined her sister—her pom-pom, frustratingly *average* sister—draped against the side of the bathtub, blood draining from her wrists. She couldn't help it. The child's grief conjured up images Kiley would rather have suppressed, and unable to control her imagination, she began to sob with the girl in unison. Tears streamed down her hot face and dripped onto the little girl's bowed head.

At the sound of the two girls sobbing, Max gulped, clenched his fists into his pockets, and scanned the campus for a sign of movement. Anything, but notice the girls and their raw emotions. He tried to will Bryan's return by imagining him turning the corner with Rachel in tow, fully equipped with boyish heroics.

After a few moments, Sage's sobs slowed to an intermittent squeak and Kiley pulled away from their embrace. Kiley's too-black mascara had melted down her cheeks in dark, inky ravines. Sage let out a tiny laugh before slouching back into a frown.

"What? Did my mascara melt? Am I pulling a Frankenfurter over here, or what?" Kiley asked, wiping her cheeks with the backs of her hands.

The child looked at her blankly.

"*From Rocky Horror Picture Show?* Tim Curry? It's a movie."

"You watch a lot of weird stuff I've never heard of," Sage said, biting the inside of her cheek as she spoke. She welcomed the distraction from the sadness circling her heart.

"Yeah. I guess so. Not much else to do when you're fiercely misunderstood, I guess. Anyway, never mind. I guess you're too young to watch stuff like that. Anyway, I'm sorry. Didn't mean to get all Rocky Horror on you. It is one of the dangers of liquid eyeliner. You'll see for yourself when you're old enough to stop dreaming it, and to start being it, kid."

Sage began to wonder if she would ever be old enough. After the events of the day, the child couldn't imagine how she'd grow up. Who'd buy her clothes? Who'd teach her to do laundry, or pack her off to college? Would there even be anyone left to teach college? Her lower lip began to tremble again.

"Hey, don't worry, chicken nugget." Kiley punched her playfully in the arm. "My sister Rachel says there isn't anything a pint of Ben and Jerry's can't fix, and doom and gloom aside, I'm forced to agree. Ice cream can follow me into the nether realm. I hear the Darkside already has cookies." She fixed the child with a weak smile.

Sage raised her eyebrows. "Are you serious? You think ice cream will fix the fact that I just watched my parents die?"

Kiley frowned. "That's not what I meant. I'm sorry. I—I meant that—I just meant that you were crying and ice cream can help tears. I was just, well—trying to say something witty to cheer you up. It's just something sunshine girls like my sister say. So, sorry, spice girl. I'll stick with the sarcasm and death glares that I'm best at."

The tension in Sage's face eased slightly. She looked at the floor. "No. It's okay. Thanks for, well, trying, I guess." She dried her face on the sleeves of her cardigan.

Max turned from his lookout position at the door. "He's coming!" he shouted. "It's Bryan. He's running up the hill."

"Is my sister with him?" Kiley asked. An unfamiliar feeling of kinship at the thought of her sister caught her off guard. Only moments before she was willing Rachel to die so she could run away with Bryan, but somehow the emotional imaginings of her sister just a second ago as she sobbed with the child had changed her perspective. The hard-edged sheen of the gothic tweenager began to melt as easily as her mascara moments ago, and now she was worried about Rachel. Almost as if she cared. She jumped to her feet and ran to the door, suddenly uncaring if the others saw a crack in her callous, gothic veneer.

She leaned to the left and then to the right in an attempt to see past Max and out the window. Max's eyebrows pulled together. Finally she pushed him out of the way and pressed her face to the glass.

Bryan jogged along the side of the building, bobbing back and forth as if he were drunk or dazed. Kiley held her breath. He paused for a moment at the bottom of the stairs, glanced back in the direction he had come, then sluggishly climbed the stairs. His hair was a mess and his face looked stained black in patches. Red streaks covered his bare arms and clothes. His hands were stretched out in front of him as he walked, as if he were afraid to touch anything with them—even himself.

"Is that blood?" Kiley asked. "Why is he covered with blood?" She reached wildly for the bar holding the door shut, but Max grabbed her arms.

"Wait," Max said softly.

"What? Why is he alone? Where's my sister? Let me open the door, damn it!"

Max held her hands tight. "We need to see if he's alone," he said.

All the muscles in Kiley's body loosened simultaneously as she slumped away from the window. Sage placed a palm on the small of Kiley's back and Kiley folded herself over the younger girl, wrapping herself in the child's embrace. Tears spilled from her already wet eyes, staining black streaks into Sage's cardigan.

Max waited until Bryan mounted the last step then pushed the metal bar open. Once Bryan had stepped over the threshold of the door, Max swung it shut quickly. The door slid silently closed behind him before he turned toward Bryan.

"You all right, guy?" he asked, a hint of nervousness quivering at the outer edge of his voice. He wasn't sure he wanted to hear the answer.

"Where's my sister?" Kiley demanded, spinning out of Sage's grip. The older boy did not meet her gaze. He didn't know any other way to say it.

"She's dead," he said quietly and slumped against the wall.

It took a beat for his words to register. When they did, the knowledge slammed into her stomach like a bag of bricks. Tears streamed down her face as she sputtered and squeaked.

"No. NO! What are you talking about? How could she be dead? I saw her just a few minutes ago. Where is she?"

"I—I killed her—" he stammered, his eyes glazed.

"You killed her? You killed *my sister?* What the hell, Bryan?" Kiley screamed. "What are you talking about? You're not making sense." Her voice gave way as she crumpled to her knees.

"She—" Bryan hesitated. "She wasn't herself, Kiley."

It was Sage who responded, her voice almost inaudible above Kiley's sobs. "She was a zombie, wasn't she?"

"A zombie? There's—there's no such thing as zombies," Bryan said and his voice trailed off.

"Was her skin all rubbery white and her veins black and sticking out?" Sage asked fiercely. "Were her eyes filled with blood?"

Bryan pinched his eyes tightly closed, tiny, white wrinkles puckering around his temples. Sage shoved his shoulder.

"I need to know!"

"And just why in the hell *do* you need to know, little girl? Who do you think you are, anyway? You're just a little girl. Go back to your Barbies and leave me alone. I just murdered my girlfriend because she tried to eat me, for Christ's sake! She was *my* girlfriend. She was *Kiley's sister*. She wasn't anybody to you. So why the hell do you care?"

"Look, I get it. Life is hard. I just killed both my parents, remember?"

Tears welled in Bryan's eyes as he dropped his gaze to the floor.

"And I'm the one who warned you about all this, right? If it weren't for me, she probably would have eaten you," Sage said quietly.

"How do you know?" Kiley asked, her voice cold and lifeless as if all the energy had spilled out of her limp hands that rested at her sides.

"What?"

"I said 'how do you know'? What if she was just sick, huh juice box? What if she was just asking for help and Bryan killed her because of your ridiculous sob story about murdering your sickly parents. Did you think of that?"

"I watched my father eat my mother's arm. That's not sickness. That's violence and danger and all the things parents are not supposed to do."

"I'm just saying my day was pretty damned normal until you showed up. Sure, school's abandoned, but there could be a logical explanation for that. Asbestos. Power outage. Gas leak." Kiley took a step toward the child, her arms folded tightly over her chest. "Then along comes Spice Girl all covered in blood and suddenly my sister's boyfriend is telling me he had to kill my sister to save his life. So tell me again exactly why we're supposed to listen to you, the youngest one here? Just who exactly do you think you are?"

"You want to know who I am? I'm a nine-year-old child prodigy. I have an IQ of 186 and I have already skipped three grades in school, six if you count my homeschooling. I could have graduated high school already if I wanted to, and be an honorary freshman at Harvard."

All eyes turned to look at Sage as she spoke. Even Max, who prided himself on taking no interest in the affairs of others, was drawn to her words. He looked the girl up and down, sizing her up the way a predatory animal assesses another in the wild. From her blood stained clothes to the fierceness in her eyes, he decided that she was the real deal. Child or no, she was a cobra. She was surely a force to be reckoned with.

Sage continued, looking each of the gang in the eyes in turn. "So, I am your best chance of getting out of here alive. I want to know if she was sick because I need to collect data about what's going on so that I can figure out what is causing this in time to stop it before it destroys the entire planet."

"Pff," Kiley huffed. "Who died and made you the world's savior?"

Ignoring Kiley's remark, the younger girl turned to Bryan. "I'm sorry you had to kill your girlfriend to survive. The people I had to kill were my mother and father, and now I have no one. We probably all have no one," she said. "Except maybe for each other. So it might be in our best interests to stop fighting and start working together so we can get out of here in one piece."

Silence fell on the group of children. They shifted uncomfortably in the quiet. Max coughed into a closed fist, his eyes gazing listlessly at the floor.

"So," he said. "You're a genius?"

"Yes."

"Oh," Max said. "That explains it."

"Explains what?"

"I've been trying to figure out this whole time how a little girl like you—no offense," Max paused as Sage nodded. "Anyway, I've been trying to figure out exactly how you managed to overpower both of your fully-grown, adult parents. And, more to the point, how you managed to do this even though they were, um, 'monsters'."

Silence filled the lobby as the young girl cocked her head to the side and tried to think of a response to Max's observation.

It was Bryan who finally spoke. "I'm sorry I yelled at you," he said, his face reddening.

Snapping out of her thoughts, Sage replied, "No problem. It's a high-stress day."

"I know what it's like. To lose a parent, I mean."

Sage eyed him warily. "And did you kill your parent?"

"In a manner of speaking, yes. My mother." The older boy paused and looked at the girl for approval. When she nodded, he swallowed and went on. "She was driving me to school when I was five. Kindergarten. I was begging her to look at me in the backseat. I was making a face, or something equally as ridiculous, I dunno. Anyway, she did. She turned to look, and when she did she got t-boned by a guy in a big rig who had just run a stop sign. She died, and I got this scar," he said, pulling back his left ear to show her a tiny knick behind the soft fold. "From where my fingernail got jammed into the skin on impact. Otherwise, I was fine. She died. I lived. It sucked."

Sage regarded him for a moment, then patted his arm. "I'm sorry," she said. "But that wasn't your fault. Even if she hadn't looked at you when she did, that other guy still would have run the stop sign. She still could have died."

"Right," said Bryan, his lips in a thin line. "Just like it isn't your fault that your parents are gone. You did what you had to do to survive, just like I did with Rachel." He stole a glance at Kiley who jerked her head away, and then he continued. "And now, you're right. We're here and we're together and we might just be all any of us has to lean on for support right now." He placed a palm gently on Sage's shoulder. A soft smile rose to her lips.

"Thanks," she said, quietly.

Max, who had retreated to his spot in front of the door, turned from the window. His breath caught momentarily in his throat. "I hate to break up our little group therapy session, but you might want to take a look outside. I think we may have confirmation on Sage's zombie theory."

The kids crowded together at the door, each trying to peer through the window to the plateau outside. Three gray-skinned people shambled up the hill toward the school. The black etching of their veins was visible as they hunched along the cement path.

"Lucifer," cursed Kiley, her breath casting a circle of fog on the glass above Sage's head. "Do you think they know we're in here?"

Sage ducked her head away from the window and grabbed the backs of Bryan's and Kiley's shirts, dragging the older kids down with her. Max followed suit. They squatted on the tiled floor beneath the window, breathing heavily, hearts seemingly pounding in unison.

"Did anyone recognize anybody?" Bryan asked.

"Too far off," said Max quietly.

Kiley patted Bryan's back. "Don't worry. I don't think it was your dad," she said. Mistaking her concern for sarcasm, Bryan grimaced and shot her a dirty look. She recoiled, confused.

"So, what's our next move?" he asked no one in particular, although they all turned to stare at Sage.

"We need a computer with internet access. We need to find out if this is just a local phenomenon, or if it's an epidemic that is affecting people elsewhere. The best way to do that is to check the media," said Sage.

"What about a newspaper?" Max asked.

"No good," Sage replied. "I think this all happened pretty fast. The newspapers wouldn't have had time to get an edition out." She paused to consider something, then added, "But, the newspapers may have printed stories about warnings. Viral epidemics. Unusual break-ins. Disproportionate intakes in hospital emergency rooms, that sort of thing."

"We could also try to find a phone and call our homes," Kiley offered.

"It's worth a shot," Sage said. "But don't get your hopes up. I'm guessing that everyone else is trying to make phone calls, too. If that's the case, we might not be able to get through to anyone. Especially if they're already—"

"How about television?" interjected Bryan. "There's one in the library, as well as newspapers and computers. But you usually need a teacher or librarian to give you access on the computers."

"That sounds like our best bet. I'm thinking if there is any information on this circling the internet, it will be local news and blogs. Anything else probably wouldn't have had time to spread the word or check the facts. I'm hoping this is breaking news," said Sage.

"Unless it's an epidemic and we're the last to get hit," offered Bryan. "Maybe somebody pulled a *Cloverfield* and uploaded a video to Youtube already, or something."

"*Cloverfield?*" asked Sage.

"It's a movie," Kiley said. "Not a very good one, either. Like, M. Night Shyamalan bad."

Sage shook her head. "I don't know who that is."

"Probably for the best," Kiley said.

"So, epidemic? Global catastrophe? Government collapse?" Bryan interrupted.

"Yeah, I'm trying not to think about that. This is happening here, so we need to look at information from here first. Outside of our little, rural dream-town and we can't isolate the variables enough to determine if what we read about happening elsewhere is the same thing going on here. Let's just go and check it out," said Sage.

Max stood up, carefully avoiding the window. "I'm going to check the lock," he whispered. Reaching a cautious hand out toward the entrance, Max allowed his fingers to close around the handle. He gave it a careful tug. The lock engaged, clicking quietly as the handle moved against the door plate.

Sage popped up on the other side of the door, eyeing the other half of the plateau. At the almost inaudible sound of metal clicking against metal, a female figure in the distance jerked her head toward the school. Instinctively, Sage ducked below the window, her eyes wide.

"There's no way she could have heard that," she said.

Max squatted beside her. "What?"

Sage nodded her head toward the door, trembling slightly. "There was a woman—one of those things—on the far side of the hill. When you tested the lock, it seemed like she heard the noise. That just isn't possible. She'd have to have the auditory sense of a dog to hear a sound that faint from so far away."

"Maybe she does," Kiley whispered.

Sage nodded, bringing a finger softly to her lips. They huddled together as Sage whispered faintly. "No sound. Bryan, can you get us to the library?"

He nodded. Sage slid silently forward on her stockinged feet, bobbing as she squat-walked across the floor. After a few paces, she waved her hand at Bryan, signaling for him to scoot in front of the group. Bryan complied, steering the slow procession toward the hallway to the right of the main office. The group bounded up and down like a long row of leap frog.

It felt like hours had passed before the group made it to the hall doors on the far side of the reception area which was hidden from the entrance window by the partition of the main office. As Bryan lifted his hand to press the bar of the door open, Max let out a soft hissing noise. Bryan raised an eyebrow and held his hands out as if to question what Max was trying to tell him.

Max pointed to a black box hanging from the ceiling, one side of which made contact with the closed hall door. Then he indicated a small sign above the door handle to the main office before swiping his hand across his throat like a knife. Bryan couldn't see what the sign said from his position, but he guessed it was a standard security system announcement. If he had opened the door just then, he might have set off an alarm alerting god knew who—or what—to their presence.

Slithering forward on his belly beneath the door, Max rose on the other side of the partition. As he slid up along the length of the door, he slipped his free hand into his pocket. His fingers jiggled around in his pocket for a moment before pulling out a plastic card that Kiley recognized as a card for the local library. She arched an eyebrow at him and he grinned down at her.

Just then, the scraping sound of fingernails on glass sounded behind them and a door rattled on its hinges. Panic shot through the children as they all jerked their heads toward the lobby. There, in the window, a creature cocked its head to one side, its black eyes scanning the inside of the school. Its gaze seemed to fall on the sole of Kiley's boot and the door rattled again.

Heart racing, Kiley yanked her leg around the corner of the partition and stared frantically at Max. She opened her mouth to speak, but Max lifted a finger to his lips to silence her.

The creature screeched loudly. The reverberations of the scream seemed to ricochet off the door and hit the creature in the face as it jerked its head backward. It slammed the entire length of its body against the door.

Kiley's eyes were wide as her fingers clutched at the linoleum floor beneath her. Sage put a hand on Kiley's leg and looked meaningfully into her eyes. After a moment, the creature smacked its palm against the glass and turned away.

"Do you think it saw me?" asked Kiley, breathless with the fear that seemed to clench off the air in her throat.

"No," whispered Bryan. "If it had, it wouldn't have left, right?"

"Right," said Sage. "That thing couldn't have seen us in this darkness. And the partition is in the way. Unless it has x-ray vision—"

Kiley shot her a look of fear.

"Which I'm sure it doesn't," she added hastily. "I'm sure it would have busted right through the glass if it saw us."

"Hey," Bryan whispered to Max, who was fishing around in his pocket. "Figure it out?"

"Yeah. I figured we should shut the hell up or they'll hear us," he said coldly.

"Can we just get out of here, please?" hissed Kiley.

Max pulled a piece of bubble gum from his pocket. Discarding the wrapper, he tossed the gum in his mouth and chewed.

"Chewing gum isn't a way to hide. Are you going to tell me why you're so cold all of a sudden?" asked Sage.

Max's mouth moved slowly over the lump of gum, softening it with each chew. He let a hot steam of breath out of his nostrils and shook his head. "I recognized that guy, is all."

"Who was it?" asked Kiley, leaning forward on her hands and knees.

"Nobody. Just my neighbor. Used to watch sports with me."

"A friend?" Sage offered.

"Yeah."

Emotionless, the boy stretched upward with the library card in his hand toward the black sensor on the ceiling. Lifting to his tip-toes, he strained to reach the ceiling. The card perched precariously between his first two fingers, barely slid between the sensor and the hall doors. Using his free hand, he plucked the gum from his mouth, squished it between his fingertips for a few moments then stretched it toward his other hand. He pressed the gum along the outer edge of the card, securing it to the side of the sensor before carefully sliding back into a squat.

Max nodded to Bryan who cautiously pressed the bar down and pushed the door open. No alarm. The library card clung to the sensor, blocking the output from registering that the door was opening, as, one by one, they slipped through the gap in the door and into the hallway.

"It might not even be on, bonehead," whispered Kiley. "I don't see any lights."

Max shrugged.

"As long as we avoid the classroom door windows, we shouldn't be seen by any of those things outside," said Bryan, ignoring Kiley's statement as he stretched his legs. "But we also have to be quiet in case Sage is right about them being able to hear really well. The library is down at the end of this hall on the left," he said, pointing toward the end of the long hallway before turning to lead the way.

Kiley ran to catch up with Max, ducking as she passed the windows in the classroom doors which were all closed along the corridor. The shock of her sister's death hovered around her, threatening to send tears spilling from her eyes. She thought about what Max had said about the monster at the door being his friend and a sudden stroke of compassion shot through her for the second time that day. She opened her mouth to say something consoling, but she was at a loss for words.

"What's up?" asked Max, unable to look her in the eye.

"How'd you learn to do that, anyway?" she asked, a hint of admiration in her voice.

"My father," he said. "My real father, he was a Special Ops soldier for the army. Toward the, um, end, he started hallucinating real bad about all these bad guys that were supposedly out to get him. Before he died, when I still lived with him, he used to smuggle me around to all these crazy places, always teaching me how to get out 'alive', as he put it. I got real good at noticing alarms and locks and movement and stuff."

"How—how did he die?"

"Suicide," he responded flatly.

"I'm so sorry," she stammered. "I didn't know."

Max shrugged. "It doesn't matter," he said, still not looking at her. "After he died, I went to live with my mom and her, um, boyfriend. They didn't really like me around much, so I used the stuff I learned from my dad to break into places for food or a warm place to sleep. I did whatever I needed to do to survive. Just as long as I didn't have to stay at home with them." He said "them" in a way that reminded Kiley of scraping gum off the roof of her mouth with her tongue.

"Why are you telling me all this?" she asked, squinting at him. Her eyes were bloodshot and she could feel the tears there, waiting for a sign that it was safe to come out.

Max blushed. "I—I don't really know," he stammered. "Maybe because the Tin Woman has a heart after all."

She was tempted to be offended, but looked at the ground instead as the tears loomed around her blurring vision. "I'm not made of metal, you know. I have a heart and feelings and my sister is gone and I never got to tell her that I loved her even if she was a polo-shirt and khakis, pep rally loser."

"Why are you telling *me* this?" asked Max quietly.

Kiley regarded Max for a moment. Why *was* she telling Max—total loser Max—her life story all of a sudden, anyway? They stopped and looked quietly into each other's eyes.

Without stopping to think about it, Kiley grabbed the sides of Max's face and planted a kiss on his lips. As she pulled away, Max's eyes were wide, his eyebrows high on his forehead.

"What was that for?" he asked, startled.

It was Kiley's turn to shrug as she cast a sideways glance at Bryan's back shrinking down the hallway. "I dunno. For a second there, I just kind of 'got' you, I guess." Tears welled in her eyes as all the muscles in her body seemed to vibrate at once. She ran to catch up with Bryan and Sage, leaving Max standing alone and speechless.

CHAPTER FIFTEEN

Max

Max stood, frozen in place. Hot blood rushed to his cheeks. He dropped his head to avoid meeting anyone's questioning eyes should they turn back to look at him. He'd never admit it to anyone, but he had never been kissed before—at least, not since first grade when he cornered a girl in the "kissing tunnel" on the playground. And, if the clumsy lips of a giggling six-year-old was any kind of comparison, Kiley's kiss had nearly knocked him out with an adrenal pumping combination of breathlessness and thrill. His heart still pounded.

He was so distracted that he failed to notice a water fountain sticking partway out into the hall. It caught him at hip level and he winced. Pausing, he knelt over the fountain and pressed the springy metal button with his thumb. A burst of water hummed from the spout, arching over the top of the fountain toward the drain. Pursing his lips, he sucked in several gulps of water. The water was just under room temperature, but it cooled the inside of his mouth and throat. A smile came to his lips as he straightened, hovering there for several moments reveling in the aftermath of his first kiss.

Something hummed at the corner of his mind. It was as though a sensor had tripped and alarms were sounding that only he could hear. He stood perfectly still. A thrill of fear suddenly raced tickling fingers over the nape of his neck. A sinking sensation weighed down the inside of his stomach as a cold trickle of sweat coated his palms. He glanced slowly to his left. The

others had somehow slipped away without him noticing—
probably to the library at the end of the hall, as Bryan had said.
Just a few yards away, beyond a closed door.

Nothing to worry about.

But something was worrying Max. Something knotted up at
the back of his mind. Something clenching the muscles of his
abdomen. And it wasn't just the leftover reactions from Kiley's
kiss.

Warily, he turned his gaze toward the door they had just come
through, but there was nothing to indicate the source of his
alarm. Just a long, glossy-floored hallway mottled by lockers and
classroom doors, all of which were closed.

Except one.

Wait a minute, thought Max. *Wasn't that door closed before?*
He fumbled in his pocket for his switchblade. His fingers closed
around a duct-tape wallet and a few pieces of gum, but no knife.

Dammit! he thought. *Bryan still has my knife.*

Then he saw it. Wedged between two sets of lockers, in front
of a fire extinguisher was a man dressed in a beige, short-sleeved
shirt and a pair of brown pants that Max recognized as the
uniform worn by the custodial staff at the middle school. In the
dim light streaming through the classroom windows, Max could
barely make out the black veins popping out on the man's
alabaster neck. The creature's hand clawed the glass over the fire
extinguisher, the pads of its fingers making long streaking sounds
against it as its tongue clicked inside its head.

Max froze. How had he not heard him? Why was the creature
even there, or, more to the point, how had the creature failed to
notice Max? *Was it when I was taking a drink? Did he sneak in
then?*

Max's mind raced. Without his knife, he felt helpless, but if he
screamed for help, he knew he risked alerting more of these
creatures. And if he ran for it, he would most certainly grab the
attention of the monster. Max glanced down one end of the hall
then the next. The classroom door that hung open at the end of
the hallway from which the creature had emerged was about five
yards away, but the library doors around the corner at the end of

the hall were a good thirty yards away. A 5 to 8 second run, at least.

Max weighed his options. Run, shout for help, or stay and fight without a weapon. He tried to calm his sporadic breath as he held his limbs tight and still. Terror crippled his legs, gluing his feet in place. If he ran, he could probably make it to the open door from where the custodian had presumably come, but what if there were more in there? From where he stood, he couldn't tell whether it was a custodial supply closet or a classroom that had been opened up.

What if this thing has a key, and I lock myself in there thinking I'm all safe, and the guy just opens it up on me?

Eyeing the expanse of hallway separating himself from the library, which he wasn't even sure was on the left as Bryan said, Max chewed nervously on his lips. For all he knew, it could be another 30 yards beyond the corner. Still, it was where he presumed the others were. If they hadn't noticed he was missing already, it was possible that they would turn back to look for him. If he went toward the classroom, he could inadvertently lead them into a trap.

Before Max could decide, however, the custodian in front of him dropped his clawing hand to his side. In that moment, Max's move was decided. Without skipping a beat, the boy took off down the hallway toward the direction of the library. A croaking screech bellowed from the creature's throat following closely behind the boy's back as its feet galloped over the linoleum-covered floor. As Max reached the corner, he skidded on the sides of his shoes for a split second before sprinting again. Sure enough, a pair of red double-doors were several yards in front of him, the silver-plated letters "L-I-B-R-A-R-Y" mounted vibrantly above them.

Puffing, he barreled forward, the exertion of his thighs clenching the muscles beneath his skin. The monster was still shrieking. From the clopping footsteps behind him, he knew it was right on the heels of his tattered sneakers. As he drew closer to the door, it swung widely open. Sage stepped into the hallway in front of him.

"We thought you—"

She looked at the two fast-approaching figures. Immediately, she backed up, holding the door with one palm for Max to come through. As Max flew over the threshold of the door like a track runner leaping over a hurdle, Sage flung the door closed. A split second before it clicked shut, the monster dove head-first through the door and rolled clumsily to its feet.

At the sound of the commotion, Bryan appeared from the bathroom behind the librarian's desk. At the sight of the creature, he hurled himself forward, vaulting over the bar-style desk, pulling out Max's knife as he landed on the floor.

Upon seeing the monster, Kiley flung herself from the computer chair on which she'd just taken a seat. The chair flew backwards a few feet before spinning around and toppling over. The noise seemed deafening. It took all her courage to keep from screaming as she scanned the room for something that could be used as a weapon.

The black-eyed zombie turned quickly on Sage who seemed to be its easiest target as she was pressed in a cramped pocket of space between it and the door. It squealed and cocked its head to one side before advancing on her. Sage pressed the sole of her foot against the library door and, pushing off with all her weight threw herself to the floor, sliding along the glossy linoleum between his legs like a baseball runner skidding into home.

The creature was slow to react, as if he couldn't tell to where the moving form had disappeared. It let out a frantic screech and jerked its head around as if searching for the girl or an easier target to sink his black teeth into. One of its hands grasped at the air in front of him where the little girl had been moments before.

Kiley spotted a pair of flags flanking the doors of the reference section. She leapt toward the door and plucked a flag from its holder. The pole was narrow, the flag only about as long as her legs. She un-looped the flag from the bar and, testing the point of the ornament at the top of the pole, she thrust the flag pole in front of her like a sword. She pointed it toward the zombie who had turned back toward the interior of the library.

Max swooped down and scooped up Sage next to Bryan, who had picked up an encyclopedia and was readying for a swing. As the younger boy turned back, the cold, rubbery fingers of the custodian closed hard around his shoulder. The points of its fingers burrowed into Max's collar bone as the thing jerked its hand and pulled the boy closer to its face. Max's tendons cracked and popped as his shoulder dislocated and hot pain shrieked through it. Spreading its blistered mouth wide, the custodian brought its teeth close to the side of Max's face, ready to chomp down with ugly, broken teeth. Max cringed, whimpering as he recoiled from the creature.

A thick hard-cover book slammed into the side of the creature's head. It shook its head and slowly turned toward the source of the blow. Sage plucked another book from the shelf beside her to replace the one she'd taken from Bryan and flung it hard into the creature's face as Bryan edged up from behind the monster, the point of Max's switchblade extending outward from his closed fist.

The custodian's hand opened, releasing Max from its painful grip. Max slumped to the floor, wincing as pain whipped through his shoulder. Grabbing the monster's ankles with the hand of his uninjured arm, he pulled quickly forward, shaking the custodian from its center of balance. The monster clattered to the floor. Sage dove forward, trying feebly to pin its arms to the ground. Bryan followed suit as he dropped to his knees and slammed the knife down toward the zombie's chest. The man's sunken torso twisted under Bryan's body and the blade struck it in the neck, spraying black blood onto Bryan's hand.

"Get it in the head," screeched Sage as she struggled with the monster's flailing arms. "You need to sever its cerebral cortex!"

Mouth slack, Bryan looked blankly at Sage.

His face contorted with pain as he clutched his shoulder, Max shouted, "The brain, Bryan. The brain! Don't you watch monster movies?"

The creature jerked its torso out from under Bryan's squatting body. Losing his footing, the older boy tumbled backward landing with a thud on his tailbone.

The blade of the knife stuck out of the rubbery flesh of the creature's white neck. Writhing wildly about, it flung Sage from its arms effortlessly and sat up, reaching for the nearest victim. It just happened to be Max who lay with his good arm wrapped around the monster's calves. Bryan rose painfully and made another dive for the zombie, grasping for the knife handle that protruded below its chin, but his shoes slid in a pool of blood and his feet flew out from under him.

Kiley stepped between Sage and Max and, lunging forward with all her might, thrust the point of the flag pole ornament into the temple of the flailing zombie. The metal tip pierced the flesh easily, as if the creature's skin were made of the dry and raspy gray paper of a wasp's nest. Blood spurted along the length of the flagpole before the beast collapsed to the floor. A pool of tar-like black blood bubbled beneath the former custodian's head as Max released his wrestler's grip on its legs and unsteadily regained his feet.

Kiley put a hand on her hip and, letting out a wild breath, said with a trembling voice, "I think that's how you slay a zombie, boys." She caught Max's questioning gaze, her hand on the flagpole shaking like a leaf in the wind.

"What?" she asked. "Like I don't stream reruns of Buffy when I'm bored? Hello?" She glanced at the creature at her feet, her knees knocking together as every muscle in her body seemed to vibrate and tremble out of her control. "That creature has been totally owned by Kiley, the Zombie Slayer," she said, teeth chattering.

As Sage and Bryan stumbled to their feet, Max grabbed Kiley's face with the palm of his good hand as if to catch her before she clattered to the ground, and pressed his mouth to hers. Their lips collided warm and soft before opening slightly, allowing the tips of their tongues to meet. Caught off guard, Kiley's knees weakened further beneath her.

"Ew," sneered Sage, turning her head away. "That's so gross." She allowed her eyes to settle on the scabby mouth of the zombie at her feet, considering it a better object for her attention than the gooey kiss of the lovebirds.

"*That's* gross, huh?" asked Bryan, following her gaze to the ground. "You're covered with the blood of human-eating zombies and you think a little spit swapping is something to worry about?"

"That's different," said Sage. "The human mouth is a cesspool of germs swimming around with just about everything we come in contact with." She gave a tiny kick to the limp hand of the zombie. Its arm rocked forward before rolling back to its original position near her toe. "Blood's just . . . well, it's somehow more, I don't know. Scientific, maybe?" She shrugged as if that closed the conversation.

Kiley pulled away from Max, her eyes wide. She blinked at him. Her hand trembled on the flag pole she was still clutching so fiercely that her fingers had gone from white to red again. As she unwrapped her wavering fingers from the pole, Max could see the red creases from where her hand had wrinkled in the fist. He reached out and touched her hand with the pads of his fingers.

"What was that for?" she asked, dazed. Max smiled.

"I just 'got' you, is all," he said earnestly, his mouth dropping open as he let out a long breath after the words. The boy turned and braced himself against the door frame of the tiny library study room.

"Now you might not want to watch this," he said, "Even if you are Kiley the Zombie Slayer." He took a deep breath and slammed his dislocated shoulder hard into the frame. A scream wheezed from behind his clenched teeth and he slumped against the wall, his eyes tightly closed, his breathing rapid and uneven.

"Ouch," he whispered and tried to smile.

CHAPTER SIXTEEN

Kiley

Kiley collapsed to the floor. Her eyes were teary and wide, and worry lines wrinkled her brow. She covered her hands with her face and mumbled something, her voice too muffled for any of them to hear.

"What's up?" asked Max. He massaged his shoulder tenderly with the tips of his fingers, wincing.

Kiley lifted her head at the sound of Max's voice, but she faced Bryan and glared at him. Black crumbles of make-up were caked around her eyes and her purple eye shadow had melted. Against her pale skin, the dark circles around her eyes made her look ghostly.

Her voice cracked as she repeated herself, this time louder than before. "Was that what Rachel looked like?"

Bryan stepped forward, a sober expression straightening the features of his face. "Yes," he whispered.

Kiley bit back a sob. Max dropped to the floor beside her and wrapped his arms around her shoulders. She shoved him off violently.

"I don't even *know you*," she said forcefully, her jaw clenched and unmoving as she uttered the last two words. Max backed away quickly, his right eye quivering slightly. He turned his back and fixed his gaze on the stacks of books beyond.

"I was just trying to comfort you," he said quietly. He bit down hard on his lower lip. *What is wrong with girls? She kissed me*

by the water fountain, and now I'm like a sewer rat to her.
"What the hell?" he asked aloud.

"I don't need your comfort," she screamed. "My sister just freaking died, okay?" She burst to her feet, her hands clenched into fists. "No. Scratch that. My sister's boyfriend murdered her. Quick, somebody call Lifetime because I have their new movie of the week." She turned on Bryan, her face twisted with rage as her neck turned vibrant red from her chin to the hem of her black and purple striped shirt.

"That's not fair," mumbled Bryan.

"Technically," Sage calmly said. "It was probably self defense."

Kiley whirled on Sage, her hands splayed out in front of her. "And you," she yelled, wringing her hands. "If you hadn't come when you did, with your blood covered sweater and your damned dirty socks, my sister might still be alive. For all we know, you brought this illness—or whatever it is—with you when you ran up that hill. You probably infected my sister! Or maybe you just made it all up like some pathological little freak, and you put this sick idea in Bryan's head, and when he saw her, he . . ." She let out a strangled sound.

"Hey," said Bryan, stepping between Kiley and Sage. Sage didn't move. She stared calmly at Kiley through the gap between Bryan's arm and hip.

"You need to calm down, girl," Bryan said vehemently as he took Kiley's shoulders in his hands. "Sage couldn't have infected your sister. If you stop and think about it, Sage didn't even join us until *after* your sister disappeared. For all we know she was already one of those things just munching away on a puppy. Sage didn't put that image into my head. Your sister was gone. She was sick and she was violent and scary. You weren't there, Kiley." His voice calmed as the muscles in his face and shoulders seemed to go suddenly lax. "You didn't see her," he finished flatly.

"So what? You killed her? Just like that?" Kiley pressed forward, her nose nearly touching Bryan's as tiny flecks of spit burst from her lips into his face. "For all we know," she started, "my sister had some kind of disease which *could have been cured,* maybe. But it's too late for that now, isn't it?"

She gestured toward the fallen custodian. "Look at him!" Her voice was so loud it was no longer recognizable as her own. "He clearly has some kind of disease. Look at his veins. Look at his eyes! They're black, for God's sake. People's eyes don't just turn black! He was sick," she cried. "He was sick—just like Rachel—and I just killed him."

Bryan's face softened. He pressed a palm into her shoulder. "Hey," he said after a beat. "It wasn't your fault. You were just protecting us from it. He was attacking us, Kiley. You had no choice."

Silence engulfed the library. Max moved away from the group, taking a seat at a computer cubicle where he remained with his head hung low. Bryan stroked Kiley's hair as she wept.

It was Sage who broke the quiet.

"I don't think he was sick," she said. Everyone turned to look at her. "I mean, at least not the 'normal' kind of sick, if there is such a thing."

Bryan looked down at Kiley who had buried her face in his shirt. He looked up, and said, "Yeah?"

Sage continued. "I mean, think about it. If he was sick. And my parents were sick. And your sis—" She paused mid-word, and looked at Kiley whose head was still buried in the boy's shirt. Nodding to herself, she turned to Bryan, and went on. "And your girlfriend was sick—

"Yeah?" interrupted Bryan.

"The point is, my parents went from peace-loving hippies to homicidal killers in the time it took me to walk from my kitchen into my bedroom and get dressed. It wasn't long. Like, four or five minutes? Maybe less."

Bryan nodded with sudden comprehension. "And Rachel was only gone for fifteen minutes at the most before I found her."

"Right," said Sage. "And she was perfectly fine before she starting masticating puppy bits, right?"

Bryan nodded gravely. "Masticating means eating, right? Then, sure, that's right."

"So?" Kiley grunted, turning to face the child.

"So," said Sage. "If they were all sick, then why aren't we?"

Max, his head still bowed, spoke first. "Natural immunity."

Sage nodded. "That's what I thought too in the beginning, but the more I think about it, well, it doesn't make sense. It was the kissing and the blood thing that made me think of it. I mean, look at us. There are four of us here now. No one else. Just us. So far, anyway. And each one of us has come in contact with their blood, their saliva, their breath. Whatever. And none of us are sick. Doesn't it seem like a major coincidence that we all happen to be immune?"

"What else would explain it?" Kiley asked. There was desperation in her voice. An ice-thin hope that there was a reason, a good reason, she had just murdered someone and that her sister had just been murdered.. Without that reason, the girl couldn't imagine what that would mean. About her. About the world. About what would happen next.

"I'm not sure," Sage admitted. "We hadn't studied viruses and bacteria in my biology class yet. I only know what I learned from home schooling and books and stuff, which isn't much."

"There's some kind of super high-powered microscope in the biology lab," said Bryan. "We examined the blood of a pig under it, and you could see all the cells moving around. Would that help?"

Sage shook her head. "I may be smart, but I'm not a biologist or anything. I'm only nine, remember?" She grinned. "All that would tell me is whether there is a virus or bacteria or something attacking human cells. To be honest, I wouldn't know if it was a flu virus or a crazy, mutating, zombie-monkey death virus. Not to mention that it wouldn't help us figure out why *they* have the crazy, mutating, zombie-monkey death virus and we don't have it."

Bryan nodded. "Okay, so what if we got blood samples from all the things around here and compare them with our own blood samples. Wouldn't that tell us something?"

"Only if I can figure out what I'm really looking at. I sort of doubt it though."

"What about the internet?" Max said quietly.

"What about it?" asked Sage.

"Couldn't you find images online of normal blood and virus blood and compare it with what you see under the microscope?" he asked.

"Why?" Kiley asked, her voice cut with sarcasm. "What difference will it make if it is a virus? Look at us. Bryan doesn't grow facial hair yet and my mom just started letting me shave my legs last freaking week. We're just kids. What are we going to do? Come up with some magical zombie cure by looking at blood samples in a high school biology lab?" She crossed her arms over her chest and leaned against the wall.

"She's right," Sage said to Bryan. "It won't do us any good."

"Unless," said Bryan, "we can get our research to someone who can help us out. Like a doctor, or something."

"Dr. Harris lives on the same street as a friend of mine," mumbled Max. "I promised I'd see him after school today." His voice was barely above a whisper.

"Except for all we know, all the doctors are zombies, too. I'm surrounded by rocket surgeons. Clearly," said Kiley, rolling her eyes.

As realization dawned on Sage, the features of her face lifted, color filling her skin with pink. A smile rose to the corners of her mouth. "That's it," she said, turning to face the slouching figure of the girl. "Kiley, you're a genius."

"No," said Kiley, not missing a beat. "You're the genius and I, apparently, am just an above-average student at your standard, cookie-cutter suburban middle school. It's like an Andy Warhol painting in here."

"Okay," responded Sage, shaking her head. "But what you said just now about the doctor. It makes perfect sense."

"Okay," Bryan said. "Care to explain?"

"Well, for all we know, *the doctors are zombies*. Just like my parents were zombies. And this janitor was a zombie."

"So?" Max asked.

"And what do they all have in common?" Sage prompted.

"Bad breath?" offered Max. Kiley snickered, wiping her tear-stained cheeks with the back of her hand.

"Uh, they're all Greendale residents," suggested Bryan as he began pacing back and forth.

"They're all dead?" asked Kiley.

Sage shook her head in frustration. "No! My point is, they were all *adults*. Maybe we're not sick because we're kids. We are naturally immune, or our DNA is good at fighting off this virus. Or maybe this virus only attacks aging chromosomes or cells, or something like that."

Kiley sighed audibly. "And she's supposed to be a genius, folks," she said, gesturing to an imaginary audience. "There's just one problem with your theory, juice box. My sister turned into a zombie, didn't she? Or did you forget that already? Like you've conveniently forgotten your dead parents." As soon as the dig escaped her mouth, she regretted it. But it was too late. Sage glared at her defiantly, then quickly looked away.

"I acknowledge that your sister is not an adult." Sage's voice was cold and even. She turned to Bryan. "So how old was she?"

"Seventeen," Bryan answered her.

"So maybe the cut-off age is seventeen. Or sixteen. Or when there's that pivotal change in the teenage brain that makes us all . . . adulty, and stuff. Who knows? My point is that we might be okay because we are younger."

"I'm fifteen," offered Bryan, a sudden realization made his stomach sink. "Am I safe, you think? Am I just going to get sick later than everyone else? Am I going to turn into one of them? Are you. . . are you going to have to kill me?"

"Or it could be that we were all breast-fed instead of formula-fed babies," said Kiley, her impatience and anger growing. "Or that we all have a recessive trait in our DNA. Or it could even be that we all share a genetic freakiness from our parents' parents drinking the rotgut water in Greendale! For a genius, you really aren't all that smart, are you?"

"Why are you so mean?" Sage demanded. "I'm just trying to figure things out. At least I'm doing something. I don't see you doing anything but demonstrating your age-appropriate angst all over everything I bring up. Let's hear your grand theory."

"Look," Kiley said, staring at the body of the custodian. "My sister just died, okay? I'm a little off my usual game, but mean is kinda my thing. Or hadn't you noticed? Besides, am I the only one who remembers our original plan? We said we were coming to the library to check the internet and the news. Why aren't we doing that? If we can keep our heads on straight and work together, we'll have a better chance of staying alive. The alternative, if you think about it, isn't very encouraging."

Max rose from his seat and walked toward the group. "She's right. Maybe we are all just kids, but we need to stop *acting* like children. If we don't use our heads and keep our cool, we're all going to die."

"Nice pep talk, coach," mumbled Kiley.

Max turned to her, struggling to keep the anger out of his voice. "That goes double for you, Kiley. You're acting worse than a preschooler. We all get that you're playing your 'nobody understands me; I'm a pre-teen goth' card, but look around. You're the only one in this room that's acting like a whiny, self-entitled brat, and we're *all* under sixteen."

Setting her jaw, Kiley turned her face as a flush of anger tingled, red hot on her cheeks. Max made it a point to ignore her, turning to face Sage and Bryan instead.

"All right," said Bryan, suddenly feeling the need to take charge if only because he was the oldest one present. "Let's do this in an organized fashion. Sage, why don't you hit the stack of newspapers in the back of the library. Scan them for the past week or so and see if there is any mention of any kind of outbreak or sickness going around or—"

"Or people acting weird and trying to eat each other?" Sage offered.

"Yeah," said Bryan. "Something like that." Sage's words brought the image of Rachel's hungry mouth back into his mind. He re-enacted the events of the morning in his head: how they had been kissing in her car just like regular teenagers and then everything changed. He still could not come to grips with the reality of everything that had happened. He sighed and stuffed his hands into his pockets—and found Rachel's cell phone. He had forgotten that she gave it to him to call his father when they realized that the school was empty.

"Phone!" Bryan said loudly. "I have Rachel's cell phone. Why haven't we tried to call people? What's wrong with us?" He held out the cell phone as if it were some magical device that they should all be bowing down before. Kiley drew closer.

"We haven't thought about it because it probably won't work," said Sage. "Remember what I said about everyone trying to use their phones at the same time? It's going to be chaos. We can call and call and it's unlikely anyone will even notice if they're all panicked on the phone with someone else. Anyway, if all the adults are dead, who's going to be answering their phones anyway?"

Bryan frowned at her. "Hey, you never know until you try, right? We're still not sure it's just an adult thing. That's just a theory. Or if it didn't affect kids under a certain age, maybe it also didn't affect old people. Who knows?" He quickly dialed the number to his father's housekeeper. The phone did nothing for a moment then a high-pitched screeching noise shot through the earpiece. Bryan pulled it away from his ear so fast, he nearly dropped it. His face scrunched in pain.

"What happened?" asked Kiley.

"It didn't work. Looks like he switched it to fax mode."

"Landline is dead, too," said Max, who sat at the librarian's desk and tried the phone there.

"How?" Sage asked, stepping toward the boy.

Max shrugged, raising his eyebrows. "I don't know. There's just this repeating message on the phone saying something about being disconnected from the network."

"They must have some kind of networked phone system. It might be tied in with the internet connection," Sage said, frowning. "We could try rebooting the router, if we can find it. Any other ideas?"

Bryan carefully closed the cover and slid it back in his pocket. "It might work later. Or I could try calling someone else. Of course, the satellite service in rural New England isn't exactly going to work in our favor. I've always had shady reception at the high school," he muttered.

Kiley rolled her eyes. "Tell me about it. A few cell towers instead of pine trees, people. It could save a life. Like, mine. Like, right now. Stupid hillbillies. Yeah, I'm sure bad cell service is really what our state license plates mean by 'the way life should be'."

"Enough, Kiley. You're not helping, okay? Why don't you check and see if the television works and if there are any news reports about what's going on, or, if that doesn't work, see if you can find a radio," Bryan said.

He turned to Max. "Max, why don't you set up shop at a computer—hopefully the internet isn't disconnected or malfunctioning, or whatever is going on with the landlines. Let's hope so, because I don't have a clue where the router might be. If you need a login, all the computers are set to 'student' for both username and password. Otherwise you can't get the internet. Scan the net for any mention of zombies in Greendale, or anywhere, for that matter. Although they probably wouldn't be using the word zombies. You know, being that they're adults, they'll call it something else for a while." He smiled. "Something like 'living impaired' or 'life challenged'. Just do some surfing and see what pops up. And I'm—" Bryan paused, sucking in a breath. "I'm going to go to the cafeteria for some food and water. We're going to need it sooner or later. And maybe the nurse's office for some medical supplies too."

"Do you think we're going to need food and water? I mean, I'm not exactly hungry," Kiley said, nodding toward the body of the custodian spread out on the floor. "This isn't the holocaust, is it? I mean, this can't last very much longer, right? Someone's going to come for us. Our parents or the police or—well, someone will come. And how about other kids? If this is just affecting grownups and not kids, then where are they?"

"Maybe they're hiding in other places," Max suggested. "Or maybe. . . maybe their parents killed them—and ate them—"

Bryan shook his head. "Thanks for the visuals, Max. But either way, no matter what the truth is, we need to be prepared."

Max stepped closer to Bryan and lowered his voice. "Listen, something tells me you'd be better with the whole computer thing and I'd be better at the reconnaissance mission. Why don't we switch jobs?"

CHAPTER SEVENTEEN

Max, Kiley, Bryan, and Sage

Bryan tugged at his left ear as he gave the proposition some thought. "I don't know, Max. You don't know the school as well as I do, and I'm the oldest and, I just think—"

"You can tell me where to go," Max interrupted. Leaning in, he whispered, "I just really need to not be *here*, if you know what I mean." Max looked pointedly at Kiley.

"Did something happen?" asked Bryan in a whisper.

"Nah," said Max, shaking his head. "I just can't stand to be around so many girls," he added, loud enough for the others to hear. Kiley caught his attention and looked him in the eyes, unblinking. Max looked away.

"Okay," he said. "I'll draw you a map of where you need to go and I'll put together a list of what I think you might need to get for us." He gave Max another scrutiny. "Are you sure you wanna do this?"

Max nodded.

"Well," said Bryan. "Bring your knife."

Sage and Kiley set off to their tasks as Bryan scribbled a hasty map on the back of a piece of paper from the recycle bin. As he drew, he explained everything he put down twice to make sure Max understood. "Now, remember to avoid the windows in case one of those things should see you. Take my backpack with you and fill it with things from the list. As soon as you have everything, come right back. Don't waste a minute. I mean it,

Max. No exploring. No heroics. I don't like the idea of you out there all by yourself."

"I'll be fine," grunted Max.

"What if there are more of them?" asked Bryan. Glancing around the library, he leaned closer. "Is this thing, whatever it is, with Kiley really worth dying over?"

"I'm not gonna die," responded Max, raising his eyebrows. "Don't you watch horror movies, man? Kids never die in horror movies. It just never happens." Bryan grinned in spite of himself, and nodded.

"Besides," Max went on, stretching his neck and twisting his shoulders from side to side. "I know what I'm doin', okay? My dad was military, and he kind of showed me how to do stuff. If I even remember half of everything he taught me, I'm the guy for the job. Don't worry about me."

Bryan eyeballed him very carefully before responding. "All right," he said. He picked up Max's tired, fallen backpack. After he dumped the contents onto the floor, he held it out. "Take this and fill it with as much food as you can. Then, if you see anything useful in the nurse's office, grab that, too." He paused. "And, Max?" Max glanced up at him as he swung the backpack over his shoulders. "Be careful." He winked. "I'd hate to be stuck here to deal with these two alone. You'd think they were the ones who were sisters the way they argue."

"Don't worry," said Max. "I'll be back before you do anything stupid." He eyed the older boy coolly. Bryan wasn't sure if Max was joking or serious from the flat expression on his face.

"Get back here at the first sign of danger. Heck, after a few more days of fighting zombies together, we might even become friends," Bryan said, shifting his hands to his pockets awkwardly. "Just remember, if something doesn't feel right, turn tail and book it back to the library. It's not like we're going to starve to death in the next few hours and there's a water fountain right outside in the hall. So don't try to be a hero. There's strength in numbers, you know. It took all four of us to kill that last zombie."

"Okay," said Max. "At least I can add that patch to my boy scout sash. I think it will look good between my 'break-into-a-school and save-a-bunch-of-wusses' patches."

Bryan raised an eyebrow. "Wuss, huh?"

"I call's 'em like I see's 'em," said Max . Then he winked, flicked his switchblade open with his free hand, and held it in front of him. "Just in case."

Bryan nodded. "Just in case," he agreed, walking Max to the library entrance. "You be careful, okay?"

"Will do, captain," said Max with a salute. "See you real soon," he added and turned to face the shadowy hallway.

"Deal," muttered Bryan, smiling faintly as he watched Max scoot through the door. He stood there for several seconds, not moving, watching the gap in the door decrease as it slowly swung shut. He wasn't sure if he felt more scared for himself and the two girls or Max out there wandering unfamiliar school corridors alone with zombies around every corner. But when he pictured a zombie version of the high school's steroid-muscled gym teacher with her square jaw and iron-clad shoulders, he had to smile in spite of himself.

Chapter Eighteen

Max

As the door clicked shut behind him, Max let out the long breath he had been holding. His mind was focused as he walked away from the door. But his thoughts weren't of the pep talk Bryan had given him or of zombies hiding behind every door.

His thoughts were of Kiley.

What was that about? Does she think she's the last girl on earth, or whatever? So she doesn't have to be nice to me? Rude. That's what she is, he thought, as he glanced at the crudely drawn map he clutched in his hands.

He was actually glad to be away from them. He didn't like being in crowds, anyway. Not that four people made a crowd, but there was something about the group dynamic that set his nerves on end. Especially with the way Kiley was so mean to him. What had he done to deserve that?

"It's not like I asked you to kiss me," he muttered under his breath, picturing Kiley's face as he said it. "Girls are crazy."

Shaking his head, he focused his attention on the map. If he was reading it correctly, then the cafeteria wasn't far. All he had to do was walk straight down the hallway, through the double doors at the end, take a left and voila: wide, open cafeteria goodness. He could hit the nursing station on his way back by heading through the science wing and then through the humanities wing to the library.

Piece of cake, he thought, his hand squeezed tightly around the handle of his switchblade. Thrusting his other hand through the strap of the backpack, Max surveyed the hall in front of him. A few basement style windows speckled the tops of the walls at the far end of the hallway, allowing a view of the grey-washed sky. A dreary light filtered in through them, casting long shadows along the lockers that lined every wall between the classrooms.

Sucking in a deep breath, he took a single step forward, pausing with his weight unsteadily on his front foot. *What if there are more of those things inside the school? The odds seem likely that there are. What if the knife isn't enough to stop them?*

For a brief moment, like a preview from an upcoming movie, he saw a wild-eyed zombie calmly chewing a human hand. *His* hand. Max forced the image from his mind. He had to trust that everything was going to be okay, that there were no more monsters inside the school. He had to believe that he would make this expedition without trouble. If they were going to be stranded without adults, without the comfort of their bedrooms or their family and friends, they'd need this stuff. It would be better not to worry about food or bandages for a while. It would be better to not worry about those things, so they could focus on the monsters outside. *Right?* he thought.

Swallowing hard, he pressed on, his sneakers squeaking too loudly against the polished floors.

As Max approached the first classroom door, he paused. The door was tightly closed, but light from the windows on the far side of the classroom trickled through the glass in the door. He watched the light dance across the floor, casting the shadows of the last few autumn leaves clinging to nearly naked trees outside in the thinly forested area on this side of the school.

Sucking in a breath and holding it as if he were about to dunk underwater, he dropped to all fours and skittered over the floor beneath the window, popping up on the other side like a submerged buoy bursting to the surface. He exhaled. His breathing seemed overly amplified in the eerie stillness of the hall. He repeated the movement two more times, imagining each time that he was training for the Marine Corps to work on submarines. He'd sink to the floor like a diver, holding his breath, only to bounce up on the other side as he swam toward the imaginary surface.

The silliness of pretending to swim kept his mind focused and less stressed as he approached the double doors that connected this wing to the adjoining hallway. As he inched closer, an uncontrollable shiver shook his shoulders and somersaulted down his back. He winced as the movement sent a jerk of pain through his injured shoulder.

He pressed his palm to the cold, metallic surface of the doors as if feeling for the heat of a fire on the other side. His fingers trembled slightly. Pressing his ear to the door, he listened for the slightest sound. He strained to hear, shutting out everything else around him, hoping to be able to detect if something waited on the other side. He imagined a hoard of the putrid creatures, all twisting their heads violently as Max stepped through the doors. In his mind, they were lumbering toward him, two creatures grabbing his wrists while two others grabbed his legs and splayed him on the cold, tile floor. He saw himself struggling as their teeth ripped open his stomach and hauled pieces of his flesh to their greedy mouths.

Geez, I've been watching too many zombie movies, he thought to himself. Fear forced his breath to come in spasms and he wanted to run back to the library to explain that the mission was impossible.

Instead, he brought his hand to his mouth, pressing his teeth against the mound of his palm. Biting with all his might, he tried to break the skin. He struggled against the pain, trying not to wince or make a sound as he pressed his teeth hard into the flesh. Pulling away, he examined the oblong of teeth marks sunk deep and red into the palm of his hand. The ridges around the teeth marks rose to a fierce, bloodless white, but there was no sign of blood.

Max shuddered, trying to imagine how hard someone or something would have to bite in order to break through the flesh. He imagined that they would lock onto a part of the body and, using their jaw and neck muscles, pull against it until it tore off or until the teeth sliced through the skin, the tendons, the muscle fibers.

Stop it! Just go back.

He glanced over his shoulder. The doors of the library were just a few yards behind him. He could slink back in with some excuse that the school was teeming with beasties. That he couldn't make it, no matter how hard he tried. That he only got back by the skim of his teeth.

They'll see through it, he thought. *And I don't think I could stand to see the smug look on Kiley's face when she believes I chickened out.*

Anger bubbled up beneath the surface of his skin. He had no intention of giving Kiley the satisfaction of, well, anything. Sucking in another deep breath, he pushed against the bar latch of the door. The metal scraped loudly as the doors opened. Max stepped quickly through, and they slowly hissed shut.

See? he told himself as a sigh of relief escaped his lips. *That was easy.*

The hallway stretched out in front of him, with one branch angling off to the right, and another one running perpendicular to the straight portion to his left. He eyed each hallway cautiously. The doors were closed as they always were before the custodians opened everything up prior to class. The walls were lined with lockers the same as the previous halls had been. Except, at the end of the hall running to his left, he could clearly see the entrance to the cafeteria, the dark blue doors open and latched to the walls on either side to keep them from swinging closed again.

Nothing here, he thought. It troubled him that the halls were so visible to one another through the rows of windows along the classrooms—it made it more difficult to be inconspicuous—but he walked on.

Who built this school? He thought, trying to imagine a bird's eye view of the helter-skelter star shape of the school's weird pattern of additions. *Charles Manson? The Middle School is just a box with two modulars. This is like some creepy labyrinth.* As soon as the thought drifted through his mind, he had to bite his lip.

Of course, his mind added. *The perfect setting for a horror movie. Maybe even one where a kid gets killed.*

The boy stifled a shudder as he drew closer to the blue doors. He stared into the empty cafeteria. Something about the vast openness of it sent another shiver up and down his spine. It seemed to be the last place he'd want to be if one of those things attacked him.

As he entered the cafeteria, the smell of lemon-scented floor cleanser wafted into his nostrils, reminding him of his mother's kitchen that one week she'd stayed away from alcohol. She'd actually cleaned. And that morning when he'd gotten up, he'd found her in the kitchen over a steaming pile of pancakes holding a glass of orange juice out for him.

That was before Ronald and his endless six-pack. Max tried to imagine what his mother was doing, secretly hoping his stepfather had turned into a beast and his mother had taken a can of hairspray and a Zippo to his head. He wondered if they were okay, or if they were even alive. He somehow knew that, even if they knew the school was closed or a zombie apocalypse had descended on the small town of Greendale, they wouldn't look for him. Heck, he could stay out until dawn if he wished and they'd never even notice.

They don't care. Even as he thought it, another, more humbling idea rose to his mind. He imagined his mother lying dead on the floor, her boyfriend dead beside her and he sobered quickly. The mental image sent a rush of emotion through his body, tears welling in the crooks of his eyes. His mother was far from perfect, but the thought of her dead, her hair in knots and drenched in blood—well, that wasn't an image he wished on anyone. And then he pictured his stepfather gnawing on his mother's heart, and he savagely wiped the tears away before they slipped from his eyes.

He couldn't even picture his mom as one of the undead. He couldn't think of any of that right now. He just couldn't. He had a job to do and that was that. He shook off the mixed emotions of sadness and anger pooling in his chest and refocused his efforts on the kitchen, the shimmering stainless steel doors of which also stood open against the back wall of the lunchroom.

As he padded lightly through the glossy-floored cafeteria of Greendale High, he surveyed the walls around him. The cafeteria doubled as a gymnasium and at each end of the room were two basketball hoops, beneath which were blue mats stuck to the walls. A red taped line ran around the rim of the floor, marking the court.

Relief washed over him when he saw the long lunch tables were folded and stacked vertically, blocking the windows in each corner of the room, but the fire exit with its red double doors on the south wall had large glass panes in them. From his angle (he stood nearly in the center of the cafeteria), he could see a grassy knoll and the low-hanging branches of a tree swooping beyond the glass pane.

Switching directions, he walked directly to the wall that housed the fire exit. Pressing himself against the cold brick, he walked along the edge of it.. His sneakers skidded softly over the linoleum as he ducked beneath the fire exit and inched along the floor. He balanced his weight on the balls of his feet as he half squatted, half walked below the bar on each door. He needed to stay close to the door to avoid being seen by anyone standing directly in the doorway, but he was afraid that if he touched the door even slightly, the sound of the metal door scraping against the frame would alert anyone outside that there might be a tasty treat waiting inside the school. His hands trailed along the ground to steady himself as he moved guerilla-style under the windows.

A fleeting memory of his father, reading him *Hansel and Gretel* one night by the dim light of a flashlight as he tried to soothe Max to sleep, filtered through his mind. He huffed, imagining himself scrunched into a bird cage growing fatter and fatter for one of the creatures, holding out a chicken bone instead of his finger for it to test each day. The dark humor of the thought brought a smile to his lips. Lost in the thought, he didn't notice a tiny sliver of glass on the floor as his fingers crept spiderlike toward it. The sliver pierced the index fingertip of his right hand and Max winced. Without thinking, he brought his finger quickly to his mouth.

The instinctive movement induced a chain reaction as he wobbled from side to side and, before he could regain his balance, his right shoulder and knee crashed into the fire exit doors. The door latch banged against the lock plate, a noise so soft, so inscrutable that it would not have been noticed by anyone more than a few yards from the door; but Max froze with fear.

A thin trickle of sweat worked its way across his forehead, creeping like a hundred centipede legs scampering over his skin. He longed to brush the sweat away, even imagined lifting his hand from his mouth to his forehead to wipe away the offending beads of sweat that rolled down toward his eyebrows, but when he actually tried, he found he could not.

As he sat, trembling beneath the door, he heard a sound that sent sickening spasms through the pit of his stomach. *Idiot*, he scolded himself. He sucked in a breath, holding it tight, afraid to release it or even to move. He focused on a piece of lint near the edging of the linoleum, unable to look up.

The sound was unmistakable: the vibrating cackle of one of the zombie creatures. And it came not from beyond the fire exit doors as Max would have imagined—as he would have *hoped*. No such luck. This sound came from the cafeteria kitchen, only a few yards from where Max sat paralyzed with fear.

Gulping deeply, he begged his legs to move, to run, to escape, but they refused to obey. He sucked air in spasms as a tear rolled down his cheek.

I'm going to die, he thought. *I'm going to be eaten alive and there is nothing I can do to stop it.*

The clatter of pots and pans as they crashed to the floor echoed across the cafeteria. Max winced, but remained unmoving, his eyes still fixed on the lint. He barely saw the scuffling feet of the creature's brown shoes as they shuffled into his peripheral vision.

The youngster's mind raced through the pages of his memory, settling on the fight he had with his mother's boyfriend a short time ago. He remembered how he'd tried to tune the man out, tried to ignore him, hoping if he could just shut off the horrible words that flowed from the man's mouth, he could somehow survive. He had focused on what?

A coffee spill. That was it. Max stared hard at the lint.

If I can just stare at this lint long enough, if I can just pay attention to this one tiny detail, maybe I'll disappear the way chameleons evaporate into the background. And maybe then, I'll somehow survive.

Maybe.

CHAPTER NINETEEN

Bryan, Kiley and Sage

As Max's soft footsteps padded away, Bryan felt less sure of himself and his decision. He briefly debated bursting through the doors, grabbing Max and forcing him to stay behind in the library, but he didn't move.

Why do we even need food and bandages, anyway? For all I know the National Guard has already been dispatched to quarantine the area, capture the creatures and rescue the survivors or isolate us here until we are all eaten by those things. His thoughts raced. *Maybe I should call him back. I mean, who made me leader, anyway? I'm not even the best qualified. Just because I'm the oldest*—he paused, the image of a mutated and bloodied Rachel flashed through his head. *Just because I'm the oldest one left, he thought, grimly. Does that mean I get to make a decision that could send a kid to his death?*

Max can't be more than twelve. And after what happened with Rachel? The kid could be dead, body parts splattered across the pristine hallway in just a matter of minutes. And for what? I'm not even hungry. He looked around at Kiley and Sage. *And I doubt these guys are feeling like nibbling on anything with this bloody corpse in the middle of the room.*

"Hey, Kiley," he called softly. She was ducked down behind the desk, rummaging through the shelves beneath the bar-style reception area for a radio. She poked her head above the table top, her eyes wide and her mouth dropped into a tiny circle.

"Yeah?"

"Can you come here for a minute?"

Kiley stood and strode around the desk. She gave the body of the custodian a wide berth, avoiding looking at it. "What's up?"

"Do you think you can help me move this guy into one of the study rooms behind the book stacks?"

She blinked. "Uh, why? I'm sure he doesn't mind lying on the floor, Bryan."

"I just think we'd all feel a little better if we didn't have to stare at the corpse of my former high school custodian, that's all," he said, shrugging. "And besides. It's probably going to begin stinking in here soon."

"I'm pretty sure the stink doesn't happen for a while. Don't you watch crime forensics shows? There's like this whole fly's life cycle thing," she said. "God. It's like you grew up in a cave."

"Whatever, Kiley. I'll do it myself."

"Wait." She tried to glance at the body of the man she'd killed moments before, but her eyes pinched shut of their own accord. "I don't know if I can touch it."

"Look, I need you to help me because Sage probably isn't strong enough to lift a fully grown adult male and lug him across a room."

"I—I really don't think I can touch it, Bryan," she repeated.

He sighed and glanced around the room. Sage sat lotus-style on the floor, a moat of opened newspapers surrounding her. He chewed on the inside of his lip as an idea formed. "What if we cover him with newspapers so you don't have to see him?"

Kiley shut her eyes, her fists unconsciously clenching and unclenching. She opened her eyes again, a look of defeat spreading across her face. "All right," she said. "I guess I can try, but don't blame me if I hurl the Technicolor that was my Mountain Dew and raspberry-flavored marshmallow fluff breakfast all over you."

Bryan smiled. "Hey, Sage! Could you bring over some of the newspapers you've already scanned?"

Sage looked up. "Sure," she said, rising gracefully to her feet. She bent at the waist, plucked the corners of a few sheets of newsprint and brought them to where they stood.

"Thanks," said Bryan.

"Why haven't you started checking out the internet yet?" Sage asked. "It seems like that would be our best bet for information. I mean, if this is happening to anyone else, it's probably the fastest way to find out. No long line at the printing press, right?"

Bryan nodded. "You can go ahead and do that if you'd like. Kiley and I are going to move—" he started to say the name of the custodian, but thought better of it. Bill. Bill Franklin. Bill had always been a chill custodian, letting the guys who were respectful off the hook for things. He'd been busted once without a hall pass one day when he was sneaking out to meet Rachel at the water fountain. He'd been caught dead to rights by Bill, but the man just smiled and waved at him, saying, "don't get caught, buddy." Bryan could easily have had detention, but Bill had been a cool guy.

Bryan pressed his eyes shut for a moment, forcing the thoughts away. This man was dead. He was someone Bryan had known, not well, but known just the same. And now, he was lying dead on the floor in a pool of sickly black blood.

"Kiley and I are going to move this man," he said at last. "It'll probably only take us a minute or so, but I think it would be better to have it out of sight."

Sage nodded. "Sure. Thanks?"

She plopped herself in front of a computer terminal. After reading the log-in code from the sticker on the front of the monitor, she punched in the username and password. Before Bryan and Kiley had even taken a step toward the body, she announced, "I'm in."

"Good," Bryan said as he began to cover Bill Franklin's body with the newsprint. "Okay, Kiley, I'm ready for you. Why don't you take the legs as they'll be a bit easier to hold. I'll get the arms. We can sort of drag and pull him instead of trying to lift him up."

Wincing at the thought, Kiley grappled with her hands beneath the newsprint. As her fingers moved over the damp cuffs of the man's trousers, her wrists bumped against the soles of his shoes. She cringed as she wrapped her fingers around the cuffs of his pants, afraid to touch any part of his body, and muttered, "Got 'em."

"Huh," said Bryan, stifling a laugh.

"What?" asked Kiley. "What could possibly be making you laugh at a time like this?"

"First, I can safely say I never thought I'd be disposing of a body with you, Kiley."

Kiley smiled in spite of herself. "Yeah. And second? Was there one?"

"I was going to say," started Bryan. "Second, for a girl who dresses all in black, like a gothic death-worshipper, you certainly do have an uncharacteristic fear of dead bodies."

"Uh, now that you mention it, yeah. I might be in love with the mystery of death," she said, glancing down at the rumpled newspaper. "But there is nothing mysterious about this, Bryan. I killed this man."

"To save us."

"Whatever. Let's just do this, okay?"

She lifted her head. Bryan pulled the custodian's arms from under the newsprint and had a solid grasp around the dead man's wrists.

"Okay," said Bryan. "Let me go first."

He swung in a wide arc so that his back was in line with the study room door and began inching backwards, straining as the weight of the custodian's body pulled at the muscles in his arms. Now he knew what they meant by 'dead weight'.

Kiley heaved with exertion as she tugged on the pant legs of the custodian, trying to keep the legs above the ground. The waist of the body bent at the middle and dragged on the ground as Bryan and Kiley struggled toward the study room. After several minutes of puffing, they managed to get the body halfway into the room. Bryan dropped the arms and, stepping over the body, walked around to Kiley's side. Kiley released the pant legs into Bryan's hands. He then thrust the legs forward with all his might, bending the man's body at the waist, and with a vicious twist, he pushed the lower half of the body vertically through the door. With the legs hoisted over his shoulder in the tiny cubicle of the study room, Bryan unhooked the metal key ring from the creature's belt loop and tossed them back at Kiley who caught them with a sneer.

"Just in case," he said as he stared at the girl under his armpit from his hunched position in the doorway.

"Yeah, okay." Kiley held the keys between the forefinger and thumb of her right hand as if she were holding a soiled baby diaper. In her other hand, she held the edge of the door tightly.

Bryan allowed the legs to drop against the wall as he backed out of the room. Kiley shut the door at almost the exact instant Bryan's feet passed the threshold. She held out her hands with the keys and placed them gingerly in Bryan's palms. He thrust them in his pocket where they bulged out widely.

"There," she said. "This pharaoh has been mummified."

"Thanks," Bryan said. "Who knew a body could weigh so much?"

Kiley shrugged. "I'm gonna go find the remote to the television," she said. "It's mounted too high on the wall. I can't reach the power button."

"Need some help?"

"No," she called out behind her. "Finding lost remotes is like my evil-vixen superpower."

"I mean I might be able to reach the power button."

"Seriously, Bryan," she said . "I can handle this."

Bryan headed to the pile of newspapers Sage had been working on. As he settled in to check the papers for any reference to an epidemic or anything else that might be of use, a weight enveloped him. He knew that Sage was right—that their best chance of finding information was through the internet or on television, but he needed to feel busy. Too much time to think about things never worked out for him.

Before his mother's car accident, she had always told him that *idle hands were the devil's playground.* As a child, he never understood what she meant by this, but after her death, he had engaged in every hobby he thought might be interesting—partly to follow his mother's cliché advice and partly to keep busy so he didn't have to think about the growing sadness which always overwhelmed him when he thought about his mother. So, he had done what any good, escapist child would do. He convinced his dad to let him take Kung Fu and piano lessons on alternating weeknights while his weekends were filled with horse-back riding and mountain hiking with the Adventure Club at Greendale High. Even when he and Rachel started dating, he managed to fill every breathing moment with something—whether it was homework or making out, he was always busy.

As he settled himself on the floor, he tried to imagine what his mother would say if she could see him now. In just a short span, he'd murdered his cannibalistic girlfriend, helped kill the school custodian, and became default leader of a small band of kids trying to survive a zombie attack. He could almost see her large brown eyes blinking at him as she shook her head slowly, her brown hair swishing over her shoulders as she said, "I warned you about idle hands. You just weren't doing enough, Bry-Bry. Not enough at all."

The image brought a tear burning to the crook of his eye and immediately, driven by instinct, he slid his fingers beneath the thin pages of newsprint and forced himself to focus on the pages of the Bingram County News. As the television whirred to life in the room adjacent to him, he refocused his attention on the black and white pages before him. He scanned the county headlines, compelling himself to absorb every word of every title on the front page. *Bingram County Cold Snap Sets New Record!* was followed by a subtitle telling readers to *Tent Those Tomatoes!* A photograph of an elderly woman with peppered brown hair and a pair of horn-rimmed glasses on her crooked, liver-spotted nose accompanied another article titled *The Face of Literacy.*

Bryan glossed past the short article describing how the local library had recently added five thousand new titles to their shelves. His eyes then slid over an article about a Doberman Pincer biting the lip off its owner of five years in the neighboring town of Chadwick. He flipped past the obituaries and inspected the local news. A short article on the recent increase in alcohol-related driver's license suspensions was nestled between a longer piece detailing the ways Greendale residents could obtain assistance with their heating bills this winter and a small blurb describing an accident where a Nanologic Technologies supply truck flipped over on Route Four's infamously sharp corner and skidded into Harpswell Creek just two days earlier.

A picture showed a bespectacled scientist with a wealth of flowing, frizzy hair standing in front of the Nanologic Technologies sign. The caption read, "According to Deidra Wallace, a Nanologic Technologies employee, the spill in Harpswell Creek was cleaned up quickly and should be of little concern to local residents." Bryan read on. "'The truck was filled with harmless fertilizers and nano-technologically enhanced water purification systems', Wallace told reporters. 'It may sound ironic, but if anything, the creek will probably be cleaner after the accident, thanks to the water purifiers released into the ground water along the creek. You might even see some wild tomatoes springing up in the area eventually.'

Bryan scratched his head. Something about the article and the smiling image of the woman in the black and white photograph gave him pause. He squinted carefully at the picture, trying to determine what was odd about it. Was it the caption? Or was it the woman? Had he seen that face before? Perhaps around town? The narrow slope of her long, upturned nose. The way her eyes were spaced just a smidge too close together and her irises were wide as planets in orbit around Saturn. The curve of her lips.

Wait a minute!

"Sage," he called out. "What's your last name?"

"Wallace. Why?"

Bryan jumped to his feet. Clutching the paper tightly, he folded it in quarters so that the woman's face was at the center as he hurried toward Sage. "Is this your mother?"

"Yes, the woman in that picture was once my mother," responded Sage. "What's your point?" Her tone was flat and unwavering.

"I'm sorry, Sage. I know this must be hard for you after all you've been through, but I think I might be onto something. Can I ask about your mom? Did she work for Nanologic

Technologies?" He shook the paper as if to coerce her to look at the picture again.

"Yes."

"Did you hear about this accident? Did she talk about it? Apparently a truck spilled a bunch of chemicals and stuff along Harpswell Creek. The creek that feeds into the lake? The town's drinking water? Do you think this could have been, well–" he struggled for words. "Could this have caused any of this?"

Sage fixed him with a cold look. "My mother believed firmly in an organic, natural lifestyle. Both she and my father were environmental activists. She took the job at Nanologic Technologies—which is paid for by research grants, by the way—because it was a company dedicated to finding healthy and natural ways of making more nutritious vegetables, and to helping end world hunger. I don't see how this accident could have been the reason why half the town has turned into a bunch of disease-carrying, crazed cannibals."

With a deliberate air of calm, Bryan said, "This whole thing just reminded me of something Kiley was telling me about this cholera epidemic in Greendale over a hundred years ago. Some corpses in the lake infected the drinking water. Anyway, the creek runs right into the lake. The same lake we get our city water from. If we can determine what caused this sudden–and I do mean *sudden*– outbreak of disease or parasite or whatever it is, I think–"

"Wait a minute." Sage cut him off, her gaze distant. "Parasite?"

"I don't know. I'm just talking," Bryan said. "I'm barely through the first six chapters in biology. I don't have any idea what turned your parents, and the custodian, and my–" His voice caught. He swallowed, and went on. "- my girlfriend into zombies, but I know enough to believe that there is no way it could all be just a coincidence. Diseases don't just materialize in minutes and take over an entire town in a single morning. And I've never heard of a disease that affects everyone except children under sixteen. It's usually the other way around. I mean, older people are usually more immune to junk because they've been around longer and exposed to all kinds of stuff. But this is all backwards." Bryan sighed, taking the computer cubicle next to Sage and sitting down on the cushioned, wheeled chair.

"Look," he said. "I know I'm just blabbering and that you're probably twice as smart as I am, but I want to figure out what happened here. And if this only happened in Greendale then I hate to think about what the authorities might do. At the very least they'll probably quarantine the area. But at the other end of the spectrum they might decide to select our quaint little suburb as the next test site for a nuclear bomb or something. Don't you watch the SyFy Channel? And even if they quarantine us, they'll send in scientists in hazmat suits to gloss over the town water supply and the town shopping plazas to determine if there were any contaminants, or whatever. The point is that those scientists won't know the first thing about Greendale. But we do. The best chance we have to ensure that this *infection*, or whatever it is, gets stopped and doesn't spread to every town in the nation—"

"If it hasn't already," Sage interrupted.

Bryan nodded. "If it hasn't already," he said. "The best chance we have to help the professionals before they get here is to gather whatever information we can and pass that knowledge onto them when they come."

"If there's even anybody left to come," Sage said .

Bryan frowned. "Try to stay positive, will you? We're literally fighting for our lives here. The last thing we need is to give up before we've even started."

"You're right," nodded Sage. "But I wasn't suggesting we give up. Anyway, before you got sidetracked by visions of atomic bombs and mad scientists in hazmat suits, you said something about parasites. That made me think about an article I read about a parasite that would get inside snails, right? And it could actually control the snail's mind, forcing it to move to the end of a branch or a leaf so that it was clearly visible to the birds. Then, when a bird swooped down and ate the snail, the parasite would take over the bird's mind, too, making it do whatever it wanted. It was like the bird was the parasite's puppet—its mind was still there, but it couldn't use it." She paused, looking at Bryan intently.

"Sure. But where are you going with all this?"

"I still believe that my mother wasn't involved with a business that would have worked with harmful chemicals." She glared at Bryan for a moment, almost daring him to contradict her, before dropping her gaze to the keyboard. "But what if in some way Nanologic Technologies was to blame, only they were just the birds eating the infected snail?

A few days ago, I heard my mom talking to my dad about some plant enzyme that had appeared overnight on her sweet potato plants. The enzyme was like this magic thing, I guess, that could make vegetables grow on a nearly dead plant without depleting the soil of its nutrients. She said that they thought it came from this other lady's experiments with sustainable tomato plants. What if that enzyme was not an enzyme at all, but a parasite controlling the enzyme? What if that truck that crashed into the creek was carrying the enzyme and, when it hit the water supply, the whole town got contaminated?"

Bryan nodded gravely, gnawing on his thumbnail. "Interesting theory," he said. "But that still doesn't explain why the thing only attacks people over a certain age. How would it know the difference?"

Sage thought for a moment. "Well, I know the adult brain is different from the brains of younger people. I don't know exactly how they're different, but maybe it's because they aren't as well-developed. Maybe they are missing something that allows the parasites to take control." She shrugged. "I don't know. I mean, this is all just speculation. It may not mean anything at all."

"Does that mean that Kiley was right? These people could have been saved?" he whispered, his eyes glazed. His mind turned quickly, and a look of horror rolled over his face. "Does that mean that when I turn sixteen, I'm automatically going to become a zombie?"

Sage did not have an answer for him.

After a moment, Bryan cleared his throat. "Have you found anything on the internet yet?"

"Nope," she said. "But I'm probably not using the best search terms, either."

"Keep working at it," said Bryan with a smile he hoped was encouraging.

"Guys?" Kiley called from the cubby behind the main desk of the library. "I think you should come and see this." Her voice was low and flat.

Sage and Bryan exchanged looks and walked over to where Kiley stood behind the desk. She was gazing blankly up at the television mounted on the wall. The screen showed multicolored vertical stripes with a black bar across the bottom.

"What's up?" Bryan asked.

"Look," said Kiley, pressing a button on the remote control. The television screen flickered to another station, but the picture remained the same. It was the same multi-colored screen with a black bar at the bottom, emitting a high-pitched humming sound. Kiley flicked again and again, rotating through 75 channels before the numbers began to repeat. Every channel was the same.

"Isn't that the emergency broadcast system? What's going on?" Her voice betrayed a squeak of fear. She turned to Bryan, her eyes red-rimmed and brimming with a thick layer of tears. She slumped toward Bryan. Bryan wrapped his arms around her shoulders and, pulling her head into his chest, rested his chin on the crown of her head.

"Hey. It doesn't mean anything, okay? It could just be that the school forgot to pay the cable bill, or the digital cable is unplugged. Don't worry about it, okay?" Bryan stroked that back of Kiley's strawberry hair slowly as she wept into his shoulder.

"Then the channels would be static, not emergency broadcast rainbow stripes," said Sage. "And you'd be able to get the basic channels in through the digital box without the paid service, anyway."

Kiley sobbed harder into Bryan's chest as he shot Sage a hostile look. "Don't you have keywords to search?" he asked.

She stuck out her tongue at Bryan and turned on her heel to walk calmly back to the computer terminal. Pressing her fingers into the keyboard, she searched for the local news stations as Bryan and Kiley had their moment.

"I don't think I ever want to grow up," she mumbled.

Chapter Twenty

Bryan and Kiley

Half-dazed, Kiley let Bryan pull her gently away. She could feel the heat of his face near her own, but she didn't dare look into his eyes. Suddenly, Bryan's mouth approached her lips, and Kiley could feel the heat of his breath mingling with hers. Her lower lip trembled as she held back tears. She sucked in a quick breath.

His lips touched hers gently and she felt it all the way down in the backs of her knees which began to tingle wildly. Her eyes closed instinctively and she held her breath as his warm, soft lips locked with hers.

Kiley felt the warmth of Bryan's palm as it pressed into the small of her back. She felt dazed as Bryan pulled away. As their lips parted, Kiley's bottom lip clung like Velcro to Bryan's upper lip before separating softly. She ran a tongue over her lips, savoring the taste of his mouth. A wave of dizziness rose from the root of her spine, causing her head to wobble on her neck for a moment before she caught herself. Sensing her swoon, Bryan pressed his palm deeper into her back to catch her.

"Wow," she moaned. "That was everything I imagined it would be." Without a word, he dropped his hand from the curve of her back and stepped backwards, looking away.

"What is it?" she asked.

"Nothing," he mumbled, staring at the floor.

"Okay, what crazy toaster-robot has suddenly taken control of your limited boy brain? I don't get it," said Kiley, anger rising in the pit of her stomach. "Is this 'kiss Kiley' day or something? Is it marked on people's calendars? Was there a memo?"

She gripped his upper arm and tried to spin him around, but failed. Giving up, she directed her question to his back. "What's going on, Bryan?"

"Nothing," he insisted, his voice louder.

"That's not gonna suffice," said Kiley, her teeth grinding together as she spoke. "I've nearly died more than once already this morning. I have killed a school employee. You've told me you killed my sister, there's a pretty good chance that my parents are dead as well, and we could easily be next. I've had it with 'nothing', and 'I don't know.' I want an answer right now. Or—or I swear I'm going to drive the steel toe of my Doc Martens so hard into your shin you'll need to buy a parrot and eye patch to go with your new peg leg. "

Bryan turned with his arms crossed tightly over his chest and regarded her coolly. "Fine," he said. "If you insist on knowing the truth, I kissed you by accident. In the heat of the moment. I was thinking of Rachel—"

Recoiling as if he had slapped her across the face, Kiley gasped. "Excuse me?"

"You heard me," Bryan said. "I looked at you with your nose freckled just like her and your eyes twinkled under the ceiling lights just like Rachel's do. Did. And I was thinking about her—your sister—and I just kissed you." He shook his head. "I'm sorry, Kiley , but it wasn't you I was kissing. I—I don't know what else to say." He searched her face. "It's been a hard day. You're just a kid," he said with a sigh. "I didn't mean to—" He stopped short, unable to finish.

Kiley's face went rigid as it drained of blood. "I understand all right." Her voice was as cold as ice. "I understand that you thought you were the only one who lost anything today. I understand that you think I owe you something for your terrible, tragic loss."

"That's not fair, Rachel! I—" Bryan halted mid-word, his mouth dropped open as the wrong name hung on the air between them. He closed his mouth. The silence that separated them was heavy and electrifying. He regarded the ambivalent expression that crossed Kiley's face, a mix of smug satisfaction and utter desolation, as he pulled a slow, deep breath into his lungs.

"I didn't mean to say that," he said quietly. "What I meant to say was that I made a mistake. I didn't mean to sound like I was giving you an excuse when I said 'it's been a hard day'. I meant to give you an explanation for the fact that I could be so foolish as to make such a mistake. I know you are not your sister. And, believe me, I know you have lost a lot today, too." Bryan reached out as if to touch her shoulder.

She jerked away and turned her back on him. "Your story is awfully convenient, Bryan, don't you think? You expect me to believe that you had a sudden hallucination that I was my sister? Your girlfriend? Mr. play-it-safe, straight-edge, good student athlete whose never sampled a magic mushroom in his life is suddenly suffering from a complete and utter brain-trip meltdown? You know I've had a crush on you since my sister started dating you, and you kissed me anyway. Look around, Shrodinger, people are dead, and we're killing them and we might even die today. This is not some dead or 'not dead' cat experiment. This is real dead. Really real dead. But you kissed me as if it was perfectly natural, Bryan, and now you tell me it was because you thought I was *Rachel*."

This time, she didn't jerk away when Bryan put his hand on her shoulder. "I know you had a crush on me," he said quietly. "And that's why what I just did was not okay."

He spun her around so that she was facing him. "I'm sorry. I don't know what to do. I miss her, Kiley. I miss Rachel a whole hell of a lot, but I don't want to hurt you either. So how about this? A kiss for Kiley, and not for her sister. Then, we can call it even, okay?" Even as the words left his mouth, he felt the guilt knot in his stomach.

What am I doing? He thought, but it was too late. He just wanted the whole thing to be behind them, to have never happened in the first place, but what was done was done. I need to make this right. *I just don't know if this is going to do it.*

He turned his attention back to the younger sister of his late girlfriend. She really did look a lot like Rachel underneath the severe eyeliner and black-Sharpied tips of hair. He looked at her face.

After a pause, Kiley finally spoke. "Sure. Because this is a fairy tale, Brother Grimm, and I'm a fairy princess who just needs a stupid kiss to snap me out of being royally pissed off at you, Mister Prince Charming. You had no right to dishonor my sister like that. I'm *not her*. I'm sorry, but I think your princess is in another castle, and—"

She didn't have a chance to finish.

Sweeping Kiley into his arms, he pulled her close to his face. This time when his mouth met hers, it was soft, less passionate. Their lips pressed together, firmly closed but mashed into the sides of one another the way a young man kisses his grandmother goodbye. Kiley blanched. This was not what she wanted at all. It wasn't what he wanted either, and she could feel it. They hung like that for a moment before they heard a call coming from the middle of the library.

CHAPTER TWENTY-ONE

Max

Max didn't dare move. He tried to stop his body from trembling, but it was no use. Instead, he focused on his breathing. It was slow and surprisingly controlled save for a nearly inaudible whimper as the creature inched into the gymnasium. Max felt like he had been crouching for hours, each minute rolling by as slowly and as painfully as he imagined what it might feel like to be eaten alive.

As each moment passed, however, Max couldn't understand why he was still breathing. The zombie had hulked into the room through the cafeteria kitchen, so Max was sure there was no way it could have failed to spot him crouching there the instant it stepped beyond the threshold. And yet, Max was still alive, the muscles in his legs screaming with strain as the pain moved from burning heat to ice-cold stabbing sensations in his quadriceps.

Though he didn't dare look, he knew the monster was still there because he could hear its scuffling feet jerking over the highly-polished floor. Occasionally, it let out a low hum that vibrated softly like a cricket and not as blaring as the screech it had emitted before.

Max tried desperately to peer out of the corner of his eye and catch a glimpse of the creature. What was it doing? And more importantly, why hadn't it attacked him yet? Beads of sweat formed along his scruffy hairline as fear began to get the best of him. Max knew he'd have to be brave, now.

Am I really going to do this? he thought, gathering every fiber of courage he could still muster.

At a snail's pace, he tightened his fingers around the handle of his switchblade and turned his head a degree at a time toward the sound of the creature. It took every ounce of his concentration to move so slowly, but after several minutes he finally caught full sight of the zombie. He nearly gasped when he realized who it was.

Squatting like a Sumo Wrestler with his head cocked backwards at a sickening angle was Rick Sigurdsson, his firefighting neighbor. The same black-eyed creature bearing the face of his only friend that he'd seen clawing at the front door of the high school just a short time ago. How the man had ended up at the high school was a mystery.

Maybe a back door was open? Maybe there were more of them.

The boy gulped as nausea tore through him. He compared the creature before him with the memory of his friend. Its flesh had turned grey with black veins pulsing against skin which seemed thin and drying as if all the moisture had been sucked away. Its dark, bloodshot eyes were unmoving in their sockets and almost sunken in with a raging fever.

As Max slowly twisted to get a better angle, the soft rustle of his clothes sent a shot of panicked adrenaline into his stomach. Faltering only slightly with the rush, it was enough to make the backpack slip an inch down his shoulder. The sound of waterproof vinyl against the flannel of his shirt was as raspy and loud as the opening of a zipper. The creature jerked its head in Max's direction, its eyes filled with black blood.

Max froze, his own eyes as wide as the sockets and skin would stretch. In that very moment, the creature seemed to be staring right at him, its back arched and its head cocked to one side. Max was going to die at the hands of one of the only people in town whom he considered a friend and confidant.

The sensation of knowing that death was possibly just seconds away washed over Max, but not in the way he might have imagined. It should have pinched his nerves, sent another rush of adrenaline through his body to thrust him upwards and running out the door, or crippled him with fear so fierce that he would simply plop to the floor and give his body up to the creature with little resistance.

Instead, it had the exact opposite effect on him. Rather than needles of panic piercing his tingling body from head to toe, a sudden calm covered his body like a veil, enveloping him with a kind of peace. He felt the tension in his shoulders fall away and his jaw, which had been tightly clenched only a moment before, loosened and went slack.

If I'm going to die, thought Max. *I'm ready. But I'm not going out without a fight, Mr. Sigurdsson, so bring it on.*

What happened next was both strange and alarming. Instead of charging Max with clutching, tearing fingers, the creature crept toward him very slowly, almost cautiously. Its head moved in a figure eight configuration as if the monster was scanning the area around Max. Max was certain that the zombie could see him, but not once had those sunken dead eyes locked on his.

It may have been grey outside, but the light trickling in through the windows around the folded tables was enough that the entire gymnasium was clearly visible. And yet, his old friend was walking toward him, moving as if he knew something was there, but wasn't quite sure what it was or where it was even though Max was squatting directly in front of him.

I don't think he can see me, the boy thought, a seedling of hope blossoming in his chest. *Could it be he really can't tell I'm here? Is he blind?*

As if in response to Max's thoughts, the creature tilted its head to the side and squinted its black eyes as if from instinct. Its mouth dropped open and that all too familiar screeching sound erupted from deep in the creature's throat, projecting the horrifying squeal at Max. The skin above the thing's blanched Adam's apple trembled with vibration for a split second before it straightened its head on its neck and, vaulting from the floor, charged full force at Max.

Adrenaline shot through Max's muscles painfully fast. He sprung to his feet and jerked to his left. The creature was unable to correct for Max's quick movement and found its arms stretching out to grasp at thin air. Max grabbed the monster by the wrist and, using the creature's momentum against him, pulled it forward where it slammed head first into the matted wall.

As the monster twisted, still off-balance from the wall collision, Max dropped his weight to his heels and lunged forward, slamming his forearms into his longtime friend's shins. The monster tumbled over Max's back and smashed face first into the linoleum floor of the cafeteria.

Max whirled around, knife clutched in his hand, and leapt onto the creature's back. He pressed his knees into the space below its shoulder blades, raised both his hands high above his head and drove the blade of the knife deep into the monster's neck just to the left of the spine.

A curdled mass of black blood spurted from around the wound like a geyser of oil bursting through the dusty surface of the earth. Max pulled the blade out, mesmerized by the blood gurgling through the hole in the creature's skin.

The wound to its neck, however, seemed to have little effect on the creature. Twisting its body under Max's weight, the monster spun its left arm around like a pro wrestler and slammed the boy into the wall. Momentarily stunned, Max felt the knife tumble from his groping fingers. It wedged between the creature and the wall.

As Max wildly shook his head in an attempt to shake out the cobwebs from the blow, the creature wailed again, the sound ear-splitting in pitch. Max brought both hands up to cover his ears just as the creature lunged forward, mouth first.

The monster's teeth sliced through the air, its mouth stretched so wide that Max could see the grey uvula twittering at the top of its throat. Its teeth closed around the underside of Max's left forearm. An excruciating pain ripped through Max's body as the creature's teeth broke through the flesh and clamped viciously around a chunk of the skin near between the thin bones of his forearm. The boy's instinct was to jerk away from the bite, but as he did so, the iron trap jaws of the creature recoiled, tearing a huge chunk of flesh from Max's arm. Blood spurted in all directions, showering the pair of them with crimson.

With a scream piercing enough to match that of the zombie creature, Max brought his free hand to the gaping wound and pressed against it, trying to quell the pain and slow the flow of blood from his arm. The creature paid him little attention as it calmly chewed the chunk of Max's arm with a half-open mouth, working its tongue and teeth over gristle and fibrous flesh.

Max fought off a wave of nausea. He bit the cuff of the sleeve of his injured arm and, taking his hand away from the wound for a moment, pulled his arm painfully through it. He plucked the dangling fabric from his left side and, wrapping it tightly around his arm, tied a strong knot over the bite using his right hand and his teeth.

Tears streamed down his face. His heart pounded in his chest and the rush of blood was so strong throughout his head that he could hear nothing but the muffled thumping of his own vascular muscle. A quick glance at the creature told him it was still preoccupied with the morsel from his arm, though the tasty snack was nearly gone.

Max thrust his hand between the creature's body and the wall, thinking to pull out the switchblade he'd lost there. The creature turned its head toward him and screamed before resuming its mastication. The sound was muffled by Max's beating heart as he searched for the blade. His fingers found the tip first as it pierced the fleshy fingertip of his middle finger.

The pain seemed minor compared to the throbbing in his arm, and he forced his fingers to trace their way up over the blade toward the handle. Hot blood seeped from his fingertip down over the curve of his palm, dribbling on his curled pinky. Max pressed on until his hand closed finally around the handle. He pulled the blade up slowly, confident the creature could not see what it was.

Hell, Max thought, *he probably wouldn't recognize what it was even if he saw it. These things seem to only care about eating.* Even as the thought flittered through his mind, he cringed at the realization that the creature was eating him. He bit his lip and strengthened his resolve.

Once he got the knife out into the open, Max positioned himself carefully below the head of his old friend and, angling the point of the blade upward, he jammed the blade hard and fast just under the brow bone and over the eyeball. The blade completely disappeared past the fleshy part of the creature's face and then slid deeper through what Max could only imagine was the brain.

The boy quickly withdrew the knife, ready to stab at the creature again. But it wasn't necessary. The creature's chewing motion ceased immediately as black ooze seeped from the eye socket and down its cheeks, dripping sickeningly from its chin. Teetering for a moment, the creature toppled backward, its head crashing to the floor.

Gasping with pain and panic, Max pulled himself to his feet. He felt cold from head to toe, as if he had been walking outside on a New England January night without a jacket. He shivered violently and threw his arms around his midsection in an effort to warm himself up, struggling to maintain his balance.

He fought the urge to pass out, though, as he stumbled toward the kitchen area from where the creature had come. Through the haze of his blurring vision, he could see the back door to the school was unlocked. Scanning the kitchen for another creature, he braced himself for another fight, but the kitchen was blessedly empty.

"Score," the boy whispered as he dragged himself toward the door.

When he reached the door, he caught sight of Rachel's fallen body through the window and blanched. The body rested between the shed's entrance and the school, a few yards in front of him. He couldn't bring himself to search for the head. Swallowing down the lump that had risen in his throat, the boy grabbed the door bar with weak fingers and pulled it shut. The door clicked into place.

He scanned the space around the door as his head swam on his neck. He couldn't see any creatures, so he turned back toward the cafeteria. He hoped no other creatures had slipped in through the open door as he took a faltering step forward. The blood throbbing in his head came in waves so strong that, for a moment, they blotted out his vision and he lurched drunkenly from side to side. He thrust his right hand out to catch him as he began to fall. A rush of wind zipped through his hair and over his face before he made solid impact with the hard kitchen floor. The boy blinked once, the edges of his vision going filmy white before transitioning to complete darkness.

CHAPTER TWENTY-TWO

Sage

Sage quickly dismissed the kissing fools as she wandered back to the computer terminal to do some additional research. Pulling up the homepage of the town's closest news station, Sage scanned it for the most recent update. A small, italicized statement at the bottom of the page indicated that the site had not been updated since midnight, meaning the six a.m. news hadn't made it to the webpage. That wasn't the best of signs. She tried another local station and found the same problem. None of the news stations in the vicinity had updated their sites to the most current broadcast, so she scanned national and then international news stations and found nothing unusual. Nothing that could tell her what might be going on in Greendale.

She exhausted every synonym, every search term, and every language her over-sized mind could process as she searched the internet for a clue, but all she found were online videos of zombie kickball and articles about epidemics in the past.

Think, Sage, think. But it was no use. It was as though her mighty intellect was taking a cat nap while the rest of her went through the motions of using a computer.

Is this what average people feel like? She reasoned.

Her eyes drifted to the clock on the wall. It was just after eleven o'clock. She found it hard to believe that they had been there for that long already. News stations, she knew, updated different sections of their web pages constantly throughout the day. There had been not one site updated since very early morning. She tapped her thumb on the space bar of the keyboard just soft enough to make it click without depressing it all the way. She twisted her mouth to the left.

What else can I look for? How can I word this?

Every time she punched in suburban zombies, she was invited to visit hundreds of George A. Romero fan sites, popular culture fiction pages and blogs. She tried "Greendale virus" and was greeted with page after page about Isaac Greendale and gravity and some computer virus in London. She tried "adult epidemic" and was informed by the search engine that nearly one million hits were blocked due to their containing inappropriate content. Sage sighed.

"I'm going about this wrong," she whispered to herself. "What should I be looking for?"

She pulled up an image of Greendale in her mind. There was the local library,–they might have something. The high school's homepage might show whether or not they closed today, and if so, why. Then there was the college across the river.

Maybe a student posted some information on one of the message boards, she thought, as her fingers drifted over the keyboard.

Absent-mindedly, she keyed in the address to her own email account and punched in her user name and password. . Her page scrolled onto the screen, revealing a tiny blinking envelope telling her she had one new mail item. She clicked on the icon. A message popped onto the screen from her friend Amanda in Chesterville.

Sage hadn't heard from her in a little over a month, but this was not uncommon. Chesterville wasn't known for its technological services. Amanda had to travel to the next town over, a few miles away from her house to connect to the internet, and she only did that on warm days since she usually had to ride her bicycle.

Sage leaned forward in her chair, her back tense and straight as her nose hovered close to the screen (*Don't sit too close to the television,* she heard her mother's voice echo in the back of her mind). The message had been posted at 9:33 a.m., which was when Amanda was usually working on her math for her home schooling program, a schedule she had rarely ever strayed from in all the time Sage had known her.

The message itself was succinct.

So it's been a rough day, old friend. Parents dead. They attacked my brother and me and we won. Everyone here is very sick and crazy, except us kids. There are twelve of us hiding out in the Bender's Grocery Distribution Warehouse. I hacked this employee's computer terminal so I could email you. His password was 'popcorn'. What kind of an idiot would use a seven letter password that could be so easily guessed by the number of empty microwave popcorn bags in the trash under their desk? Weirdos. Not that I'm complaining.

Anyway, the warehouse was closed today, so we're alone. Got some weapons. Don't know if this will get to you or not. I hope so. We tried using the phones, but they don't work. If this isn't already happening in your area, then you should know what to look out for, just in case. If someone is sick, his eyes will get filled with blood and his skin will turn white like an albino frog. And, believe it or not, he'll try to eat you. This is not a joke, Sage. I know it sounds funny, but you have to believe what I say.

The only way to stop them is to hide, or hit them in the head, otherwise they just keep coming for you. If you do get this, Sage, please let someone know and see if they will send us help. Hopefully they will believe you. Or if this is happening to you, too, then you should try to get yourself to Chesterville. We've got food and supplies here in the warehouse and we could use the help. Strength in numbers, you know, and we need all the help we can get. There's a dozen of us here, and not a one of us is even old enough to drive farm equipment, let alone cars.

I hope you're all right. Love, your spirit sister, Amanda.

###

Sage leaned back in her chair, swallowing deeply. Her face

drooped as all the color drained from her skin into her neck and chest, which glowed a faint pinkish color.

So it's not just happening here, she thought, as she scanned the desktop in front of her. *Whatever this thing is that's turning our adults into mindless cannibals, it's already reached Chesterville. Or maybe it started in Chesterville.* Sage tugged on her hair. *I just don't understand this. I'm so tired.*

Sighing, Sage rolled her eyes to her hands. There was a bit of dried blood caked under her fingernails, and she looked away. Near the computer terminal to her right was the newspaper article that Bryan had dropped. A thought occurred to her and she opened a new search window on her computer.

After a few keystrokes, she was looking at a satellite image of Greendale and its surrounding towns. She scanned the map until she found the tiny chicken scratch image of Harpswell Creek bending and curling across the screen. She traced it with her fingertip. Sure enough. At about half its length, the creek forked. One end of the fork fed into the lake and town's water supply, and the other end fed into Possum River. A quick scroll through the map's screen and she found what she was looking for.

Possum River ran right through Chesterville.

A river would spread a parasite much faster than stationary water. Even if that stationary water happens to be a town's well. People need to travel to spread illness, but rivers travel all on their own.

She flipped back to her email screen. She wanted to compose a letter to Amanda right away, but she wasn't sure what to say just yet. *My mother's company may have poisoned us all?* No good. Maybe *Don't drink the water?*

Sage sighed. Her eyes drifted from the finger-shaped cursor hovering on the screen over her inbox to the room behind the desk. Bryan and Kiley were still standing where she'd left them, only their faces were mashed together like two mounds of play-dough, their lips lost in the mush.

God, that girl kisses everybody, thought Sage. *I better keep my mouth shut or she'll be kissing me next.*

"Hey," she called softly, testing the power of her voice over the smoochers. They did not respond.

"Hey," she called a bit louder. Still nothing.

"Hey!" She shouted this time and suppressed a giggle as the two faces broke wildly apart, their breath coming in gasps and their faces flushed with red. They turned their heads sharply toward her. Bryan wore an expression of distaste, Kiley one of swooning daze.

"What?" Bryan called back.

Sage glowered at him. "I just thought you might like to know that Greendale isn't the only town being taken over by zombies. My old town looks like they are experiencing the same problem. My best friend emailed to tell me she and eleven other kids are holed up in a grocery store warehouse in a neighboring town. No phone service there either, but it looks like they still have net access, or at least they did when she wrote the message. And that's not all. It looks like you might be right. That Nanologic spill into the creek could have carried the parasite to Chesterville through Possum River. If it's moving that fast, I don't know how anyone can stop it."

Bryan and Kiley rushed over to stand at her back. They gazed down at the email message on the monitor.

"Why didn't you call us right away?" demanded Bryan.

"Technically I did call you right away. I just finished reading this a moment ago, and it took me a minute to figure it all out," Sage said, irritation flooding her voice. She twisted at the waist, gripping the back of the chair to look them both in the face. "And besides, you two looked a little busy from where I was sitting."

Kiley glared at them defiantly, her left foot angling in front of her instinctively. "*He* was," she grumbled.

"Kiley was scared," said Bryan coldly. "I was just comforting her. That's all." He looked at the little girl, daring her to ask a question. He went on quickly. "Where is this place? How far away is it and do you think we should try to go there like she suggests?"

Sage's head shook from side to side, her eyes widening. "I'm not sure where we should go or what we should do. Why are you asking me?" Tears welled at the corners of her eyes as she bit her lip to keep from crying.

"I am nine-years-old, Bryan. I may be smarter than a fifth grader, but frankly, I don't know what the heck to do. I—I still miss my mommy." As she said the word 'mommy', the tears she had been stifling poured from her eyes, spilling down her face and spattering the backs of her hands.

"The world I live in has changed overnight and everything I used to think was safe—the people who I thought would always protect me—are dead and I'm all alone. And now it's apparently children against monsters. *Monsters!* Not adults, mind you, but actual, real-life monsters and they are trying to eat us and it will hurt and I don't want to die!"

She sobbed uncontrollably, her voice coming in spurts as her chest heaved. "And what about the tiny babies? Have they just been eaten by their mothers? And the little, little ones? Did they get away, or were they ripped apart by their father's hungry hands? We got away. The four of us got away. But those tiny children, those little babies probably didn't get away and it's awful! It's just awful." Sage broke down, unable to command her voice anymore as the sobs overtook her. She couldn't get the horrific images out of her head.

The solemnity of her words hung like hot, humid air draping over the hapless trio. The weight of it pushed the corners of their mouths low on their faces, chins sagging, and a thick sweat beaded their palms.

"Look," Bryan said softly. "You can't think like that, okay? It will just drive you bonkers. We need your help, Sage. We don't know that this is happening everywhere. Maybe it's localized. Maybe places like Los Angeles or other cities are still okay. Where is Chesterville, anyway?"

Sage pressed her face into the cradle of her arms as she leaned against the computer keyboard, sobbing.

"Three hundred miles away," she mumbled. "That means this crazy virus is epidemic. If it's happening three hundred miles away, then it's probably happening much farther than that. Everyone has it, Bryan. Everyone! Don't you get it? If they don't have it yet, they will. We don't know how it spreads and we don't know how to stop it, and if the government isn't here with their tanks and their soldiers ready to drag us out to safety, then they either don't know, don't care, or they're dead already. This happened in Chesterville. It's happening here. Don't you think someone would have noticed by now if there was anyone alive to notice it?" She lifted her head to glare at him through tear-stained eyes.

"The whole world is probably affected and overrun by zombies. And that creek you were talking about? Well, it runs straight into Possum River. And that river runs across four states in New England including Chesterville. If Greendale is where the thing started, then it's spreading super fast. It's only a matter of time before we're all a bunch of orphans. Or worse. Dead orphans."

The girl's face scrunched up, hot red with emotion, as tears streamed down her cheeks. "But I guess by then it won't matter much, will it?"

Bryan struggled for something to say, but no words came to him. He patted her shoulder softly. "It's going to be all right," he intoned as if he were reading the text from a greeting card. The sound of the words triggered the memory of his mother's funeral. All of his aunts and uncles, even his grandparents had said the same phrase to him at some point or another that evening, and every time he heard it, he had grown angrier and angrier.

It wasn't true, after all. His mother had died. Nothing would ever be all right again. And yet, here he was saying it to this young girl who was sobbing not just for the loss of her mother, but the loss of all mothers everywhere—saying the same things that had made him cringe when his own family had said it to him.

The thought that every one of them were probably dead by now caused a shiver to shake his body from head to toe as if he would never get warm again. Or, if they weren't dead, they were mindless zombies, which he guessed was basically the same thing.

In his mind's eye, he saw his Aunt Victoria clutching her newest baby boy to her chest, bundled in a blue receiving blanket that was as soft as a goose's underbelly. He could imagine her holding the hand of her other son, a lanky, tow-headed toddler no more than three. Then, he imagined her skin turning paper white and rubbery, her eyes filling with blood, her mouth opening to sharp grey teeth. He shuddered, pushing the thought from his mind.

We grow up so fast, don't we? He thought. *I'm not ready for this. I'm just a kid.*

As he snapped back to reality, he found himself still patting Sage listlessly on the shoulder while she sobbed heavily into her arms. Kiley hovered behind him. Carefully and deliberately, Kiley stepped forward, pressing a palm into Bryan's wrist. He looked at her, an eyebrow raised, and she nodded at him. He hesitated for a moment. Kiley tugged lightly on his wrist and, with a look of regret, he pulled away. Kiley gave him a penetrating look, before leaning over Sage. Placing both hands on Sage's shoulders, she tugged slightly.

"Up," she said calmly. Sage didn't respond. Kiley gave her a fierce jerk, pulling her face away from her arms and thrusting her upper body upright against the chair.

"I said, up, juice box! As in, now," Kiley said with more force, pressing her hands firmly against the girl's shoulders and pinning her against the back of the chair. Fixing her gaze on the computer monitor, Kiley ignored Sage's whimper and weak protest as she went on.

"Now, the way I see it, you have two options. You can either stay here and cry your little heart out about how you survived and all the babies of the world have died, or you can get out of your chair, count your blessings, and get on with your life.

I lost my sister–probably my whole family–and you know what? I'm just grateful I'm still breathing. I'll sort all that stuff out when I'm safe and sound. Until then–" she fixed Bryan with a look over her shoulder. Sage's whimpering had silenced, her tears slowed.

"Well, until then I'm only going to worry about staying alive," Kiley said. "And you should too. And the best way you can do that is to wipe those tears off your sappy face and grow up. Hopefully the internet is still working. If it is, why don't you email your friend and tell her we'll try to get there as soon as we can. Or you can just sit here and wait for the monsters to come and get you. Your choice."

Silence fell over the library. It was so quiet that Bryan thought he could hear his blood moving through his veins. Finally, Sage lifted her head and wiped her eyes.

"All right," she said quietly. "But how are we going to get there?"

The corners of Kiley's lips lifted slightly into the faintest glimmer of a grin. "Easy," she said. "My sister's car. Bryan can get the keys from her—um, off her body and we can probably be at the warehouse by nightfall. Get the address, chica. We can use the internet to plot our route to the warehouse. We'll grab everything we think we'll need including weapons and exit stage right before this show gets any freakier."

"What about Max?" asked Bryan, glancing at the clock. "He should have been back by now. You don't think he ran into trouble, do you?"

Kiley shrugged. "We can look for Max on our way out," she said. To Sage, she said, "Get those fingers moving, Spice Girl. There's no time to waste."

"What are you two going to do?" Sage asked, eyeing Kiley uneasily. There was something about Kiley she didn't like, but she was unsure exactly what it was. It could be the way she was all smoochy-faced with Max one minute, then Bryan the next. Or maybe it was the way she spoke to her. Half the time she talked to her like a drill sergeant with bad hormonal moodiness, and the other half like an angry but maternal teenager babysitting a tiny infant.

Kiley met her gaze, unwavering. "We're going to split up. You're going to stay here and work on the net. Bryan is going to get the keys and I am going to find some weapons and, hopefully, Max."

"I don't like the idea of you wandering around a school that is possibly infested with zombies all by yourself," said Bryan with a hint of condescension. It also bothered him that she was suddenly taking charge. After all, he was the oldest and should have already thought about all of this.

Kiley scowled. "Max went out alone and that didn't seem to make a dent in your plastic leadership pin. That's nice, by the way. Did you get that in a cereal box? I like how it already says 'Hello, My Name Is Your Unassigned Leader' all printed out for you. Those guys at Staples think of everything." She flicked his chest above his right pectoral where a name badge would be.

"Or is this a boy-girl thing?" she went on. "Has Cro-Magnon man whipped out his club to whack me over the head with his manliness? It's okay for Max because he's a boy and boys are supposed to be valiant knights, while little, helpless girls like me have to be protected like the frilly princesses we are. Is that it?"

"No, I just meant—" Bryan stammered.

"It doesn't matter what you meant. News flash, superhero. This girl is a self-saving princess, so you can take your heroics and shove them down your throat. I'm perfectly capable of protecting myself, thank you very much. Or do we need to open the door on Mr. Janitor over there to remind ourselves how Kiley has super strength?" Kiley gestured toward the study room where they had stashed the custodian's body.

"You're not a supernatural zombie-killer, Kiley," Bryan said.

"Whatever," Kiley said, retrieving the flag pole she had used to penetrate the custodian's skull. "I've got my weapon. I suggest you two find your own. We can set a time and then we'll all meet up—" Kiley stopped short. She looked blankly at Bryan. "Where?"

"Oh, all of a sudden big, bad Kiley needs some help, does she?" asked Bryan sardonically. Kiley held his gaze. "We meet back here since Sage is staying," he added firmly. "That way, if none of us bump into Max along the way, we can be sure that he finds at least one of us. He'd head back here anyway."

Bryan gestured toward Sage. "As long as you don't mind holding down the fort?"

Sage looked around the library, uncertain.

"The library doors open inward, right?" she asked. "What if I barricade one side of the door so that no one—or, no *thing*—can get inside at least one door while you guys are out. Then, we'll wedge something else against the other door so that it only opens wide enough for one person to enter at a time. That way I won't have to worry about defending a whole fort by myself."

"What if we need to get inside in a hurry?" asked Kiley, slapping the flag pole against her palm.

Sage tucked in one corner of her mouth as she thought for a moment. "I guess we could angle a book shelf so that, with enough force, the door would swing open. I don't think these zombie creatures are smart enough to figure it out."

Kiley looked doubtful, but Bryan spoke up before she could.. "Sounds like a good plan to me. And then we won't have to worry about you while we are away."

Sage glanced at Kiley, not certain that the girl would worry about her under any circumstances. After a pause, she said, "Do you really think we should split up?"

"We need to cover a lot of ground and get a lot done if we want to get out of here before dark," Kiley said.

"What about the blood samples? I mean, if kids really are the only survivors, then the only way to make sure we don't all become infected with this thing, or–" She turned to Bryan, pointedly, and added, "to make sure you don't all of a sudden turn into a zombie, is to figure this out for ourselves. We've got to learn what we are dealing with and how we can stop it. From the sounds of it, everybody at the warehouse is pretty young. I think, except for me, everyone here is older than that group is. So I think we need to take the lead in this and be proactive."

A wry expression wrinkled Kiley's face. "And how do you propose we do that, hmm? It's not like any one of us is a doctor."

"Maybe not, but we could run into one if we're wrong about this thing not affecting kids. Or, with enough study, maybe we can figure it out. I don't know," Sage responded. "But I do know that, sooner or later, we're going to need to find out what started this whole thing and how to stop it. We have to assume that burden will be left to us. Based on what we've seen so far, it's likely there aren't any adults left alive. What do we do then? No mommies to kiss our boo-boos; no daddies to sling us over their shoulders and walk the rest of the way for us. In other words, it's going to be up to us kids to make sure that this disease thing is taken care of and doesn't spread to the rest of us as we grow older."

"So, now you're saying we should try to save the world?" asked Kiley, sarcasm dripping from every syllable.

"Exactly," said Sage, the hint of a tear threatening the corners of her eyes again. "Somebody has to."

Kiley rolled her eyes. Bryan wedged himself between them. Facing Sage, he asked, "What do you propose?"

"Let's see," said Sage. "I think we'll need clean, original samples. I remember something about viruses mutating, or something like that. So it seems we should have blood samples from individuals we know were infected in the first round."

Bryan nodded slowly. "Like Rachel," he said softly.

"Exactly," responded Sage.

"Right," said Bryan. "I think the nurse's station has syringes locked away for those kids with diabetes. We can break into the supply cabinets if Max hasn't done that already. Sage, we can help you barricade the door before we go, but you'll probably have to finish. Are we ready, then?"

"And a microscope," Sage added.

"What?" asked Kiley, blankly.

"We'll need a way to view the samples and, I doubt that a grocery warehouse has a microscope tucked away somewhere. We need to think ahead."

"Good idea," interjected Bryan. "The science hallway is opposite the corridor we just came up. I can go out the back door in the chemistry lab in that hallway, which should give me a straight shot to—to Rachel's body. I'll get the microscope on my way back through after I grab the car keys."

"What if this doesn't work?" asked Kiley.

"What are you talking about, Kiley? This was your idea, if you recall," said Sage.

"Yeah, but what if Bryan goes out to get the keys and is attacked by a bunch of those zombie creatures?"

"'That's not gonna happen," came a soft voice from the doorway. The words were so faint that the trio might not have heard them at all if it were not for the dense silence of the library. In unison, they turned toward the library door.

Chapter Twenty-Three

Max

Max stood hunched in the doorway, one elbow pressed into the door frame as his free arm dangled limply from his shoulder. A pulpy backpack, stuffed to the brim with jagged edges clung haphazardly to his back before it fell from his shoulder and clunked to the floor. His face was the color of dried glue, a purplish tint dappling the corners of his eyes and around his mouth.

"What happened? You haven't turned into one of those things, have you?" asked Kiley. She looked around for an avenue of escape.

"He just said something," Sage said as she rose from her chair. "Our zombie friends don't speak so much as screech, in case you hadn't noticed."

Bryan rushed forward and caught Max as he began to slide towards to the floor, still half wedged in the doorway. Sage was at the door a split second later. Only Kiley hovered back.

"Can you walk?" asked Bryan. He grabbed him by the wrist and pulled the boy's arm over his head and around his shoulder for support.

Max cried out in pain and at the same moment Bryan realized the younger boy was clutching a drenched, red arm wrapped tightly in a flannel shirt. Bryan quickly adjusted his stance, dropped to a knee, and pressed his shoulder into Max's armpit, averting the pressure from the injury.

"Are you okay?" asked Sage.

"What happened?" asked Kiley.

"My old neighbor. The firefighter I saw at the window this morning," Max huffed, pausing between breaths.

"He—he was in the cafeteria—I don't know how—he attacked me. Bit into my arm real good," he said with a weak grin. He gestured to the backpack on the floor by his feet and winced at the jerky motion.

"I passed out, but when I came to, I remembered to get the food."

"It looks like you've lost a lot of blood," said Sage warily.

"Yeah, but I found something out that could be important." Max gulped, sucking in a breath as Bryan helped his struggling legs push past the doorway. Sage wrestled herself under his good arm and helped support the other side. The difference in weight was dramatic, and he leaned on her. They stumbled weakly toward the closest chair. Max gratefully took the seat, his body sagging into the chair as Bryan and Sage released him.

"We need to look at that arm," said Sage.

"In a minute," responded Max . "I need to tell you something first. In case I lose consciousness again. Or in case I die."

"Don't say that," Sage said. She turned to Bryan and whispered in a low voice. "But there's a chance he could turn into one of those things, I think. Depending on how the disease is spread. Maybe age doesn't matter if you get bitten. I don't know."

Max grunted. "I heard that. Thanks for the vote of confidence."

Sage and Bryan exchanged a look. "All right, buddy. What is it that's so important?" asked Bryan.

"When I was attacked, I noticed something," Max said. A hacking wheeze cut him short. He sucked in a breath and went on. "I was frozen on the floor, right? I was so scared I couldn't even move. And this thing lumbers into the room and looks right at me. I swear, guys; there is no way he could have missed me. But he did. He walked right past me and didn't know I was there until I made a sound."

"What are you talking about?" asked Kiley as she finally joined them.

"He's trying to say that the creatures are blind," said Sage.

"Blind?" asked Bryan, his voice fading to a whisper.

"Well, not blind exactly," said Max. "He seemed to see me when I moved. Or he sensed it. I made a noise or something. I don't exactly remember. But at that exact moment, it turned to face me and—"

"—and it let out a screech, right?" said Sage, finishing his sentence. Her voice was filled with certainty and awe.

"Exactly," Max said excitedly. "It was like he was seeing me with the sound, like a bat does."

Max caught Kiley's eye. Her eyebrow was arched. "What?" he asked. "I've had a science class, you know."

Sage ignored the exchange, her mood suddenly lightened by this new input of information. "I can't believe I didn't see this before. That's why my father didn't charge me earlier this morning. He didn't know where I was until I moved. It's not that he didn't think me a threat. It's that he didn't even realize I was there. It makes perfect sense. And Mom—" her voice tripped for a nearly imperceptible moment before she continued. "She didn't notice me either until I yelled out a greeting."

"It makes perfect sense," Bryan chimed in. "Rachel didn't turn around either until I called out her name. And every one of them have this black blood stuff over their eyes. They must not be able to see through it!" The realization seemed to lift an invisible weight from the shoulders of everyone in the room except for Kiley, who stood staring incredulously at each of them in turn. Max was the only one to return her gaze, but offered her no words.

"All right. I get that genius girl has had a sudden jolt of brain juice, but how does this help us exactly? Who cares if they're blind if they can still *see us with sound?*" she asked.

"Are you serious?" asked Bryan.

"Don't be a tool," said Kiley. "I just don't see how this little tidbit of information is very useful, okay? I mean, so what if they can't see us with their *eyes*. They can still hear us and they can still bounce their bat-like sonar waves thingy at us to figure out where we are. So, what difference does it make? They can still find us. They can still attack us. They can still turn us into lunch meat."

"The question I have is how does the echolocation thing work for them?" Sage said, turning to Kiley and tilting her head as if she were discussing things with a two-year-old. "That's the bat-like sonar waves thingy, Kiley."

Kiley snorted, started to say something, then stopped and turned away. A hint of a smile curled at Sage's lip as she looked back at Bryan and Max.

"The reason it works for bats is partly because their ears are big enough to gather the sound waves. Human ears just aren't equipped for that sort of thing." Sage's voice was quiet and thoughtful as her eyes drifted over the book shelves that lined the central lobby of the library.

"Maybe we can jam the frequency!" Bryan suggested excitedly

"And how would we do that exactly? With our top secret, multi-billion dollar lab equipment, Lex Luthor?" Kiley asked.

"Echolocation works using sound waves, right? That's the way bats do it, anyway. They emit a sound and interpret the data the same way sonar data is interpreted."

"The Doppler Effect," Sage added.

"Right," Bryan said. He turned and spoke directly to Kiley as if she were the only one in the room who needed educating. "All sound is waves, right? That is, all sound moves from the source in waves the same way water ripples out in circles away from a rock that has just been tossed into it. The rings spread out from where the rock hit the same way sound ripples from its source."

"I know what sound waves are, Einstein, but thanks for the free physics lesson," Kiley said.

"Then you know how waves react to other waves," said Sage. "Let's say you are at the beach and you see this gigantic wave coming full force at an angle toward the shore, and at the same time, another wave is coming at an opposing angle toward the shore so that the two waves almost form a V-shape. What happens when the two waves crash into each other?"

Kiley looked at Sage blankly. "There's usually a geyser or something—some big spray of ocean water that shoots upward as the waves hit and then start to fizzle out," Max said. He sat a little more upright in his chair, the look on his face half alert with interest and half sagging with pain.

"Have you ever been to a rock concert?" asked Bryan. "You know when you stand on the floor near the speakers, how you can see the speakers bouncing as the music belts out of them? And you can feel the blast of each note from the bass guitar as it slams into your body like a surge of energy?"

"Got it, thanks. Why does everyone think I have the I.Q. of spam all of a sudden?" Kiley asked.

"So let's say these things use screechy noises to try to see where we are. But at the exact same time, they are being blasted by the loudest rock concert sounds ever to come from this school's intercom system. We just find some loud music on Pandora and run it through the system. Then, the entire school is a sonar disruptor," Bryan said.

Max pushed himself weakly up in his chair as a grin overcame his face. "The waves would crash into each other and, to them, it would seem like there was a huge wall of something in their way. They wouldn't know which direction to move." Max, pale and slumped, looked pleased in spite of his agony.

Sage smiled at him. "Something like that," she said.

"So in a sense, they wouldn't be able to see us. For all intents and purposes, they would really be blind. We could make it to Rachel's car in a snap." Bryan snapped his fingers for emphasis.

"Hold on a minute, there, Professor X," Kiley said, holding her hands up with the palms facing out. "If you were listening, Max said that his old neighbor noticed him when he moved. And bats aren't really blind, you know. Hello? Lady Darkness over here is kind of an expert on creatures of the night. And I *knew* what echolocation was," she said, snapping at Sage. "Anyway, my point is that these things can't be completely blind, or at least, they aren't completely bat-like. So what if these things can see, just not really well? What then?"

"I said it turned toward me when I moved and made a *sound*," corrected Max.

"But I didn't make a sound," said Sage, her brow furrowing as she slowly shook her head. "I'm afraid Kiley might be onto something here. When my father noticed me, I was quiet as a mouse, pressed against the wall. He noticed me when I made a sudden movement—I don't think I even made a whisper of noise. They must be able to detect movement through their eyes or some other sense. Or, at least, we should probably assume that they can so we don't make a really stupid mistake."

Bryan's shoulders sagged. "So what do we do, then?" he said.

"We simply distract their auditory and visual senses at the same time," said Sage. "I've got it. What if we hit the gym? You guys have a soccer team, right?"

Bryan nodded slowly, waiting for the idea to click in his mind. "Yeah."

"Ready? Okay," Kiley said in her best cheerleader voice. "Go Team Spirit!"

Without looking at her, Bryan raised an arm fiercely and quickly to silence her. She bit her lower lip.

"So," said Sage. "We wrangle a soccer net and fill it with as many soccer balls as we can. And basketballs, and whatever else will roll and possibly bounce. Then, we rig the system to blast the loud noise at the same time as we let the balls fly. We're on a *hill*!"

"Holy crap," said Bryan as her plan sunk in. "The balls will bounce all the way down the hill, giving them something to look at while we—" He paused, his eyebrows knitting together.

"While we what?" he asked. "Slink slowly down the hill? The balls will make it to the end of the hill before we do and when they realize that they've just got a bunch of sports balls, they'll turn back and see us trying to make a break for it."

"That's why we run." Sage's eyes were wide and bright, dancing in the glow of the fluorescent lights embedded in the ceiling. "All of us. In different directions, zigzagging as fast as we can down the hill. If we are fast, we might be masked in the camouflage of all the moving and bouncing spheres. It will be chaos. They might not know what's what."

"They *might* not?" Kiley muttered. "That sounds wonderfully encouraging."

Max slumped. "It does sound risky," he said, pressing his palm into the flannel-wrapping around his wounded arm. "Besides, I might be too weak to run, I think. Right now I'm almost too weak to sit in this chair."

"I'll help you," said Kiley, quietly. His eyes turned quickly on her, wide with surprise.

"And we can each be holding something like a super bouncy ball, or something else that we can throw if we're spotted. If we throw an object that is big enough just right and hold perfectly still, they might forget we're there and go for the thing we threw. When their back is turned, bam. We're outta there," said Sage.

A wide smile lifted the corners of Kiley's mouth, her cheeks rising as she looked at Sage. "Attack a vicious hoard of cannibal zombies with a soccer net full of balls and really loud music? Sure. Best plan ever," she said. "But let's not forget the original plan either. We need to email Sage's friend up north, gather up some weapons, balls, nets, music, health supplies, microscopes. I think you'd better tell your friend not to expect us until well after night fall, maybe even early morning. We have some serious work to get done around here, so get to work, Cinderella. This wicked stepmother's got to go to the balls."

Sage grinned. "Can do," she said. "I'll e-mail my friend right now if you want." Sage gave the older girl a mock salute.

"Let's wait until we figure out our new plan," said Kiley, grinning, finally feeling better about herself as well as their situation. She turned back to Max who was now slumped so low in the chair, he was only being held in place by his healthy arm which was slung haphazardly over the back of the chair. His eyelids fluttered as he looked weakly up at her.

"Now," she said calmly. "What are we going to do about our injured friend here? Who wants to play doctor?" she asked with a smirk.

CHAPTER TWENTY-FOUR

Sage, Bryan, and Max

Grimacing, Sage stepped forward and gently took hold of Max's wrist. She waited for some kind of sign from the boy. After a moment, he looked her in the eyes and took a deep breath. His eyelids slid slowly closed.

"If you're going to look at it, do it now while I'm not looking, please," he said quietly.

Sage unwound the blood-soaked flannel bandage from his arm. As she reached the last layer of flannel—the layer which was in contact with the open wound itself— the flannel stuck to his bloody flesh, and she had to peel it away from his arm. Max winced with pain, but only released a tiny gasp. Sage peeled off the final layer of fabric and the skin and tissue fibers of his wound stuck greedily to the shirt like threads of saliva to a hungrily opened mouth. Sage had to fight through her instinct to recoil with disgust at the sight of the wound.

Kiley closed her eyes, tightened her lips and looked away. She admitted, if only to herself, that she would never be able to do what the younger girl was doing in spite of her hardcore veneer. Bryan took a deep breath and stepped forward to help Sage as much as he could without getting in the way.

The only way Sage could think to describe the wound in Max's arm was to use the word *crater*. The side of his forearm was largely missing, leaving behind a bloodied gorge of swollen skin, tendons and muscles. Even part of the thinnest bone in his forearm was visible, though slathered in the black and red jelly of his slowly coagulating blood. For some reason, Sage thought the wound was reminiscent of her breakfast: strawberry rhubarb jam on toast.

She swallowed back a hot burst of bile rising acridly to the back of her throat. "It's not that bad." She hesitated, then added, "Really, it isn't," as if the extra words would sound more convincing, but they did just the opposite.

Max's face was flushed with pain. His features pinched tightly together as he tried not to look at the open canyon of his forearm.

"Think we can do anything about it? It's not like I can go see the school nurse." He tried to chuckle, but the motion of his chest quickly turned to a cough and the smile faded quickly from his strained lips.

"Can you move your fingers?" Sage asked.

"I can't tell," said Max after a beat. "Are they moving now?"

Sage watched as Max tried to wiggle his fingers, but there was no motion. She frowned. "We're going to get you better, Max. I'll be right back, okay?"

"Okay," Max said in a barely audible whisper. As Sage tugged on Bryan's sleeve and began to walk away, Max added, "Are you going to leave it open like that?" Sage laid the flannel softly over the wound before dragging Bryan into the cubby behind the librarian's desk. Kiley, unable to stomach the blood, was all too eager to join them. Max shifted uncomfortably, trying to take deep breaths. His eyes were still closed.

"I don't have a clue what to do," said Sage in a voice barely above a whisper. Her voice was uneven and breathy. "I don't think we can sew it up and, even if we could, my being smart doesn't mean my fine motor skills are heightened or anything. I can barely sew a straight line on doll clothes, let alone a person's skin."

Bryan lifted a hand. "No one could expect you to sew up his arm, Sage. And besides, I agree with you. That wound is beyond stitches."

"So what will you do?" asked Kiley. Sage stole a quick glance at her, noticing her marked use of the word "you" rather than "we".

Bryan had watched enough movies to come up with his own suggestion. "I think we have to cauterize it," he said.

Sage flinched. She fell quiet for a moment as her mind processed the idea. "With what?" she finally asked, coming up with no alternative of her own.

"A lighter and something hot." Bryan thought for a moment, and then snapped his fingers. "Max's knife. It's got a handle that we can hold onto and the blade itself is probably long enough to cover the opening—well, most of it at least. And doesn't he have a lighter?"

Sage nodded. "I think so. I have some fishing wire in Squiggly, too, if you want to take a stab at stitching up the smaller cuts around the opening of the wound."

Bryan raised an eyebrow. "You have fishing line in your stuffed bunny? You don't happen to have an AK47 in there as well, do you? Or a helicopter?"

"Rock on with your girl power, Sage. And here I thought only bio-boys could be boy scouts," said Kiley. Her genuine enthusiasm was mistaken by her peers for sarcasm.

Sage shot her a look. "I just finished reading Huck Finn," she said as if that were all the explanation they needed.

"Whatever, juice box. I meant it," muttered Kiley.

"Okay. But I'll need a needle too," said Bryan. "You don't happen to have one of those in here, do you?"

Sage shook her head.

"I saw one of those little dollar-store sewing kits in the desk when I was looking for the television remote. Nothing like getting sutured by a child wielding a second-rate needle and thread," offered Kiley.

"Good. Could you get it, please?" Bryan asked.

Kiley nodded and edged out of the alcove. Bryan held out his hand and accepted the wad of fishing line from Sage. "And you, young lady," he said, trying his best to adopt a fatherly tone. "I will need you to do the most important job of them all."

Ignoring his condescension, Sage asked, "What would that be?"

"I think he's going to scream. I know I would and I'd rather not alert the entire collection of monster people that might be in the vicinity to our location. I need you to find a book or a stick he can bite down on because I think this is going to hurt. Bad."

Sage nodded, slowly, a thought buzzing through her mind. As Bryan turned toward Max, she grabbed him by the arm and pulled him back.

"What is it?" he asked.

"Aren't you worried?"

"About what?"

"You know—the bite. I mean, apart from what all the movies and books say about zombies biting people and turning them into zombies too, we could still be dealing with a viral pathogen. It is possible that Max has been—" She paused, struggling for the right word. "—*infected.*"

CHAPTER TWENTY-FIVE

Max

After the group had gathered the necessary materials to attempt the first medical procedure in their adolescent lives, Sage laid them out on a linen napkin Kiley had found in one of the desk drawers. They had decided that, since Bryan was the oldest and had the steadiest hand, he would perform the procedures and Sage would be his assistant, handing him whatever he might need as the occasion arose.

Kiley, meanwhile, had asserted her desire to be elsewhere during the operation; and, after much fussing with Bryan waxing on about safety and *look what happened to him all by himself in this school*, he reluctantly let her go.

She'd fetch syringes for blood samples, medical supplies, and, after a quick explanation and a hastily drawn map, she would fetch the microscope from the science lab on her way through the school.

She reasoned it would save them time to send her out alone

"I've got my zombie-killing flagpole," she told them. "Who can stop me?"

But the truth was, Kiley knew she didn't have the stomach to be anywhere near them as they worked on Max. She emptied a backpack and strapped it on her back before leaving without so much as a "Goodbye and good luck" to the boy about to be operated on by a pair of children.

While Bryan sent a wary glance toward the door swinging shut after Kiley left, Sage felt relieved to see her go. From what she had seen, Kiley was more trouble than she was worth, more twists and bends than an emotional rollercoaster.

Doing something as delicate as minor surgery using rudimentary tools in a setting like a high school library is going to be trouble enough, reasoned Sage. *Why add to it with an unsteady, hormonal pre-teen?*

"Okay," Bryan said to Max, feigning an air of calmness that thinly masked his tension. "While Sage and I are fixing you up, I want you to look the other way. Under no circumstances are you to look at what we are doing, understand?"

Max nodded, relieved at the idea of not watching the inner workings of his own bloody, organic body. He trained his eyes on the thermostat beside the library doors.

Is it hot in here? he thought, but the sweat on his face felt like tiny icicles.

Sage pressed a thin paperback book into his good hand. He looked down at it. The title read *Smile Today Because You Might Not Be Here Tomorrow* by J. S. Becker. He looked up at her as if to say *are you serious?*

She smiled nervously. "I thought it was fitting," she said. Max smiled faintly and, pressing the book as far back into his mouth as he had been instructed to do, bit down on it firmly.

"Okay," said Bryan as Sage walked around the back of Max's chair and joined him on the other side. "I need you to hold the lighter steady underneath the knife. I think it's going to get covered with soot and that can't be helped, so we're going to hope that it doesn't matter and go for it anyway. I expect we'll need to heat it up for a good few minutes. It's going to have to be very hot and we want to get this right the first time."

He pointed a finger at her in a friendly, almost brotherly fashion. "Now, don't you go burning your fingertips on his Zippo, there, either. If it starts getting too hot, just take your thumb off the button."

Sage nodded. Pressing hard on the silvery button, she felt the click and catch of the Zippo's flint making contact with the striking surface as the flame burst through the tiny hole like a geyser of fire. Holding her hand as steady as she could, she flicked the tear drop of flame under the blade in the middle, pressing the flame closer to the surface of the metal to spread its heat. The fire fanned itself out a few inches, lapping the underside of the knife with an orange glow. After a few moments, black soot began to collect on the blade as the smoke rose around the knife in black swirls.

After several minutes, Bryan licked the pad of his middle finger and tested the blade for hotness. He recoiled quickly, shaking his hand to free it from the pain. He nodded at Sage and she reached for the moist towelette still in its paper-coated wrapper that they had found in an empty lunch bag in the librarian's desk. Biting down on the corner of the wrapper to brace the packet, she tore it open with her teeth. Then, flipping the package over and biting on the closed end, she pulled the towelette out with her fingers and let the package fall from her mouth to the floor. With two quick motions, she flicked the lighter off and wrapped the sooty knife blade with the napkin, wiping as much of the black off the metal as she could in one stroke.

It happened in a flash.

Bryan, afraid of losing the heat, quickly pressed the blade flat on its side at an angle against the opening. All the muscles along Max's arm immediately tensed as he clenched his teeth against the book. A guttural moan rose from his mouth, the sound filtering out around the edges of his makeshift bit. The room filled with a sickening scent of burning blood and fat. Sage imagined it smelled kind of like fried cat box litter, but she didn't dare say it out loud.

When Bryan finally pulled the metal away, sweat was beading heavily around his temples and his hair line. The skin and tissue where the blade had been laid now rippled like sand dunes and was an angry red and pink color.

Bryan turned back to Sage and nodded at her. She flicked the lighter again. They repeated the process to cauterize the remaining half of the bite. By the time it was over, Max was slumped, pale and whimpering, barely conscious. He was either so used to the pain at that point or half out of it as he barely acknowledged the uneven sewing needle and fishing-line stitches traveling up his arm in two places along the top and bottom of the bite where the gash was most narrow. When Bryan had finished stitching, Sage wrapped the wound in strips of an old, clean T-shirt she'd found in the librarian's bottom drawer.

Sage pulled the book carefully from Max's mouth. His jaw creaked and he could hear it inside his head as his teeth separated painfully from the book. Tooth depressions created a crescent moon around the front and back covers. Toward the front of the crescent on either side were craters where his canines had pressed sharply through several of the pages. Sage looked at it and winced before tossing it on the floor beside them.

"You did great," she said. "Can I get you anything?"

Max shook his head. "Naw," he said, his voice thin and weak. "I just hope I don't get fined for damaging that book."

Pressing into the arm of the chair with his good hand, the weakened boy tried to push himself out of his seat. "We can't waste any more time. We have to get out of here." But he couldn't back up his words with action as he faltered and collapsed back into the chair, grimacing with pain.

"Maybe you should just sit there for a minute," Sage said, eyeing him closely. "Losing blood and going through a lot of pain can make you really dizzy. Sit tight for a few minutes. We'll clean up, and then when you're ready, we'll go. Hopefully Kiley has found some aspirin and you can chug a few down, shortly."

"No," Max said, his voice a little stronger than before. "I want to get out of here now."

"Okay. But you really should let us get you some water or something to boost your blood sugar, like a candy bar from the vending machines outside, because if you pass out—"

Max cut her off. "We have to get out of here now." He fixed her with an intense look, his gaze unwavering. Sage nodded at him after a beat and he relaxed again, dropping his gaze. "Kiley's out there," he mumbled. "Alone."

Sage stared at him blankly for a moment, then turned away. *I wonder if you'd still be so eager to play the white knight if you knew that she'd been smooching with Bryan a few minutes ago while you were getting eaten by your neighbor. Boys are so weird. When I grow up—if I grow up—I don't think I'll like boys very much.*

With a shrug, she returned to the computer terminal where she had read her email from Amanda, re-logged into the system and wrote a hasty reply. In it, she explained their plan to escape and meet up with Amanda and the others at the warehouse later that night. She said she was pretty sure she knew the warehouse Amanda was talking about; but if she could find a computer between here and there, she'd love to get a reply with some landmarks describing it, just in case. Just for kicks, she added a post script. *Teenagers are crazy, Amanda. I'm not sure I ever want to be one. Ha, ha.* She stared at the words on the screen. The cursor blinked in and out after the period several times before she backspaced over the message.

Better not jinx myself, she thought. *I definitely want to be a teenager some day.* With that, she clicked out of her email and turned back to Bryan and Max.

"Ready to fight some bad guys?" she said. Max smiled weakly at her.

"You bet," he said.

"Good," said Bryan, grabbing Sage's backpack and slinging it over his shoulders. "Because we've got a lot of ground to cover and I'd rather get it done before nightfall. I don't imagine running around after dark with a bunch of echo-locating, child-eating zombie things running around would be very much fun."

"Agreed," said Sage.

Max fumbled to a stand. His knees buckled briefly before stabilizing beneath him. A grin curved the features of his pallid face. "Let's roll!"

Chapter Twenty-Six

Kiley

When Kiley first found herself alone in the hallway, she was too caught up in her impenetrable gothic-girl fortress act to really notice the magnitude of her situation. Alone. In an abandoned school. Surrounded by flesh-eating monsters who viewed tender, teenaged skin as a pre-packaged meat snack.

"Great," she mumbled to herself. *My first real kiss falls on the same day I get eaten by undead creatures of the night. Not exactly the glittering vampire romance story I envisioned, but at least the undead creature part is right.*

She remembered kissing Max in the hallway. How he'd seemed so vulnerable and heroic all at once. She had wanted to know what it was like to kiss someone before she died and, given that she might very well die at any point today, she took her chance. But as she reflected on the kiss they'd exchanged after she'd murdered the custodian, she couldn't remember how it had felt. Had she been sickened by him? His mouth all jammed up against hers, getting his spit and his breath all over her lips and chin.

It was kind of gross, she thought, trying to squash down the memory of her weakened knees at the touch of his lips. *Kissing over a fresh corpse. That's sick, right?*

Then Bryan kissed her and it was equally weird. She'd wanted her knees to go weak. She'd wanted to see fireworks and hot air balloons. And just as she began to process how he'd made her feel, well, nothing, he told her that crap about thinking she was

Rachel and then planted a kiss on her that reminded her of the way she used to kiss her cat's head goodnight after she'd slathered her lips with lip balm, all careful not to get fur stuck to her mouth.

What was that about? she thought. Her mind raced. *Didn't I feel a little knee-knocky when Max and I kissed?* She strained to remember.

It took her several minutes before she realized she had been wandering around the halls of a school with which she was only slightly familiar. She'd only been here a couple of times when she had been dragged to Rachel's parent-teacher conferences. The reality of it hit her like a blast of lightning on a dark night. She was alone and there were flesh-eating zombies wandering around outside and maybe even inside that would just love to wrap their teeth around her. Kiley slowed to a stop, took a deep breath and looked around, forcing her thoughts to remain on her mission.

Without realizing it, Kiley had wandered into the central corridor of the school where all hallways intersected into one, dome-style mini-lobby. From her history books, she remembered this was the oldest part of the Greendale High School, having been built first as a kind of conservatory for the female students to learn horticulture. From where Kiley stood, she could easily see out several windows. It occurred to her that, if she could see out, then the creatures might be able to see inside, too—at least, they might notice her movement through the glass.

She froze in place, her head turning so slowly on her neck it seemed almost animatronic as she looked out each window in turn. There were hundreds of those creatures, all shambling around the top of the plateau, wedged into the gap gardens. Some were visible near the bottom of the hill, stumbling around the parking lot or meandering up the hill that led from the middle school. There were so many of them, it looked to Kiley as though the entire town had shown up for an undead rights meeting at the high school.

Kiley's jaw dropped open at the sight of them all. Where had they come from and why had they come here?

What if they came here because they figure there must be more meat here? What if they already cut through whatever kids showed up at the elementary school this morning and now they're looking for fresh food? I mean, schools have pretty much turned into the drive-thru at McDonald's for these things, haven't they? Kiley shuddered. *How am I ever going to get out of here?*

Carefully, she began to lower herself to the floor, so slowly that the tension that rose in her thighs and calves quickly turned to pain. Her eyes darted from side to side, seeking the most efficient way out of the window-lined conservatory that wouldn't put her too far off track in her search for the science lab or the Nurse's office. A layer of sweat began to coat her face and back. The lower she got, the harder it was to remain steady. Her legs threatened to give out, but Kiley focused all of her attention on slow, controlled movement as she eyed the dozens of blanched-skin, black-veined creatures lumbering around the school grounds.

Just as she was about to reach the floor, she collapsed flat onto her butt. Her instinct was to check to see if any of the creatures had noticed her, but she fought the urge.

No sudden movements, she told herself as she forced her head to remain motionless. She held her position, panting, for several moments. A thwapping noise against the window pane to her left caught her attention. She turned her head ever so slightly toward the sound. There, pressed against the window, was the grotesquely disfigured, bloated and grayed face of her history teacher. Her horrific mouth, smeared with a mixture of blood and slobber, was open wide and her tongue was pressed against the glass.

It looked to Kiley like a horrible abomination of a kiss.

Like I said earlier, she thought. *It must be 'Kiss Kiley Day' at school.*

She closed her eyes tightly and willed the beast in the window to leave. The flagpole that hung loosely in her hand suddenly seemed like it was just a pointy piece of wood against an army of warrior beasts. She sighed inwardly.

Here goes nothing.

CHAPTER TWENTY-SEVEN

Sage, Bryan, and Max

Sage and Bryan thought it was best not to leave Max alone again. Max mumbled some protests, declaring that he'd rather intercept Kiley and work with her; but Bryan kept asserting that he knew the school better and would probably find her a lot faster. Max finally agreed, and he and Sage set off to find the principal's office to access the intercom system while Bryan headed off to find Kiley and get her help with the second part of their plan. They would tackle retrieving the car keys from Rachel's body, then they'd head for the gym to look for soccer balls or whatever else they could find there to implement their plan.

With a sense of foreboding seeping through his body, Bryan jogged lightly down the hall toward the central corridor. Armed with what they now knew about the monster's limited sense of perception, he felt a little more at ease in the hallway. If the monsters did sense movement, it was unlikely that they would notice anything through the glass of the classroom windows and then the glass of the classroom door windows beyond them. If he happened to round a corner and find one of those things standing in front of him, however, well, that was a different story.

He slowed as he approached the doors to the adjacent hallway and cautiously pulled the door open. No alarm sounded. He headed toward the next set of double doors which opened into the central corridor. Unfortunately, that corridor was flooded with windows, but it was also the most direct route to the cafeteria and nurse's station. If he wanted to find Kiley in a hurry, he could use that as a kind of home base since it connected to all the main corridors in the school.

He quickly reached the next set of doors and pulled them open, jogging through and down the short ramp descending toward the corridor. As he approached it, he slowed considerably and dropped to a squat over the floor. He figured his best bet would be to press against one side of the lobby to minimize his chance of being seen while he waddled toward the door to the hallway that led to the nursing station.

As he began to circle the octagonal, window-lined corridor, his eyes swam over the hordes of creatures now patrolling the plateau outside the school. His breath quickened. Part of him wanted to run. Part of him simply wanted to sit down and give up. How did they stand a chance? How many of these things roamed the town? Hundreds? Thousands? And wouldn't the next town be the same? He closed his eyes for a moment and then shook the images from his head.

From his angle on the floor, he could only see the upper half of their bodies, and only those that were close to the windows, but he counted at least a dozen of them as he rounded the corridor. All he could think of was that these poor, hapless creatures had been humans only this morning. And they were now likely hording around the school looking for what? Their children? If they hadn't eaten them already. Or fresh meat. Or maybe just something familiar. Who knew?

He tried to suppress the rising images of children and babies being consumed by their black-toothed parents. His slow, steady movements afforded him maximum self-control and, though he panted heavily with fright, he made it to the intended corridor without seeming to stir up the crowd outside. Leaping to his feet, he broke into a brisk jog down the hallway.

As he approached the nursing station, he slowed. The door was flung wide open and sounds of rustling boxes and metal clinking in drawers could be heard from the outside. His first thought was that it must be Kiley, but what if it wasn't? He suddenly regretted his failure to bring a weapon with him. He approached the door cautiously, edging toward it at an almost sideways angle. Abruptly, the sounds inside the station ceased.

Had he made a noise? Was there a creature standing on the other side of the entrance running a gray tongue over broken, bloody teeth?

He halted and held his breath. After a moment, he crept forward on the balls of his feet and peeked around the edge of the door. He couldn't see anything, so he crept a few inches forward and slowly stepped into the room. He scanned the nursing station. Drawers had been pulled out of their rollers and boxes had been pulled off their shelves and tipped open, their contents strewn about the room, but there was no sign of Kiley.

"Ha!" The shout came a split second before the stout pole cracked hard across the crown of his head. He cried out in pain, dropping to his knees as he grabbed his head with both hands.

"Oh nuggets!" said Kiley , dropping to her knees to help him. "I'm so sorry, Bryan! Oh Goddess, I am so sorry! I totally thought you were one of those things!"

Rubbing the top of his head with both hands, he glared up at her. "Yeah. I really look like a zombie, don't I?" he muttered.

"Really, I mean it. I'm so sorry. I was crawling on the floor back there when I thought I saw one of those creatures. Then, it was you. Really, you should have some kind of bell around your neck. What the hell are you doing here, anyway? Checking up on me to make sure I'm doing my job?" Bryan raised a hand to hush her.

"Please be quiet," he said. "It's fine, okay? But we gotta go."

She opened her mouth to stammer more apologies and explanations, but he held his hand up to insist she remain silent.

After a beat, he asked, "Did you get the stuff?"

"Mostly," she said . "I broke the lock off a couple of cabinets and the refrigerator and found some syringes and a bunch of bandages, some alcohol swabs, ibuprofen tablets, antacid tablets, peroxide,—" She continued to list materials she had collected, but Bryan tuned her out. The pain in his head throbbed from the top of his skull to the inner pockets of his ears. He grabbed the backpack from her hands and pulled it open, peering inside. It brimmed with medical supplies, everything from cough drops to butterfly sutures.

"Good job," he said. "What about the microscope?"

"Last time I checked, superhuman speed was not one of my many talents, Bryan. I just got here, and there was the zombie teacher thing, which apparently was a non-issue. But, good gods, it took forever for me to crawl through that damned central lobby low enough so those creatures couldn't sense me through the glass. Seriously. Who designed this place? King Minos? Anyway, I just got to the nursing station when you interrupted me before I—" she said.

"Interrupted you?" Bryan demanded.

"Yeah. I had things under control, Captain Underpants. Sir, yes, sir," Kiley said, fake-saluting.

"Whatever. Did you get the microscope or not?"

"Not."

Bryan zipped up the backpack and flung it over his shoulders. "No problem. I need to go through the kitchen to get to the back of the school where your sis—where the car keys are anyway. We'll pass the lab on the way. We can go together."

Before she could respond, he turned around and jogged from the room. "Try to keep up, girl," he called back to her. Her mouth dropped open for a split second in protest but, seeing that he was already out the door, she let out a sigh and followed him.

"Sir, yes, sir," she repeated softly as she tried to pad lightly behind him in her chunky-heeled boots.

CHAPTER TWENTY-EIGHT

Max and Sage

Sage and Max found the door to the principal's office in the lobby off the humanities corridor near the hallway where they had broken into the school. Having stuffed her backpack with medical books from the library, Sage's bag had grown too cumbersome for her tiny frame. Max offered to carry it for her and slung it carelessly over his good shoulder.

While Max's wound slowed him down, he still managed to pick the lock on the office door in less than a minute and, in the dimness of a shaded window, they snuck past the receptionist's desk to the principal's office door. Sage was able to just make out the first letters on the plaque reading "Principal" before Max set to work popping the lock.

Beads of cold sweat rolled from his hairline down over his brow and into his face. The salt in his sweat stung his eyes and he squinted slightly with the pain, but in truth, he welcomed it. He was ready to take any distraction he could get from the burning and throbbing torture of his arm. His body begged for him to find a corner somewhere and just lie down for awhile.

Lie down and die, right? Plenty of time for that later, he told himself and thought of the old saying: 'I can rest when I'm dead.'

Once inside, Sage bee-lined for the principal's desk and set to work hacking his computer. After a few rounds of "guess the password" from objects around his desk, she pursed her lips and lifted the keyboard. Sure enough, there was a sheet of paper taped to the bottom. She smiled. She now not only knew the principal's login and password for the computer, but the password for disabling the fire alarms, for engaging the fire drill, for accessing the intercom, and even for entering employee evaluations. She shook her head.

She tried the login and password and, sure enough, it worked. "What an infant," she said quietly to Max.

"What?"

"The high school principal apparently has the memory of a goldfish. Well, maybe that's not fair to the goldfish." She tipped the keyboard up and pointed at the piece of paper taped there. "He wrote down all his passwords and kept it in the most obvious place imaginable."

Max chuckled. "That's where my dad kept his when I lived with him. I used to break into his computer all the time to play video games whenever he left me at home."

"Grownups aren't as smart as they think sometimes," Sage replied. "Either that or they're just lazy." She thought for a moment, and frowned. "*Were* just lazy, I guess."

As she looked at the computer monitor, a thought occurred to her. "Hey, what if we just blare the fire alarm and route it through the intercom system as well? I mean, instead of music? That way, it would emit one steady stream of sound. We could even project it from the speakers on the sides of the school."

"There's speakers on the sides of the school?"

"Yeah. I noticed them when we walked up to the school this morning." She turned her attention back to the keyboard, logging into each system one at a time.

"You did?" he asked, raising an eyebrow.

"Yeah. I guess I just notice everything," she responded, swinging her legs off the side of the principal's chair. "For once that particular talent is going to pay-off big time."

Max coughed lightly into his closed fist as he muttered the word "genius," the cough swallowing up the word.

She stared at him for a moment, then, turning her attention back to the keyboard, announced, "I'm in."

"Already?"

"No biggie," she said . "Definitely easier than patching up a half-eaten arm." She grinned and pushed herself off the seat. She found herself wedged in a corner. On one side was a shaded window, and the other was Max leaning across the large, faux-mahogany desk, half blocking her route around the desk and back to the door.

"Maybe you can show me how to hack into things sometime?" he said. A gut-clenching cough rose up in his chest.

Sage eyed him for a moment. "Are you all right?"

"Yeah," he said, trying to catch his breath. "I just—well, it just hurts like hell, is all. It's hard to breathe. Hope they find some aspirin or something."

He straightened up, but still half-blocked her behind the desk. "Did you email your friend?"

"Yeah, back in the library. I hope the web's still up and she gets the message. I don't want to get mistakenly shot as zombies when we arrive," she said.

"You think they have guns?"

"Sure. It's the middle of Chesterville. Nothing but pine trees, hippie communes, and members of those pro-gun-rights movements. Even my parents talked about getting a shotgun when we lived there. For the bears, if nothing else." She stepped forward to try to get past Max. He hesitated before stepping back out of her way so she could slide by him.

"We were supposed to meet here, weren't we?" Max asked, changing the subject as he glanced at the clock on the wall.

It had only been ten minutes or so since they left the others. But he was right; they had agreed to meet in the principal's office due to its location near the exits and the need to access it during the evacuation. Someone would need to press the button to initiate the music over the intercom before the others could release the decoy sports balls.

For some reason, though, Sage was suddenly feeling rather uneasy alone in the principal's office with Max. She wasn't certain of her hypothesis that the virus only affected adults. What if Max was going to turn on her? What if it was like rabies and the virus or parasite only needed to get to his brain to take it over and then there was nothing but a narrow principal's desk separating her from a creature of the undead? It was all she could do to keep her breath steady and her legs from bolting while she waited for the others to show up.

"Yeah," she said, leaning against the wall nearest the door. "Let's just chill out here for a while."

Max grinned. He took the principal's seat and, cradling the back of his head with his one good hand, he stretched his legs out and rested his heels on the desk. "Sounds like a plan. I could use the rest anyway." But his eyes were wide open, following even her slightest movements. A moment ago an exhausted, pained Max had been covered in a thin, cold sweat. Now he was as alert as if he'd been pumped full of espresso beans and let loose at a roller derby.

"You seem awfully alert all of a sudden," Sage said cautiously. Instinctively, she moved her body away from the wall and rested her weight evenly on her feet as if readying to fight or flee at any moment.

Max took note of her stance and cocked an eyebrow. "Second wind," he said dismissively. "What's up?"

"Nothing," said Sage, avoiding his gaze. "Just checking your status, I guess. That's a doctor term, right? Status? I'm pretty sure I've heard doctor's say that before."

"Right," said Max, nodding slightly. He eyed the girl. "You're scared I'm going to turn into one of those things, aren't you?"

Sage forced a laugh. "No, of course not. How could you? You're a kid, remember? I'm pretty sure, I mean, I'm positive you have to be an adult to get this virus thing. You're going to be fine."

Max let out a derisive laugh. "Right. Fine. Killed my best friend today. Stuck in a school surrounded by flesh-eating killers and I plan to escape with a bunch of soccer balls and some loud music. Not to mention this gaping wound in my arm."

"Which should have stopped bleeding by now. No seepage, right? Does the burn hurt?"

"Like hell," said the boy. "I'm just not much of a complainer, you know?" He squinted at the girl. "Besides, it's not like I'm going to turn into one of those zombies and try to eat you, right? I'm just a kid."

"True," Sage said, eyeing the door. "You're just a kid. Just like me."

Sage crossed her hands protectively over her chest. *All right, guys*, she thought. *Whose bright idea was it to split up and where the heck are you?*

CHAPTER TWENTY-NINE

Kiley and Bryan

After stuffing the microscope they found in the chemistry lab into Kiley's backpack, Bryan decided the best way to get to the shed was to go through the back door of the kitchen. The distance between the two was only a dozen feet at the most. Kiley stood poised at the back door of the kitchen, peering out the window at the bush-lined path toward the shed. Her sister's sneaker-clad feet were the only part of her clearly visible. The rest of her body was heavily shadowed by the interior of the dark shed, which was a blessing for Kiley.

That's my sister, she thought. *Or, was my sister.*

Bryan handed her his book bag which now contained a few granola bars and some bottled water. Absently, she pulled it over her arms and onto her shoulders. He held out his hand for her to pass him her book bag in return, but she didn't seem to notice him. Her eyes were glazed.

Sighing, he glanced over his shoulder. He caught sight of Rachel's hand through the window and nodded. "I'm sorry, Kiley," he said quietly.

She said nothing. After a moment, Bryan walked around Kiley and unzipped her backpack. He plunged a hand inside and retrieved a plastic-sheathed syringe from the medical supplies she'd pilfered earlier. Shoving it in his pocket, he walked back around Kiley and looked her in the eyes.

"Okay," he explained. "I'm going to sneak out this door. It'll lock behind me. You stay right next to the door and get ready to open it as soon as you see me coming, okay? I might be in a hurry." He smiled lamely. "I'll make a dash for the body, find the keys to the car and run straight back. If you see one of those things, freeze. It will probably get distracted by my actions anyway. If it doesn't, you keep that door shut unless you see I have a clear pathway back. If I can't get back in this way, I'll meet up with you guys in the parking lot near the car. Got it?"

Kiley's eyes were still trained on the body of her sister as she nodded. "Uh huh," she mumbled, not really hearing anything he said.

"Okay," he said. "Here we go." After a short pause, Kiley stepped back from the door to give Bryan plenty of room to exit.

CHAPTER THIRTY

Bryan

Bryan took his time scanning the area around the shed. After all, his life and possibly the lives of the rest of the rag-tag group depended on it. He couldn't see any signs of the creatures wandering around the plateau, but that didn't mean that they weren't on the other side of the mound, outside of his line of vision.

He glanced again at Rachel's body. She was slumped on her back, her legs bent at right angles and her feet were darkened by the shadows of the shed door. Bryan let his shoulders drop as he exhaled out one long breath of air that said more than words ever could. A tingling sensation rose from the base of his spine and in moments it felt like an avalanche of huge boulders tumbled down through his abdomen. The fear built itself up from tiny rivulets and then became streams and, before long, were roaring rivers. His knees buckled slightly, and he hoped Kiley hadn't noticed.

I don't want to die today, he thought and quickly forced the image from his head. "Now," he said.

Kiley flung open the door and Bryan dashed through it. He was halfway to the shed before she even thought to pull the door closed behind him. She watched through the window feeling helpless as Bryan screeched to a halt and froze at the near side of the shed. His breath spiraled out of his mouth in a crisp, white mist for a few beats before he moved again.

Now that he was outside, Bryan had an unobstructed view of the area and could only see two of the creatures stumbling around behind the school. One was near the side of the plateau, shambling toward the river. The second was about thirty yards to his right, facing away from him. Even though the creature seemed not to have noticed Bryan, there was something troubling about him that the boy couldn't quite put his finger on. He hoped he figured it out before he found himself being slowly eaten alive.

Mustering up enough courage to plunge ahead, Bryan carefully planted one foot in front of the other and eased forward, moving as imperceptibly as he could in spite of the trembling that rattled his knees with each step.

After several excruciating minutes, Bryan slid closer to Rachel's body. The two visible creatures had still failed to notice him. His breath grew rapid as he pressed a tentative fingertip to the shed door and swung it slowly open. The door creaked like achy bones. Bryan would have bet the sound was heard clear on the other side of town, but a quick glance told him the creatures were too distracted by the movement of each other to seem to care.

His hands trembled as if they were as old and decrepit as a ninety-year-old man.

He tried to slow his heaving breath as he peered wide-eyed into the building. If a creature had wandered into the shed since the gang had gotten inside the school, Bryan would have no way of defending himself. Plus, he would have no way of knowing if a creature was inside until he made his presence known. What really troubled him, however, was the position of Rachel's corpse. He would have to step over her to reach her pockets and, once inside the shed, he'd be unable to keep an eye on the creatures wandering around outside.

But then, he reasoned, *they won't be able to see me either.*

A tremor rippled down the length of his body. He froze in place for only a moment, but it felt like much too long. Collecting his courage, he poised on the balls of his feet and prepared to spring into a sprint at the slightest hint of movement from the shed or the doorway.

As he lowered his hands to Rachel's body, his gaze accidentally (or perhaps simply subconsciously) drifted to her head. The detached head lay in line with her body. It resembled a tribal woman from Africa he'd once seen on some educational channel whose neck had been elongated by several golden rings, pressing her head almost a foot and a half above her shoulders. Rachel seemed to be a sick, almost carnival interpretation of this memory with her black-bloodied face and ashy skin. Bryan gulped as his stomach flip-flopped and threatened to project its contents.

He shoved his fingers into Rachel's pants pocket, digging for the keys. Even though she was clothed, Bryan felt as if he was touching a piece of cold stone wrapped in cloth. All the fleshiness and warmth of the skin beneath had vanished. It unsettled him more than he thought it would. He managed to gulp down a throat full of bile.

His fingertips found the key ring and looped through it. Wrapping his fingers around the keys to prevent them from clinking together, Bryan quickly retrieved them. He thrust them into his own pocket and took out the syringe he had brought along. Squatting above the fallen body of his girlfriend, he sighed.

At least your death might save some lives, Rachel, if we can figure out how to examine your blood.

He had to insert the needle into her left arm several times before he finally found a blackened vein. He pulled back the plunger. A thick, tar-like substance oozed and bubbled into the syringe. He filled it completely before extracting the needle. Putting the protective cap back onto the syringe, he thrust it into his other pocket with her cell phone, leaving the keys in a pocket by themselves.

As he stood up, a thought occurred to him. *There were a lot of garden tools in that shed. We sure could use some weapons right about now.* He hated having to hang around any longer than necessary, but knew they were going to need weapons sooner or later. As he hovered in the doorway of the shed, he lifted his head to face the kitchen door. Catching sight of Kiley in the window of the kitchen, Bryan held up the index finger of his right hand as if to say 'one more minute'. She looked wide-eyed. Her mouth dropped open in muffled protest, but Bryan simply turned around and entered the shed, into the darkness and out of her sight.

Scanning the array of garden tools and maintenance supplies along the shed's back wall, a couple of things caught his eye. Hanging from a hook in the corner was an iron pickaxe. Next to it hung a rusty hatchet, a matching spade and a metal-pronged rake.

He walked to the back wall and pulled the pickaxe down. It was surprisingly weighty in his hands. There was no way any of the others could wield this weapon without significant trouble, but he eyed the points on either side of its head with a smile. His lips curled upward. He could definitely use this. He pulled down the hatchet for Max and then surveyed the utility table next to the hanging tools. On the table was a long-handled hammer that he suspected Kiley could use with little effort.

The hooked end of the hammer would probably do more damage than the flag pole she used, he thought. He grabbed it and slid it awkwardly through one of his belt loops.

One more, he thought. *Something light and easy to handle for Sage.*

A busted spade rested on the table at the far end, the iron spade end having separated from its wooden handle. The broken end of the handle was sharp and jagged where it had broken off.

Perfect, he thought, scooping it up and glancing around one last time. His arms laden with bulky tools, Bryan approached the entrance with a new sense of confidence.

At least we'll stand a chance with these, he thought as the faintest glimmer of a smile lighted on his face. *Maybe we'll make it through this after all.*

He lifted his gaze to the window where Kiley's face was visible. Her face looked strained, the skin of her forehead creased against her hairline. Her eyebrows were raised and her eyes were wide. As soon as she caught sight of him, she shook her head violently. The smile dropped instantly from Bryan's face.

He held perfectly still.

What is it? Where is it? Bryan clutched the axe, pickaxe, and handle to his chest; his free hand gripped the hammer tightly.

From where he stood, he could only see a small section of the green between the shed and the back door. Sweat covered his forehead as he scanned the ground fervently. Something had spooked Kiley, but he could not determine what it was. He couldn't see anything different than when he had entered the shed. He returned his gaze to hers, searching her eyes for the reason for her fear.

Bryan watched as Kiley lifted a hand behind the glass and extended her index finger downward. Bryan followed the direction her finger pointed toward his shoes. It took several minutes before he realized what was wrong. He slowly lifted his head to look Kiley in the face, his mouth slack and a crease of skin pulsing between his eyebrows. Several four-letter words echoed through his head.

Rachel's head was still right where he'd left it, but the body was gone.

CHAPTER THIRTY-ONE

Kiley

Kiley watched helplessly as the mutated man hobbled toward the fallen body of her headless sister. Soundlessly, the creature turned its back to Kiley and stooped over the body's shoulders, his foot kicking the edge of her sister's limp hand which extended above her neck. Curling its fingers around her colorless wrist, the creature dragged the body from the entrance.

Rachel's feet, which had been invisible in the darkness of the shed, slid over the wooden threshold. No sooner did the creature drop the body's arm than two smaller, grey-bodied mutants jerked out from one of the gaps along the edge of the school and ambled gorilla-like toward him.

The first creature twisted and snapped Rachel's hand off at the wrist effortlessly and lifted it to its dry, leathery mouth. Kiley's eyes widened at the ease with which the monster tore apart her sister's body.

Acid rose up in Kiley's stomach and she swallowed back a lump of vomit, fighting her urge to thrust open the door and attack them for defiling her sister's body. The other two creatures took turns poking and scooping at Rachel's abdomen, pulling out long grey strands of guts and ripping through it with their blackening teeth.

One of the creatures jerked its head in her direction and she froze. Had it seen her? She couldn't be sure, but she held perfectly still, afraid to even angle her eyes back in its direction. In her peripheral vision, she saw the creature's head return to the body of her sister as it scooped another handful of viscera into its sickening mouth.

Where are you, Bryan? Her knees trembled. She strained to see around the opening of the shed for a glimmer of Bryan, but he had disappeared into its shadows and not returned.

What if there is a creature in there? What if he's already been eaten? Icy fear clawed at her insides, then another thought occurred to her. *No. I would have heard something. He'd have screamed. These other guys would have gone running after the sound. He's fine. I'm sure he's fine.*

In spite of her self-assurances, however, her instinct was to turn and run, but her body wouldn't let her. It was frozen in place. Kiley knew she had to stay put. Bryan was counting on her, but it took every ounce of power within her to do so. Her hand trembled on the door latch as tiny bursts of electric adrenaline shot through her.

No, she thought. *I will wait here for Bryan. He's not dead. He's not going to die. I just have to hold out for a little while longer. Only, please hurry, Bryan. Please.*

Chapter Thirty-Two

Bryan, Rachel, and Kiley

Straining his neck, Bryan slowly arched his head around the doorway of the shed until he caught sight of the creature's back and side. The thing appeared to be eating Rachel's hand one finger at a time.

Finger food, he thought immediately and reprimanded himself. The mind worked in crazy, weird ways.

Concentrate! He edged his way back into the shed and out of sight, fighting with himself to calm his breathing. He looked down at his arms. If he dropped the tools he was holding, the clatter would instantly alert them to his presence, but his arms were so overloaded he would need to set them down before he could make a break for it. Bryan scanned the tool shed helplessly.

There must be something, he thought. He caught sight of a few strips of spongy, mattress-like material that resembled yellow insulation piled beside the tool bench. Beads of sweat formed on the line of his brow as he worked his way to the pile. One at a time, he dropped each of the tools softly onto it, keeping only the pickaxe tightly in his grasp. He imagined himself swinging the axe in a constant, tornado-like circle as he zipped forward from the shed, slamming the sharp end of the pickaxe into the creature's soft skull before bursting through the kitchen door, just in time to shut out a throng of them.

Ridiculous, he thought, his eyes skimming over the shed's interior one last time. *This isn't a video game.* He gulped hard. *I'm going to die. It's that simple. Martial arts and a pickaxe aren't going to get me out of this. These aren't tree stumps or sparring partners. They're monsters. And they've got me cornered.*

Suddenly, he caught sight of a familiar object—something he hadn't seen since his last fishing trip on his dad's boat last summer. It was the handle of a flare gun.

What if these creatures can see, just not well? What would happen if a sudden burst of light glared in their eyes? Would it confuse them?

Moving quickly, he stuffed a handful of flares into the front pouch of his hoodie. Grabbing the flare gun in his free hand, he shut his eyes for a moment and held his breath.

If this works, he thought, *I'll be safe inside in no time. And if it doesn't—well—*Bryan's eyes snapped open, cutting off the thought mid-sentence.

Not gonna happen today, he thought. Mustering his courage, he lunged for the open door. As his gun-toting hand swung through the entrance, he fired the flare gun toward the creature ravaging Rachel's body. Bryan bee-lined for the kitchen door as the flare struck the monster in the shoulder. The two creatures near the monster immediately jerked their leathery hands up to cover their faces while their companion staggered backwards, roaring. He seemed oblivious to the pain in his shoulder. The shriek echoed out and the creature twisted, suddenly homing in on Bryan. A moment later the monster lunged in the boy's direction, still shrieking wildly.

Bryan was about three feet from the door when he saw out of the corner of his eye the creature rapidly coming at him. The boy knew he wouldn't make it to the door before the creature was on him. They were fast and they already had a location on him. He swung around, trying to lift the heavy axe high enough to get the creature in the head, but was unable to lift it above his waist. The pointed end of the pickaxe curved around in a wide arc until it met resistance. The end of the iron pick wasn't exactly sharply honed, but it still made a sickening wet sound as it penetrated the fleshy side of the creature just above the hip. Bryan released the handle so the monster didn't pull him along as it staggered from the blow.

It gave Bryan just enough time. He sprang forward, lunging for the door. The creature recovered quickly, and ignoring the pick axe still sticking from its side, it stretched out a leathery arm.

Kiley flung open the door and Bryan dove over the threshold like a football player diving for the end zone. The monster's hand crashed against solid metal as Kiley slammed the door shut. It shrieked wildly and clawed at the sturdy door as it clicked into place. Bryan jumped to his feet and grabbed Kiley's arm. The warmth of her flesh was comforting. He took her hand in his. They turned to stare out the window as the creature continued to scratch at the door, the long handle of the pickaxe still hanging from its side.

The creature shrieked, jerking its head around, its blind eyes still seeming to stare at the kids through the glass. The other two monsters reached its side and joined in the shriek-fest, also beating their hands on the walls and door until their fingers and knuckles turned black and bloody from the battering. They seemed not to notice, however, as they continued their bloody, wild barrage.

"Let's get out of here," gasped Bryan. "That noise is going to attract more and more of those things."

"Already gone," said Kiley. The two turned and skidded down the short corridor and into the empty cafeteria.

"Hold on," Bryan shouted, pulling on Kiley's hand so she was forced to stop. "We need to get into the gym storage closet and grab as many balls as we can. Don't forget the rest of the plan, Kiley, or we'll never make it out of here alive!"

"I'm not going to get eaten by a mob of monsters so that we can get a few soccer balls." She fixed him with a desperate look.

"Do you have a better idea?" asked Bryan, panting.

Pursing her lips, Kiley rolled her eyes. "We could turn on the sprinklers. That might create enough commotion to stop them," she said.

"We'll do that, too," said Bryan. "You know the best way for a plan to fail?"

"No, what?"

"Change it in the middle."

Bryan turned toward an unmarked door at the back of the gymnasium. Kiley sighed heavily then followed. To their relief, the door was unlocked and Bryan shoved it open. Kiley immediately spotted a box in the corner marked 'soccer' and, pushing past Bryan, tore it open. She pulled out a thick-roped net.

"This is heavier than it looks," she said, wrestling the net out of the box.

Bryan had moved to the rack near the doorway. It was filled with dozens of balls of every size and shape, from the bright-red, rubber dodge balls (that used to leave red welts on his arms during gym class) to the easily recognized white and black, sectagoned and pentagoned soccer balls. He turned quickly back toward Kiley and, helping her untangle the soccer net, spread it out on the floor in front of the rack.

"Hold the corners on your side," he said as he clutched one corner. Gripping the rack with his left hand, he grunted as he tried to move it away from the wall. The rack teetered near the top as it came about a foot away from the wall, each of the balls dropping and bouncing on the net. A few of them rolled off, but Bryan caught the stragglers with his feet and herded them back. Grabbing the remaining corner of the net, he pulled his two corners together tightly, closing the net over the top of the balls. Kiley did the same.

Twisting the net in his hand, he turned toward the door. "I can just drag this thing. The floor's smooth enough. Just hold your end closed, okay?"

Not waiting for an answer, he shoved his way back through the door and toward the hall. The balls, caught up in the net, pressed around the opening of the door before shuffling together and, with a tight squeeze, popped through the door.

Bryan could still hear the monsters banging on the doors and walls. If nothing else, they were determined creatures. He knew it was only a matter of time before they managed to get inside. He jerked the netting forward and pushed his way into the hallway, Kiley struggling to maintain her grip on the net as she stumbled along trying to keep up.

"Hurry," he shouted, no longer worried about the volume of his voice. "There's another locking door beyond this hallway. We can shut them out in layers. It should buy us some extra time."

Kiley grunted what Bryan took as approval. He did not look back.

The girl cast a wary glance over her shoulder toward the kitchen, her eyes rolling quickly over the fallen body of Max's neighbor. She jerked her head forward again. Strengthening her resolve, she clenched the netting tightly in both fists and waddled behind the netting as fast as she could to keep pace with Bryan.

CHAPTER THIRTY-THREE

Sage and Max

"We should probably cue up the music or fire alarm," said Sage, casting a wary glance at the clock. "Or both. They've been gone almost forty minutes. It'd be good if we were ready the minute they return."

Slumped in the chair, Max jerked his head up from where it was resting on the desk. He lifted his eyebrows high, pulling the lids of his eyes up with them. His face was ashen. "Huh?"

Sage held her breath, eyeing his face carefully. His skin was pale and the purple circles around his sunken eyes made him look like some kind of a macabre clown. She suppressed a shudder, cleared her throat and said, "The music. We should cue it." She gestured toward the computer.

Max looked at the monitor blankly. After a beat, he said, "Oh. Yeah. We can do that. Music."

"Are you all right?" asked Sage. Tightness clenched at her jaw. *Is he going to turn into one of them? Was I wrong about the child thing? Could this disease simply be spread through blood?*

Stepping back, she pressed firmly against the door, her fingers secretly seeking behind her for the doorknob. Max was looking hazily at the spiraling light of the screen saver and not at her.

"You don't look so hot," she said softly.

Max swallowed drily, shifting his hands under his armpits. Blinking slowly, he said, "Yeah? Well, let's see how you look when you have your arm almost bitten off by your best friend."

"He was really your best friend?" asked Sage. Her fingertips grazed the edge of the doorknob panel.

"Yeah," said Max. "He was kind of like my dad, I guess." He shot a quick glance at Sage. Her body went rigid as she nodded at him to continue. "I mean, the dad that I would have picked instead of my mom's boyfriend. You know, since my real dad died."

Even though Max was trying to conceal the sorrow in his voice, Sage could tell he was heartbroken. From the slump of his body in the principal's chair to the arms crossed hard over his chest, she could see that he really missed his father. And now this whole thing with his best friend/father-figure made her feel bad about second guessing him. Her hand stopped moving along the door behind her. She made a quick decision she hoped she wouldn't regret.

If he is sick, then I'm going to risk it. She folded her hands in front of her at her waist. *Besides, I managed to kill both my fully grown, zombified parents*, she thought, her breath catching in her throat at the memory, *I think I can handle one adolescent boy if I need to.*

Still, she was afraid and she knew she'd have to handle the situation. *Best to keep him occupied.*

She stepped away from the door. "Come on, Max," she said. "Why don't you see what kind of music you can find on the internet? Got any good names of death metal bands you could try out?"

Max grinned. Wheeling into the desk with a slight wince, he dropped his fingers to the keyboard and began typing. "Do I ever," he said, a little color returning to his face.

Sage smiled faintly. Glancing at the clock again, she said, "Well, see what you can find. They could be back here at any time."

Chapter Thirty-Four

Bryan and Kiley

Bryan tugged on the netting in his hands, pulling the bulbous bundle through the doorway of the hall. The cross-hatched ropes of the net dug into the flesh of his palms. He ignored the pain and kept pulling. Kiley stumbled along behind. She gripped the corners of the net so tightly that her hands had gone from numb to pins and needles, from tense white to violent red again.

"Hold up," she said, scrambling to maintain her grip.

"Hurry up," said Bryan. "We have to lock this door. Those things could already have gotten into the building. It's like all they want to do is eat fresh meat. Did you see the way it dropped Rachel's hand to come after me? It's like these things know what's alive and what's dead. What's us, and what's them. And what's worse, they seem to have superhuman strength. I don't know how long these doors will hold them out."

"Then we're already dead," she said drily. "So what difference does it make if I need a second here?"

Frowning, he watched her gather more net into her hands and hoist it off the floor again. He jerked on his end and moved back as she waddled through the doorway. Pressing the corners of the net into one clenched fist, he pulled the doors closed and lifted the handle. Taking out a hexagonal key from a jumble of keys in his pocket, he pressed it into the bar latch of the door and turned it.

Kiley snorted. "I'll bet Sage and Max could have used that dead guy's keys."

"Sage and Max can handle themselves," he said. Turning his back on her, he dragged the bag further down the hallway.

"Come on," he said.

Sighing, Kiley followed.

The process of dragging the soccer net full of sports balls from one end of the school to the other took them much longer than Bryan had anticipated, but they finally made it to the front lobby. As they turned the final corner, Sage slipped out the door of the office to greet them.

"How's Max?" asked Bryan.

Sage frowned. "Not good. He's a little weak. I'm not sure–" She stopped.

"He'll make it," said Bryan sternly. "He's just lost a lot of blood."

"Of course!" said Sage, striking a palm against her forehead. "His blood sugar must have bottomed out. That's why he was acting all weird. He just needs a candy bar or something. All Max brought was canned goods. Did you find anything in the nurse's station?"

"Maybe," said Kiley, jerking her head toward Bryan. "He's got my backpack. His is full of bottled water and stuff. Mine is chock full of microscope and bandages. You know, I only pack the essentials when planning a zombie apocalypse vacation."

Sage unzipped the pouch hanging on Bryan's back and stood on tiptoe to peer inside. She nudged the microscope to the side and plunged a hand to the bottom of the backpack. Her fingers curled around a bottle and pulled it out. Cough Syrup.

"This should do the trick," she said. "My mom never let me use this stuff because she said it was full of sugar."

"We should probably hurry," Kiley interrupted.

"What happened?"

"We ran into some trouble," Bryan explained.

"And that trouble may have followed us into the building," added Kiley.

Sage looked from each of them to the net full of balls. "Well, guess we shouldn't stand around here talking," she said. "We need to move."

"What about Max's blood sugar? Is he going to slow us up?" asked Kiley. "Well, you know what I mean." No matter how hard she tried to sound sincere, everything that came out of her mouth sounded like sarcasm.

Sage glared at her. "He can chug this," she said, holding up the cough syrup. "The longer we wait, the less our chances of getting out of here. And—" her stare never wavered from Kiley, "We are going to make it out of here. *All* of us."

A clunking noise echoed down the hall. The sound cut through the moment like a saw blade through flesh. Three pairs of eyes widened with fear.

"They're inside," whispered Kiley.

Sage nodded, loosening the fear that threatened to flash-freeze her mind. "Then we have no time to lose."

Bryan nodded in agreement. "Let's get going," he said. "Sage, go inside, grab Max. Kiley and I will get the balls ready to toss down the hill the second you guys are back in the hall with us. Guess we'll have to do it without music."

"Guess again," Sage said. "Max and I cued an online music video. We can start it just as we leave the office. And a fire alarm, too."

"How long will it give us?" Kiley asked, with a furtive glance down the hallway.

"Max said about four minutes for the song. The fire alarm should give us uninterrupted sound for a while, but I can't guarantee how long."

"Hey, can you turn on the sprinklers while you're in there?" Kiley asked.

"Probably. They must be on the principal's computer," replied Sage. It dawned on her what Kiley was asking. "Oh. Good idea. The movement might distract them, and who knows how the sonar works on droplets of water."

"Okay, Super-genius, now how long will it take you to get the sprinklers going?"

"I don't know. I'll have to find them in the files on the computer," Sage stammered.

"Then go!" urged Bryan. "Hurry."

Sage spun around and dashed back into the office.

In the distance, a metal door rattled against a lock. To Bryan, it sounded like shotgun shells rattling inside a cardboard box. There was no doubt the things had made it inside. And if they had made it that far, it was just a matter of time. He would have given his left pinkie finger for a shotgun right about now. Or the pickaxe he hoped was still stuck in the side of the beast he'd injured and that the creatures hadn't suddenly started carrying weapons. He could almost hear slamming against the metal door with every buckle and shove. He shuddered, dropping his gaze to the net full of soccer balls.

How could our fate be so twisted that we have to rely on the contents of a high school athletic department for survival? The thought nearly made him chuckle.

"What?" asked Kiley. She tried to sound cold and bracing, but her voice quivered as she spoke.

"Nothing," said Bryan, a smirk rising uncontrollably to his lips. Clearing his throat, he gestured at the net full of balls. "Let's get these things ready."

Bryan and Kiley wrestled the assortment of balls toward the center doors, each placing a hand on one of the metal-bar handles and pulling the net up to the doorway with the other. The coolness of the metal against Kiley's skin sent a shock through her palm and she jerked away before cautiously placing it on the handle again.

"I guess we're about to see if that little girl is really a genius or not," said Bryan through gritted teeth. The sinewy muscle beneath the skin of his jaw was nearly pulsing, pulled taut and white against the bone. His eyes seemed to tremble in their sockets as the muscles around them wrinkled tightly together.

Kiley sucked in a breath and bit her lower lip. "I'm really scared, Bryan." Her voice was quiet.

Her fingers had turned bloodless and white against the tugging loops of soccer net wrapped around them. A cool trickle of sweat worked its way down the crook of her underarms. She fixed Bryan with a frightening look that made her seem even younger than her actual age.

"Are we going to die?" she asked.

CHAPTER THIRTY-FIVE

Sage, Bryan, Max, and Kiley

"Time to fly," said Sage, plucking her backpack from the chair beside the door. She flung it awkwardly over her shoulder. The bag hung heavily on her back, throwing her weight off balance as she staggered toward the desk.

"No time like the present," Max said in a soft voice. He rose weakly to his feet. "Let me take that for you," he offered, reaching tentatively for the backpack.

"Don't worry about it," said Sage, tossing the bottle of cough syrup at Max as she pushed past him. "I need you to move. I told Kiley I'd look for the command for the sprinkler system on the computer."

"What? Why?" Max asked, a hint of anger in his voice.

"I don't have time to explain. Just drink some of that," she said, indicating the bottle. "I've got work to do."

"What's this for?" he asked, turning the bottle over in his hands.

"Drink it. It's got sugar. We need you to stay alert for this," she said, looking up at him.

"Since when does cough syrup keep you alert?" asked Max.

"Since it has sugar in it and you need it. Now drink," she said, turning her attention back to the principal's desk. She scanned the computer's mess of icons for something identifiable. She spotted a raindrop icon on the desktop and clicked it.

"And Bingo was his name, oh," she said to herself, stealing a glance at Max. His eyebrow was raised, his face lifted into a smirk.

It was the first time Sage remembered seeing any emotion on the boy's face since meeting him earlier that day.

"What?" she asked.

"So you are a real child. I was starting to think you were a Sage-bot," Max said.

"Drink your cough syrup, young man," Sage said dismissively. "It's time to make some noise out there."

Max opened the bottle and chugged half the contents. His lips twisted away from the spout. "Disgusting," he said, tossing the bottle into the wastebasket next to the door.

Sage ignored him. Reaching out her index finger, she pressed 'enter' on the computer keyboard. A loud crackle of static and feedback exploded from the intercom at an almost deafening pitch. A split second later, the walls of the school vibrated to the incoherent rasping of an unidentifiable industrial song punctuated by the reverberations of one mind-numbingly loud fire alarm. Sage raised one eyebrow at Max as she plugged her ears with her fingertips and pushed past him.

"What?" he asked, his voice drowned out by the incoherent noise pollution now filling the school. "I thought you wanted it to be loud." The boy stumbled to catch up to her. As Sage and Max burst into the hallway, neither Bryan nor Kiley acknowledged their return.

Their eyes were fixed on something moving just beyond the windows of the doors, their mouths gaping open. Sage followed Bryan's gaze through the thin pane of window and saw it. On the plateau, all the way down to the parking lot at the bottom, hundreds of inky-skinned creatures were cupping their ears. Some were doubled over at the waist, bashing their heads into the cold earth below. Others were flailing their bodies, rocking back and forth so violently at the waist or knees that they looked more animated than real.

"Where did they all come from?" Kiley said. "Are we really going to do this, Cinderella? Are a net full of balls, a little M. Night Shyamalan sprinkler action, a fire alarm, and some angsty music really the way we get out of this?"

Sage met her gaze. The look in her eyes was uncertain, but she nodded at the older girl. Kiley set her mouth into a firm line and nodded back.

"Then we should let these monkeys fly," Kiley said in agreement.

"How much time again?" Bryan shouted.

She held up four fingers in reply.

Nodding, Bryan clenched the soccer net in one hand and lifted his other, signaling for Max and Sage to each take a door. Sage positioned herself next to Kiley and Max ducked under Bryan's arm. Each braced their hands against the door lever.

"On three," shouted Bryan. "One. Two. Three."

Max and Sage shoved open the school doors and dropped to a squat beside Kiley and Bryan. With the doors wide open, the sound of the music blasting through the megaphones on the school's roof was almost deafening. Max had turned up the volume to full blast. The thick bass line and the pounding drums vibrated through Sage's temples as Kiley and Bryan dropped one side of the net and lifted the other.

The balls bounced down the front steps of the school. Some rolled slowly off to the side while others bounced high against the cement. A pattering of sprinkler water darkened the ground and glistened on the surface of the balls as they rolled and bounced against it. The grass looked treacherously slick where the spouts had emerged and begun pelting the grass with a halo of water.

Sage and Max flung themselves through the door while Kiley and Bryan pulled the net back out of the doorway and let it fall to the floor. Bryan pushed Kiley out behind Sage and Max, who were standing dumbfounded on the porch.

As he looked behind him, he saw the trio of creatures that had been chasing him and Kiley previously. They had obviously broken through the second set of doors. They came stumbling into the lobby, but now seemed off balance, not quite sure in what direction they were headed as they shook their heads violently against the sound of the music. One of them ran repeatedly into one of the brick walls lining the hallway. The monster that had attacked Bryan tangled a foot in the crumpled soccer net and crashed to the floor, its arms flailing in frustration against the linoleum.

For a second—only a second—the quartet of children stood motionless, packed tightly together on the cement steps of the school. The throng of creatures separating them from Rachel's car in the parking lot below seemed like an impervious roadblock, a sea of mindless, thrashing creatures presenting no visible path to their desired destination.

Several of the monsters near the top of the hill clutched their inky hands over their cracked and reddened ears. The sun had dropped low in the sky, setting the clouds above the trees ablaze with orange light. A thick blanket of grey hung coolly over the parking lot below, and mingled with the spattering drops of the sprinklers. It cast the entire scene before them with the feeling of a rainy day.

A single creature near the top of the stairs, dressed in a dirtied terry cloth bathrobe, lashed her hand out against a basketball that bounced off one of her legs. No sooner had she pulled her hand away from her ear than she let out a pained screech and quickly clapped her hand back to the side of her head.

The glimmer of a grin crossed Sage's mouth as Bryan, shouting so loudly that his voice cracked, wailed "Go!" As if they were marathon runners awaiting the sound of the starting gun, they each broke into a sprint.

Slow equals dead, Bryan thought, but he fell to the rear of the pack, protective of the younger kids.

Kiley leapt over the cement stairs that led up to the building and weaved her way through the mob of creatures bobbing along the path down to the parking lot. Their gnarled fingers clipped at her hair and clothes as she whipped past them. Sage, her backpack tightly fastened to her shoulders, ducked and wove her way at waist-level, twisting and turning her way past the wriggling adult-sized creatures with ease, less of a target than the older kids. Max, still faint from his loss of blood, pressed forward at lightning speed, his arms pumping as he barreled down the plateau-side ahead of his companions. An explosion of adrenaline aided his efforts.

I'm gonna pay for this later, the younger boy thought.

Bryan took up the rear, kicking a ball here and there that had spun to a stop as he too, charged down the edge of the plateau, narrowly missing several writhing creatures' gnashing teeth and hands. He fought the panic that floated through his body.

The momentum of the runners as they sprinted down the hill limited their ability to maneuver or even halt their hasty progression. Sage, for one, was moving so fast with the extra weight of her backpack pinned to her shoulders that if she needed to change her trajectory through the crowd of flesh-hungry fiends and the slick grass-covered hill, she would stumble, slip and fall. It would only take one misplaced or uncertain step on the now wet grass to make her tumble, but the pelting droplets of water did seem to be affecting the creatures, which were turning in every direction and grasping at the air around them as she fled past.

Her heel caught a patch of wet autumn leaves and she skidded a few inches before recovering. She tried to push her center of gravity back to her heels, pressing them firmly into the ground with each footfall as she dodged past a cluster of cracked-mouthed creatures clawing at the sides of their heads with the hooks of their fingers. One younger, female monster sent scraps of flesh showering to the ground as it clawed at its ears. Oozing black blood began to seep down the sides of its head.

On the other side of the plateau, about twenty yards from Sage, Kiley struggled to veer back towards the car below. She had twisted and turned to avoid the thick throng of monsters and was now inadvertently headed toward the lake behind the school, away from the direction of the parking lot. But every step closer to her sister's car seemed to put her in the path of an open and hungry mouth. She stumbled, caught herself and sped on, her heart seemingly lodged in her throat.

As her eyes locked on the parking lot and the single car parked there, her feet scrambled to stay steady beneath her. She plummeted down the hill at breakneck speed. Panic set in, telling her this was all impossible and death was but moments away.

Clouds of white film curled like smoke at the corners of her vision as her breath came in shorter and shorter gasps. She shifted her weight to her left leg and swung her hips backward to avoid the reaching fingers of the former town librarian. She barely avoided the creature's grasp, but stumbled into the path of a man who had to have been in his nineties. Her momentum knocked the frail monster flat on his butt before she even had time to react.

Luck, she silently pleaded as she continued her flight toward the car below. *I know we haven't always been on the best of terms, but now would be a good time to make it up to me. Please stay by my side.*

The balls seemed to be doing their job, as the few creatures that had noticed the movements had lunged at them in vain. Out of the corner of her eye, Kiley saw her old Spanish teacher gnawing uselessly on the diamond-patterned, rubber skin of a red dodge ball. A cluster of creatures closed in around it, thinking their mindless cohort had found food.

The sun radiated a violent red-orange behind the trees near the lake, casting a thick shadow along the grassy slope. A knot worked its way up Kiley's chest, clenching the muscles around her heart and lungs.

If I stray too near the trees, there is no telling how many of those things will pop out at me, she thought, immediately trying to compensate by twisting herself once again in the direction of the parking lot. She was moving so fast it was difficult for her to maintain a straight line down the hill.

Swinging to the right, she found herself face-to-face with a grey-fleshed, bald man wearing a bloody tank top and a pair of soiled boxer shorts. She screamed as the zombie's fingers coiled into her hair, clenching a thick clump of it in its greasy, white fingers. The creature jerked her head backwards and she lost balance, tumbling awkwardly to the ground. The creature fell with her, screeching its high-pitched squeal as its cracked mouth snapped at the air, trying to find fresh meat.

As the creature's shoulder collided with the ground, its grip instinctively tightened and a golf-ball sized clump of hair tore painfully from her scalp. Blood poured from the circular tear on the top of Kiley's head, tiny bits of her scalp littering the ground as she screamed down the plateau for several feet. The monster, his hand still clutching the clump of Kiley's now-beet-red hair, rolled along behind her. Kiley and the beast abruptly collided with the legs of two other creatures and she found herself entangled in a pile of the monsters.

Terror shot like ice bullets through Kiley's blood as she scrambled to get up. She imagined that, from a distance, she might look like one of them, covered with blood and flailing wildly about. Hands touched her and the two creatures she had bowled into now grabbed hold of her, clawing at her as they clawed at each other, unable to tell who from what in the chaos that surrounded them. One had her ankle in a death grip while a black-haired female wound the back of Kiley's shirt around her fingers in one hand, and tore at the hair of a creature in her other. The bald man grappled for her heel as Kiley kicked and thrashed against them. She twisted her body against their grip, pressing herself forward on her forearms and elbows as if adopting a cobra-like yoga pose.

Digging her fingernails into the frosty ground of the plateau, blood rushed to her face as she pointed herself down the hill once again and tried to drag herself from the grip of the creatures. Her eyes faltered as she focused on the crowd below her which was still fighting against the noise of the metal song vibrating through the air.

There were so many of them!

Her eyes came to rest on Sage, who was easily dodging past a group of school teachers. She stretched her hand out helplessly toward the child as salty tears boiled to the corners of her eyes, but Sage did not see her in the tangle of bodies, in fact, might have thought she was one of them. A hot, piercing sensation exploded through her ankle as the teeth of the black-haired woman tore into the flesh below her shin. The nerves of her ankle both burned and froze all at once as hot blood pumped from Kiley's leg into the mouth of the gnawing zombie. A scream rose to the back of her throat as a wave of dizziness washed over her and her vision faded into whiteness.

I'm dead, was the single thought that blasted through her mind. *I'm dead.*

toward the car, swung himself under her free arm and pulled it over his shoulders. They barreled on down the hill, past several more wriggling, clutching creatures, as they closed the final thirty yards to Rachel's car.

CHAPTER THIRTY-SEVEN

Max, Bryan, Kiley, and Sage

Reaching the bottom, the trio found Sage standing on the roof of the vehicle, a soccer ball cradled in one arm while a brick-red dodge ball rested on the palm of her other hand, ready to be thrown. Over the din of music and screeching zombies, she shouted a greeting.

"Glad you finally decided to quit playing around," she screamed with a wink. A middle-aged man wearing the white collar of a clergyman, his lips cracked and bleeding, spun around towards Sage at the sound of her voice and was promptly met with a face full of dodge ball. With a quizzical look on its leathery face, it scrambled after the ball, which rolled out of his grasp each time he stooped to pick it up. Any other time, Sage would have yearned for a video camera. She cued the next ball and inspected the area again.

Bryan fumbled in his pockets for the key to Rachel's car. As his fingers closed with relief over the cool metal, he rolled his eyes at Max.

"Can you get her?" he asked loudly.

Max grunted an acknowledgment as Bryan ducked out from under Kiley's arm and lunged toward the car. Kiley stumbled and Max struggled to hold her up. He hadn't been sure if she was dead or alive until he felt her hot breath against his neck.

Bryan pressed a button on the key chain, and sighed at the sound of the doors unlocking. He pulled open the driver's side door and clambered inside.

"Get in," he shouted as Sage tossed another ball over Max and Kiley's heads. Sage dropped to her bottom and slid off the car until her feet jarred into solid ground. She grunted, opened the front passenger side door and motioned for Max to stuff Kiley in. Without waiting for him to respond, she opened a rear door and flung herself into the back seat.

As carefully as possible under the circumstances, Max pushed Kiley into the front seat and slammed the door shut as Bryan fumbled with the girl's seatbelt. He then dove into the back seat next to Sage. As he pulled the door closed behind them, the car sprang to life and Sage clicked her seatbelt into place. Max lifted an eyebrow, smirking.

Sage shrugged. "Don't you think it would be a little ironic to escape all that and then die in a car accident?" Bryan snapped the car into reverse and stepped on the gas. The moment the car rolled into motion, dozens of zombie heads twisted toward it. They immediately began shambling after the moving vehicle.

Without hesitation, Bryan shifted the car into drive and stomped his foot hard against the gas pedal. The car jerked forward, lurching with a stomach-turning crunch as the passenger side front bumper collided with the knee of an elderly creature with half of its face torn off, knocking it easily to the pavement. The music droned to silence as the gap-mouthed group tried to catch their breath.

The song had ended and the creatures surrounding them screeched, with nothing now on their minds except the moving vehicle. The elderly monster thrust a helpless hand toward the vehicle, its fingers clutching on to the car's rear bumper. Sage swallowed with much effort, her mouth dry, as the creature scraped along the asphalt for several yards before losing its grasp. The other half of its face disappeared in a bloody pulp. Bryan didn't even glance into the rearview mirror as he sped out of the parking lot and careened onto the vacant road separating the two schools.

The roar of the car's engine echoed through the valley and hundreds of creatures burst from the woods and scrambled toward the moving vehicle. Kiley, who had finally regained consciousness, slammed her hand down on her door lock only moments before the dried, cracking claws of her math teacher snatched at the window. Its fingers thumped loudly against the glass as they cruised by, leaving a smear of blood on the pane.

"Lock your doors," Max yelled. Sage and Max pressed their locks in place. Sage reached her arm between Bryan's shoulder and the door and pressed his lock down as both of his hands were locked tightly on the steering wheel. He jerked the car left and right as they rolled down the stretch of road. He smashed into some of the creatures, but tried to evade them for the most part as he was afraid the impact might damage the car.

"Th-thanks," stammered Bryan when he heard the door lock click into place. His shoulders were high, close to his ears and his hands were alabaster white on the steering wheel.

"Kiley," Max leaned forward and placed a hand on Kiley's shoulder. "Kiley, are you all right?"

The girl's face was ashen. Her mouth lolled open and her eyelids hung limply over the center of her pupils. She nodded dumbly, her eyes rolling under her slinky eyelids. Her skin was fiercely pale. This scared Max and he wondered if that was how he looked earlier to his compatriots.

"Where did it bite you?" he asked, panic edging his voice. Sage straightened in her seat, leaning forward against her own seatbelt to look at Kiley.

"It didn't bite me," she said softly. "Chewed my shoe. Like a teething dog." She let out a smile-less giggle, her eyes wide but unfocused as Bryan twisted and turned to avoid the stumbling creatures.

Blood filled her sock.

Max pressed forward, his voice urgent. "I saw blood, Kiley," he said. "When Bryan picked you up, I saw lots of blood."

"I'm fine," she said, her voice thin as a slip of paper. "A scrape. That's all. I don't need a prince to come rescue me, you know. I'm a powerful force. I'm Kiley the zombie slayer." She was stammering and Max moved in to look more closely at her.

She turned her head to face him. Worry etched lines across the boy's forehead and crinkled the edges of his eyes. She reached her hand into the backseat with a grimace from the pain as she twisted and closed her fingers around his.

"Thank you for saving me," she said quietly, a smile on her mouth. She blinked up at him. "And I promise I'm not being sarcastic right now."

"Bryan helped," he said, gulping. "I just want to make sure you're okay. You might need stitches."

She laughed softly. "And we're going to do that in a moving car while dodging flesh-eating zombies? I realize you probably have profound little Suzie Homemaker skills, Max, but I'm thinking stitches can wait until we've found a safe place to stop for a while, thanks."

"So you did get bit," said Max with concern. He still hadn't fastened his seatbelt and his body was halfway between the front seats as he tried to inspect her body for signs of injury. She turned her head and planted a soft kiss on his lips. Max was so light-headed he nearly fell backwards onto Sage's lap, but grabbed the side of Kiley's seat. He told himself the light-headedness was from his own loss of blood as he searched her eyes. They were wet and sparkled with gratitude.

Sage rolled her eyes and opened her mouth to speak. Without looking at the girl, Kiley thrust a hand in the child's direction to silence her. She shot her a cold, dark look before turning her gaze back to Max.

"Shh," she said to the boy. "Don't say a word. You saved the girl, all right? Sure, Mr. Permit may have helped, but you're the one getting the kiss. So I'd avoid complaining and not make such a big deal out of it, if I were you."

Just then, the car thudded hard and fast as it bounced over a bump. Sage rose and crashed into the seat, held in place by the seatbelt. Max's head collided with the rooftop and he rubbed it gingerly, thinking maybe he should buckle his seatbelt.

"What was that?" asked Kiley, whipping back to face the front and pressing a hand against the dashboard.

"Body," said Sage. "One of theirs." She didn't even realize she had already divided the world into two categories. Us and them. Young and old. Dead and alive.

Bryan nodded. "It was definitely an adult," he said, gulping as the car curved around the bottom of the hill, snaking through the school roundabout toward the main road.

"And no more kids anywhere to be seen," Max muttered, blinking as his gaze faded out of focus on the back of Kiley's seat. "What do you think happened to them all?"

"Dunno," said Bryan, jerking the wheel to avoid a dark-haired woman dressed in army fatigues with one arm missing.

"You know what happened to them," said Kiley coldly. She craned her head to look back at Max. "Eaten like an appetizer sampler at a pizza place."

"Lovely image, Kiley," Bryan groaned.

"What? You were thinking it," Kiley said.

Sage shook her head. "No," she said. "There must be more of them out there." She turned to look out the window at the middle school's parking lot. A cluster of creatures squatted, huddled together over something she couldn't see, while one of them gnawed on the stump of a severed arm.

"They're out there somewhere," she said softly, her breath fogging a small area on the glass of the window. "Surviving just like we are. If only we could get a message to them, we could—" she let the sentence trail.

"There she goes again. Saving the world," Kiley mumbled.

"We could what?" asked Max.

"I don't know," shrugged Sage. "We could tell them to meet us at Amanda's warehouse, I guess. Safety in numbers. And it's like a fortress with cement walls and high windows and tons of food and they have weapons—" She caught herself and took in a breath. "Or we could tell them what we know. Maybe if they knew about the echolocation and about only the adults being infected— I don't know. Maybe they could do something. Protect themselves. I feel like we're abandoning them somehow. I know we can't save everyone, but—" Sage's eyes flooded with tears. She slumped forward in her seat, pressing her face into her lap as the sobs wracked her body.

"Hey," said Max softly. He let his hand rest on her shoulder. "We would all be dead without you, you know. You saved all of our lives."

Sage sobbed harder into her lap. Hot tears warmed the bottom of her shirt, dampening the skin on her face. "My parents are—they're—" Sage's voice cut short, muffled by her crying.

Kiley arched her body in her seat again and tapped the crown of Sage's head with her index finger. "Hey, Einstein," she said. Sage lifted her head weakly. Her eyes were streaked hot pink with tears and little beads of red had blossomed on her cheeks.

"What?" breathed Sage, expecting a sardonic remark from the girl.

Kiley fixed her with a hard look. Her mouth twisted downward and she bit the inside of her cheek. "I get that you want to be all 'save the world', or whatever, but right now I'd settle for saving us. We're still not out of the woods, you know. A flat tire or zombie mob could shut this little operation down, and then where would we be? Can't be a superhero without your Bat Cave," she said.

"Makes sense," Max said, nodding. "Gotta recoup and regroup before we plan our next move."

"I just want to get to the warehouse and be safe for a while," Bryan chimed in, his fingers still white on the wheel as he jerked it to avoid hitting a creature that had lunged into the middle of the road. He gulped as the tires gripped the pavement of the hill again and continued to barrel forward.

"Safe. Where's that?" Max asked. "I think we should kiss 'safe' goodbye."

"What about the warehouse? It's gotta be safe, right?" Sage asked.

"Maybe for a little while," Bryan said. "But who knows for how long. Who knows how far this thing reaches?"

"He's right," Kiley interjected.

"Huh?" asked a surprised Sage.

"Max, I mean. Max is right. You gave us direction, juice box." She looked the little girl in the face and corrected herself. "I mean,

Sage. We'd probably still be in the library right now, sitting ducks for those zombies to gnaw on our vulnerable flesh."

"Right," breathed Bryan. "And now we're just meals on wheels."

A trail of black rubber snaked behind the car on the pavement as Bryan spun the car onto the main road. He turned the wheel and headed toward the highway. Kiley glared at him.

"All I'm saying is, we've got each other," she said. "And that's more than I ever imagined."

"Hey," said Max, bolting upright in his seat. "We should turn on the radio."

Kiley's eyes widened. "Good idea," she said, reaching for the dashboard. She rolled the station indicator slowly across the dial from left to right. Sage quieted her tears as she listened to the static rolling through the car speakers. Kiley's fingers rolled over a station where the static silenced and was replaced by the low bell tone of the emergency broadcast system. She dialed right past it and had to backtrack to find it. After a moment, a recording proceeded to loop over the stereo, filling the car with its crackling voice.

Citizens are urged to remain inside their homes and lock their doors. We have dispatched military support to assist with this crisis which started on the Northeastern seaboard and is now rapidly moving inland. The recording looped again and repeated the same message.

Sage slumped back in her seat, the fast drying tears on her cheeks tightening the skin of her face as her mouth fell open into a perfect "Oh" of shock.

"That was the president's voice," she sighed, but they had all recognized the distinctive voice.

"So, it's the whole country," Max said. "Or if it isn't yet, it soon will be." No one responded as the radio announcement repeated itself.

Kiley finally turned the radio off so they wouldn't have to hear the same ominous message over and over. The car rolled through the lifeless town of Greendale, past cars abandoned on the side of the road. Past black-eyed, black-veined creatures mobbing nearby sidewalks as they searched for breathing food. Past the bloodied front lawns of so many suburban houses, before finally rolling through a stop sign at the edge of town and onto Route 136, a squiggly, coastal shot toward Chesterville.

Sage quietly reached a hand into the front pouch of her backpack. She dug her fingers down to the middle of the overstuffed bag until they closed around the familiar, fluffy leg of her stuffed bunny. She pulled Squiggly from the bag and looped its arms around her own, hugging it close to her body as her head tapped absently against the side of her window. A few flakes of snow feathered to the ground from the gray-clouded sky.

"It's early for snow," said Sage quietly.

Kiley and Max looked at Sage then they each pressed their heads to their car door windows and looked out.

"Sure is," grunted Max.

"Look at that," said Kiley. "Funny how peaceful snow seems after all that blood we left behind at the high school, you know? Hey, maybe all those zombies will freeze to death."

"They're already dead," Max mumbled.

"Well, Captain Pep Squad, how's that for some team spirit? Maybe they'll at least freeze until next spring," she replied.

Bryan flicked on the windshield wipers. The blades sprung to life, batting away the tiny flakes as they floated down against the windshield.

"I've never driven in the snow," he said.

Sage leaned forward in her seat and touched Bryan's shoulder lightly with the tips of her fingers. "Just take it easy," she said. "I'm sure you'll do just fine after everything else we've been through."

A slow, steady grin overtook Bryan's face. "Sure," he sputtered. "Guess it can't be any harder than slaying zombies, eh?" His shoulders dropped away some of the tension that had been there for what seemed like forever and his hands loosened on the steering wheel.

"You guys should get some sleep," he said, affecting his best dad voice. "It won't be long before we're home, now."

"Home," sneered Kiley, crossing her arms over her chest and pressing her palms deep into her armpits.

"Well, it will be soon enough. At least for a little while, I guess," sighed Max.

"Is this going to be our life now?" Kiley asked.

Shrugging, Max said "Maybe. I dunno."

"Hey, Einstein?" Kiley called out. "Have you given any thought to what's gonna happen when we get there and find your little friend has become zombie kibble?"

But Sage didn't hear a word Kiley said. She pressed her face against the cool glass, her eyes lulled slowly closed as the car whirred and glided over the pavement. A cloud of fog rolled out of her mouth along the window glass as a tiny snore sputtered from between her lips. Outside, snowflakes had begun to collect on the cool surface of the ground, blanketing random patches with a thin layer of white as the sun sunk lower in the sky.

And she dreamed.

BIOGRAPHY

Araminta Star Matthews has her MFA in creative writing and teaches postsecondary writing and literature in Central Maine. Compelled to write from an early age, Araminta has always been drawn to the supernatural and macabre in literature. As a child, her father read to her from J.R.R. Tolkien every night and her mother kept a bottle of tomato juice in the refrigerator labeled "fresh blood". While vampires enthrall her, it's only zombies that freak her out. She hopes these zombies give you as much of a chill as they gave her when she was dreaming them up. This is her first full-length novel.

Photo by Lynda Hurd Goodman

CPSIA information can be obtained at www.ICGtesting.com
Printed in the USA
LVOW111819170512

282187LV00010B/231/P